## PRAISE FO

*"Orphaned boys cling to each other through stories of loss, love and life. You will laugh. And you will cry. But in the end hope is palpable."*
- SUSAN JIMISON, AUTHOR OF *DEAR MARK*

*"With* Another Long, Hot Day *Stan Waits joins the ranks of great Southern storytellers. Set in rural Georgia during the turbulent 60s, this powerful coming-of-age tale begins with an unspeakable crime that leaves a young boy filled with hate until an unlikely friendship with two older men, one white, one black, shows him the redemptive power of forgiveness. Highly Recommended."*
- RONALD AIKEN, AUTHOR OF *DEATH HAS ITS BENEFITS*

*"Chilling yet heartwarming....Charles Dickens in west Georgia. A tough coming of age story that tromps through hate to love and loyalty of family and friends."*
-JENNIE HELDERMAN, PUSHCART PRIZE NOMINEE AND AUTHOR OF *AS THE SYCAMORE GROWS*

*"This is a book of love and hatred. Love triumphs.... Highly recommended."*
-CHARLES OLOF JOHNSON, AUTHOR OF *RAINBOW IN A LEMON FIZZ TIN*

*"Our most treasured stories—in literature and in life—are about either redemption or forgiveness, depending on whether the storyteller is the sinner or the one who was sinned against. Stan Waits has written the latter: a memoir about his journey from anger and hate to making peace and discovering happiness. He tells of his childhood with courage, intensity, and heart. An old Southern adage is to forgive but never forget.* Another Long Hot Day *is a story you will remember forever and a guide for those who need to absolve so they can become the people they were meant to be."*
- GEORGE WEINSTEIN, AUTHOR OF *HARDSCRABBLE ROAD* AND *THE FIVE DESTINIES OF CARLOS MORENO*

*In the South, every generation produces a writer whose literary gifts, honed by life's hardships, conceives stories of simplistic yet unforgettable verse. With* Another Long Hot Day, *author Stan Waits joins illustrious literary company: Welty, Conroy, Morrison and Bragg.*
—JEDWIN SMITH, AUTHOR OF *OUR BROTHER'S KEEPER*

*Another*
*Long*
*Hot*
*Day*

For Lynne
I hope you enjoy
my humble story!
Take Care &
God Bless,

Steven Day

6-13-15

*Another
Long
Hot
Day*

Stan Waits

DEEDS PUBLISHING | ATLANTA

Published by Deeds Publishing
Marietta, GA
www.deedspublishing.com

Library of Congress Cataloging-in-Publications Data is available upon request.

ISBN 978-1-937565-99-2

Books are available in quantity for promotional or premium use. For information, write
Deeds Publishing, PO Box 682212, Marietta, GA 30068 or
info@deedspublishing.com.

First Edition

10 9 8 7 6 5 4 3 2 1

*To my wife Mary*
*You believed in me and made me better*

# Contents

# A word from the author...
# and a few fond memories

This is a story about love, but it doesn't start out that way. It begins with hate, even before I knew what hate was. When I was a child, all I knew about hate was that it didn't feel good.

And not just any hate—a deep-seated, stomach-churning hate that arose from the knowledge that someone who was charged with loving and protecting my three brothers and me—the man who fathered the four of us—failed miserably.

It was a soul-shattering betrayal of four young hearts and spirits, a betrayal that for many years I believed was unforgiveable.

There are those who excuse a man's behavior because he has certain afflictions. Maybe that's valid if some incurable disease has laid waste to a father's senses and he's unable to protect and care for his children. Most folks can understand and sympathize in such a case.

But I believe that plying yourself with whiskey until you hurt so much that you're willing to end your life in some violent fashion isn't one of those valid circumstances.

I need to tell you that I understand pain, though. I now understand my father's pain, the horror he experienced during the Second World War and what that did to him. Life can throw things in our direction that overwhelm even the strongest of men. I accept that premise.

But being overwhelmed by anything is temporary. Even the most painful experiences one might encounter, such as the death of someone we hold closest to our heart—a wife or husband or one of your children. Or all of them, all at once.

I've known folks who have experienced such tragedies and survived—saddened of course, and changed, but alive. And with the love and compassion of friends, they have persevered and discovered that life is still worth clinging to.

So hate drove me and hardened me and kept me alive. And even though I came to understand and accept pain as an everyday companion, I couldn't forgive my father's transgressions.

But that's only the beginning of my story. I mentioned that the story is also about love. Not romantic love, mind you, but love in its purest state—the unselfish, even anonymous, caring for one's fellow man.

At some point, I was blessed—that's what I believe it was, a blessing.

Equal to the events that created hate are the blessings that create love. In my case, these blessings came with names—two men of different colors, Luke and Buddy. They were, and still are, the sole cause of my resurrection from that hateful abyss.

Both have passed on now, their lives having left a nice furrow in the hard, unfertile ground of hate they discovered in me when we met and our lives became entangled. Luke and Buddy ploughed and sweated until my earth became fertile. Then their seeds of love were sown and took root. It was all their doing—the two of them together, in an uncalculated, persistent display of reaching toward the finest, most honest and pure ideals that most men can only speak of.

For nine years I was their student while they filled the void left behind when my parents died. The seeds they planted a long time ago, when I was a troubled, hate-filled child, are still growing, and for that I'll forever be grateful.

So come join me as I tell you the story of how these two old men altered the course of my life.

When this book was finished, I realized that I'd cast my father, "Big Mark" Waits in a terrible light. Before the insanity of alcoholism invaded our household, he'd been a good, nurturing father and there are memories of him when I was very young that

I still hold dear. I penned a few of them here for you to read. God rest your soul, Big Mark.

## Story 1

The field behind our house is ablaze. The wind has whipped the waist-high orange flames into a frightening spectacle that has threatened to overtake our foxhole.

Danny and I spent all day scooping hard clay with post-hole diggers and Dad's entrenching tool to dig a foxhole—the kind of holes we had seen the Marines lying in, in the combat photos Big Mark brought home from the war. We had swiped a can of our Dad's Sterno and some stick matches and were busy cooking grasshopper legs over a piece of screen-wire, pretending to be Marines surviving in the field during the war with the Japs. Danny tipped over the Sterno can, and the dry grass erupted into the blaze that now had us surrounded.

Momma, having spotted the fire, is frantically waving her arms above her head and screaming something to us from a distance, the flame's ferocity preventing her from coming any closer.

Through the wind and the crackling of the fire, we hear sirens approaching. Big Mark arrives in his '49 Ford moments before the fire engine, and I see him bolt from the car and sprint in our direction. Fearlessly leaping through the flames, he reaches us quickly, tucking Danny and me under different arms and racing back through the fire toward the safety of the crowd of firemen, whose hose is now busy spraying the out-of-control blaze.

Our faces are smudged with black soot from the fire. Big Mark sits us on the edge of the back porch while Momma cries as she strips us to our underwear to make sure we aren't burned.

Lying in bed tonight with my eyes closed, my perception of my father's abilities knows no boundaries. He will be here when we need him. He will save us from anything and anybody.

As my sleep gently tugs me toward my dreams, I smile and feel safe under the blanket of protection and security of my father's love.

# Story 2

"Where we goin' Big Mark?" I ask, my five-year-old curiosity getting the better of me.

As we wait to board the massive train we stand beside, it occurs to me that my Dad hadn't said anything about our destination.

"Well, Charlie, we're goin' to meet some folks we've never seen before. Every man has a different story to tell and the learnin's in the listenin', so we're gonna be learnin'. Life's all about people, son."

When we board the train, Big Mark leads us straight to the club car and orders a whiskey for him and a Coke for me. A man in a suit sits beside my Dad and orders a beer, and Big Mark introduces both of us. So, I think, this is gonna be the first story we're gonna hear, and sure enough, Big Mark and the man strike up a conversation that lasts through three more whiskeys and beers and Cokes.

We meet a lot of people and listen to their stories. Big Mark is like that—he does crazy stuff, like hitch-hiking with us or riding trains, just to meet people and listen to their tales. Then he writes about them in the column he pens each week in the *Cedartown Standard*.

He writes for hours with me on his lap, sitting at a beat-up oak desk with his typewriter clattering, spitting out page after page of stories of folks we'd met and listened to, his ever-present cigarette and glass of whiskey close by. The drone of the keys lulls me to sleep.

I awake, still in his lap. Big Mark nods his head in satisfaction at what he'd put down on paper. Just some down-to-earth story of someone's joy or pain, a snapshot of some ordinary traveler's day. But to my father—well—to him, that day in their life is special enough to write about.

I pretend to be asleep still. I know he'll carry me to bed and tuck me in beside Danny.

"Sleep tight, little man," he says before shutting our bedroom door.

# Story 3

Skull Murphy is featured tonight in the wrestling match at the Cobb Auditorium in Marietta.

Big Mark is working for the *Daily Journal* and gets passes for us to all sorts of events. Neither Danny nor I have ever been to a wrestling match before, so tonight's a big deal—especially so because Paul Anderson, "The World's Strongest Man," is gonna be here too, in an exhibition of strength. I'd heard a lot about him, but I'd never seen him.

Sure enough, we have seats by the ring, on the front row. I watch in amazement as Skull pounds his masked opponent into a bloody pulp. Danny and I wonder how anybody could lose so much blood and still be fighting. Skull, having made quick work of his foes, yields the ring to a tag-team match, but he re-emerges in the middle of their match and proceeds to whip all of them, too.

Then, as advertised, Paul Anderson is introduced. "The World's Strongest Man" declares that if fifteen men from the audience will be so kind as to enter the ring, he will lift the entire ring, with them standing on it, off the ground.

Big Mark places us on the platform with the men, and with the entire auditorium holding its collective breath, we feel the ring lift into the air. Danny and I cheer as the building erupts into wild applause and screams. Paul Anderson has delivered!!!

Soon, the night's festivities are over.

"Come on with me boys," Big Mark says. "I have a surprise for you."

He leads us to the back of the auditorium, and—wait—can it be? Yes, holy cow, Paul Anderson is standing there in his wide, shiny weight-lifting belt, motioning for Danny and me to join him.

He flexes his muscles, and my Dad takes a photo of Danny and me doing a pull-up on his arms. The picture is in the next day's paper. Could there ever be a better Dad?

# Story 4

High in the North Georgia Mountains is a place called Warwoman, where a crystal-clear stream teems with rainbow trout. "It's a spiritual place," Big Mark always says, and it is a location that he finds irresistible. Nearby is Jesus Creek, and when the stocking truck rolls by and dumps copious populations of hatchery-raised slick rainbows into the ice-cold water, he makes sure we're there to harvest our share.

Fishing with him is an early morning event. Once the morning's catch is cleaned and iced down and Momma makes sure we were fed well, the day's hiking begins. We stand at attention and salute, proud to be following in the footsteps of our Marine Corps leader.

Big Mark teaches us how to survive here, in the open wonders of some of "the most beautiful mountains in the world."

Long before John Barleycorn would lay him to waste, Dad encourages us to examine every detail in our surroundings, from the wild orchids in Tallulah Gorge to the undersides of leaves that contain "an intricate beauty hardly anyone ever takes notice of."

Big Mark marches all four of his sons—though we are hardly old enough to navigate the steep trails—until we reach the top. The birth of one of the creeks below can be found erupting from the ground, a crystal spring pouring from the earth and cascading downward. We strip down naked, and he tosses us one-by-one into the heart-stopping cold water.

Back at camp that night, after finishing the last of the rainbows we'd cooked over the open fire, the ritual begins. We rub our skin down with the oil from the fish remains.

Just as Big Mark finishes his bottle of whiskey, he loudly exclaims, "It's the way of the Indians, boys. Rub that grease in real deep." While Momma sits at the picnic table nearby, shaking her head at Dad's drunken nonsense, we dance around the fire, our skin glistening with greasy fish oil until we collapse in exhaustion, dreaming of tomorrow's adventure.

# Story 5

Big Mark carries me into the officer's club bar at Dobbins Air Force Base. He takes a seat on a stool and gently sits me on the bar beside him, my four-year-old legs dangling over the edge of the bar in front. Recognizing my father, the aproned bartender heads toward us.

"Hey Major. What'll it be?" the man asked.

"Give me a double Wild Turkey on the rocks, Barney, please."

"Who's the little Marine you got with you?" the heavyset bartender asks, smiling and nodding his head in my direction. The man pours brown liquid from a tall bottle into an ice-filled polished glass then places it on the bar in front of Big Mark.

"He's the toughest little first-born son you ever laid eyes on, Barney," my Dad replies, as he grabs my slight shoulders and pulls me to him, kissing me on my cheek and ruffling my blonde hair. My Dad's blue eyes sparkle with pride as he looks at me, grinning.

I'm embarrassed because of my Dad's kiss, because I am tough, just like he says. He made me tough. But I'm proud, too—proud because so many of Big Mark's friends speak of my father as the war hero I imagine him to be.

The cracks in his hero's façade aren't evident when I'm four—he's what I want to be when I grow up. He's a hard Marine, a battle-tested survivor, and everything his first-born son needs.

Yeah, when I grow up I want to be just like you, Big Mark. My small chest is swollen with pride. Being your first-born makes my head spin, knowing you're here to protect me.

God, I love you, Dad.

# Story 6

The fat black water moccasin suns itself on a bed of pine needles close to the bank of Tift's Lake, in South Georgia. When the sun-warmed snake moves, Big Mark warns us away.

We'd been taught to be cautious, but none of us are afraid. Our Dad has taught us well. Fear "would keep us alive and safe," he'd told us, just as his "fear had kept him alive in the Pacific."

He calls us his "men" and his "platoon," and as soon as we are old enough to walk, we're proud to follow him anywhere. We are his men, even though Little Mark and Jeffrey are still in diapers. We are a platoon, whatever that is.

"Stay back, men," Big Mark says, "and I'll show you something."

With a piece of pine limb in hand, he approaches the slow-moving reptile from behind and pens it to the ground with the stick, right behind the animal's head. Carefully replacing the stick with his hand, he lifts the poisonous snake into the air for us to examine.

The snake is massive, as thick as Big Mark's arm.

"Charlie, break me off a green limb and bring it here," Dad requests.

He inserts the small branch into the snake's mouth and pries open its jaws, revealing a glistening white interior.

"This is a cottonmouth, men, and he'll kill you with his bite. And let me show you something else."

Gripping the snake firmly behind its head, he gently pries downward until inch-long, needlelike fangs reveal themselves, drops of clear venom dangling from their sharp tips.

Big Mark gently places the moccasin down on its bed of pine boughs, and we watch as the massive snake slides back into the safety of the lake.

There is no doubt amongst us that our Dad is the bravest man alive. We're four proud sons.

# 1. The Beginning

WHAM!

I jumped when the back screen door slammed hard. This was quickly followed by Big Mark screaming at my mother to get up.

I was sitting up on the bed I shared with my little brother and had just watched as my Dad's '53 Ford turned into our short driveway, the tires crunching the gravel underneath as he approached our small, white-frame house and then disappeared out of sight around the side. Until that frightening outburst, I was listening to a whippoorwill somewhere off in the distance beckoning a mate and the cicadas' ear-piercing clatter in the tops of the pines, thinking about how hot it was this late at night.

It was late July 1959 in north Georgia, and steamy nights like this weren't unusual. The exact date escapes me now. I was only nine years old. I didn't keep up with the date—I just knew it was summer. It was late, though. I think I'd been asleep for a while, but the oppressive heat had caused me to stir and I'd been sitting there in front of the open window above the bed hoping, to no avail, for a breeze to cool the stifling summer night.

I could see the beads of sweat on my brother Danny's forehead glistening in the thin shaft of light from the streetlamp out front. As usual, the small fan humming quietly in the hall fought a losing battle as it struggled to move the thick air through the house. Across the narrow hall, our two youngest brothers were fast asleep in the bed they also shared.

Our father was known to all of us as Big Mark—mainly to differentiate himself from Little Mark, the second youngest of my brothers—and when he arrived home this late it usually meant that something bad was about to happen.

My brothers and I were unaware of the demons that possessed our father. What we were aware of was his violence, especially when he was drunk. He would lash out at anyone or anything close by, so we learned to stay hidden from him. Even though we were often subjected to his drunken rage, we still loved him. He was our dad.

Some of his Marine Corps friends had told our mother that the war was the reason our father was like he was, and many times she tried to explain this to us. I had often wondered what he'd seen and done in the war and how bad it must have been for him to end up this way.

Big Mark screamed for our mother again. She answered sharply for him to keep quiet so as not to wake up the entire house. This had become a common occurrence—her staying up late, waiting for him to stumble in drunk while trying her best to insulate us kids from his drunken insanity.

Sweat had begun to roll down my forehead, so I stripped off the damp T-shirt I was wearing and used it to wipe my face. Their talking quickly turned to shouting.

I was wide awake now. This night was infused with a foreboding, and my fear suddenly became paralyzing at the sound of the wooden chairs being knocked around on the floorboards in the kitchen. I'd heard them fighting hundreds of times, but tonight felt different.

Suddenly I heard mother shriek, followed by a loud wailing plea.

"MARK, PLEASE, NO, PLEASE NO," she screamed, and then it happened.

I saw a bright flash of light in the hall, accompanied by a deafening roar. I instantly recognized the sound. Big Mark had taken us shooting many times and the terrible explosion of his service .45 was unmistakable.

As the concussion shook the walls of our small house, I also began to scream. My brothers, all jolted awake by the gunshot, were in my room now, crying and holding onto one another, their eyes wide with fear, wondering if this was just a collective nightmare.

For a brief moment there was only silence as we all strained to hear any other sounds from the kitchen. But the only sound was my brothers' whimpering.

As sick with fear as I was, I had to find out what happened. I whispered to my brothers to stay in the room, and then I peered down the hall and slowly began to creep toward the kitchen, fifteen feet away. Halfway to the kitchen door I heard Big Mark expel some horrible, guttural noise.

When I reached the end of the hall and hesitantly peeked around the doorjamb, I could see my mother's feet—her painted toenails pointed toward the ceiling. As my eyes traveled up her body, I was momentarily paralyzed at the sight of her blood slowly creeping outward, creating an ever-widening crimson halo around her. When I looked at her sweet face with her eyes closed, I felt the hot tears streaming down my cheeks.

I remember my knees buckling as I turned my head, seemingly in slow motion toward Big Mark. It was a scene that was difficult to comprehend. He had the barrel of the pistol in his mouth, and I couldn't understand why.

The second explosion drowned out all reality as most of my father's head disintegrated and his blood and flesh spattered my face and chest.

Later, people would tell us that it was Guadalcanal or maybe Iwo Jima that had caused Big Mark to crawl into a bottle of whiskey. That war destroyed him and now had destroyed his family.

I didn't much give a damn about that now. Our mom and dad were dead, and my three brothers and I were alone in a big world.

# 2. Fear

THIS NIGHT WOULD REMAIN IN OUR memories, forever replayed over and over again in our young minds. We had gone from being part of a family to being orphans in exactly the amount of time it took for our father to decide to pull that trigger twice.

For a while, we were alone in the house. I had recovered somewhat, only because my first thought was about taking care of my brothers. I stood and looked down the hall. Danny, the next youngest, was standing there trying to see what had happened. I told him to get back into the room with Little Mark and Jeffrey, who at four was the baby. I told Danny to look after them for a minute, and then I'd be there. I leaned against the wall in the narrow hall and stood there, crying. Time seemed to stop.

I watched my tears dripping onto my chest, weaving trails through my Dad's blood as they ran down my belly before being soaked up by the top of my underwear. I didn't want my brothers to see me covered in blood, so I stepped back into the kitchen and grabbed a dishtowel and tried to clean up some.

"Charlie," I heard Danny say, from down the unlit hall.

"I'll be right there," I answered, and headed toward them. Entering the bedroom where Danny was holding both little Mark and Jeffrey, I sat with them on the bed. I decided that I couldn't tell them what had happened, only that Big Mark and Momma were hurt and that they needed to stay in the bedroom. I made them swear they'd do so—hating that I didn't have anyone to hold me, and hating that I was the oldest and had to do what was expected of me.

I knew I had to cover my parent's bodies, so I went into my Momma's bedroom and stripped the sheets from her bed. The scent of perfume from her pillow touched my nostrils—it was a smell I would never forget.

The force from the pistol had propelled Big Mark's chair backward, coming to rest propped at an angle against the wall with him still sitting in it. I took one of the sheets and, without looking directly at him, draped it over the upper half of his body. Quickly, the blood began to soak through the sheet and I imagined that it would soon be completely red.

Taking care of my Mom's body was easier. There were no visible wounds other than a small ragged hole through the front of her nightgown. If not for the pool of blood surrounding her, she looked as if she were asleep. I knelt down beside her and kissed her, my tears falling onto her face, as I told her I was sorry that this had happened, before I covered her. I desperately wished that I could have stopped this from happening—that I could have protected her somehow.

Mother had repeatedly told us that if anything bad ever happened we were to pick up the phone receiver and dial zero for the operator. I told the operator who I was and what had happened and where we lived and then gently put the receiver back in its cradle. Slowly I walked down the dark hall to my brothers. I was afraid and desperately wanted someone to come quickly.

# 3. Confusion

I HUDDLED ON THE BED WITH MY brothers, and for a moment, we were all quiet. Although he had no idea what had occurred, Little Mark, who was just five at the time, asked, "What's gonna happen, Charlie? Is it okay now?"

I doubted that anything would be okay for a long time to come. I could taste and smell my intense fear—kept at bay only because of the need to care for the only thing I had left in this world—my three brothers.

"Yeah, everything's gonna be okay," I said, turning my head so he wouldn't see my tears. It was all I could do to sit there, knowing that my Mom and Dad's lifeless bodies were just twenty feet away, and I thought that if I could get five-year-old Mark and Jeffrey to go back to sleep, that whatever was coming would be easier for them if they were rested.

"Why don't we all lie here and close our eyes," I said, and they laid their heads on the pillows. Danny and I put our arms over them, and soon they were sound asleep.

I motioned for Danny to follow me into the hall. I whispered that Big Mark and Momma were dead, and I held him tightly while he sobbed on my shoulder. He asked if he could see them—I told him I didn't think that he should. From where we were standing in the hall, he could see Momma's feet and much of the blood. He leaned back against the wall for support and then slowly crumpled to the wood floor. I sat beside him and put my arm around him, and he leaned his head on my shoulder and wept silently. The only sound in our little house was the small fan, still struggling to do its job.

Shortly thereafter, I heard sirens coming from far away, steadily growing louder. Soon, flashing red lights from the police cars reflected into the house, splashing onto the hallway walls, the color a grim reminder of the carnage in the next room. I stood, helped Danny to his feet, and asked him to stay with the others. I went to the front door, opened it and was met by a policeman who, not knowing what to expect, was standing with his gun in his hand. This startled me. When I began sobbing, he holstered his pistol then picked me up and held me tightly. He asked me if I could tell him what had happened.

After describing what had occurred and telling him about my brothers back in the bedroom, he asked me to go stay there with them while they investigated.

Several cars were at the house by now, and I could hear many different voices. My reality had been dealing with the carnage and my work in that regard was finished. I lay back on the small bed with my brothers and drifted away into anything that would help me dispel the images of the past hour. I began a process, unconsciously, of allowing most of what I'd seen to slip down into a place from which there would, for a very long time, be no retrieval. A place where I could survive at any cost—because I had my brothers to care for and that, I knew, I would always do.

Because of Big Mark's drunken tirades and abuse, we were already well-schooled in denial, and now, more than ever, that denial would be called upon again. The uncertainty of all our futures began to claim its place in my psyche. I could only wonder what direction our young lives would take.

I glanced out the window as a black hearse pulled into the drive, followed by another car. I heard a woman's voice as she made her way down the hall to our room. She was the neighbor lady from next door. When she saw us she came into the room and hugged Danny, then me, and told us how sorry she was about what had happened. She stayed, trying to comfort us as best she could, whispering because Little Mark and Jeffrey were still sleeping.

One of the policemen quietly asked the lady if she would begin to pack our belongings into whatever containers might be available, and the undeniable truth of our situation was at hand. We couldn't stay here, in this house, any longer. Where we were headed, no one would say—only that the life we'd known here was finished.

There were only a couple of suitcases. Our family had never really traveled much. We moved frequently, though, for Big Mark to find a new job in a new town, where inevitably, his drinking would get him fired again. He had risen to the rank of major in the Marine Corps during the war, and he still had friends who would come to his aid, helping him find new employment in a different town. Then we'd be on the move once again. He had been a promising writer once, with a degree in journalism from the University of Georgia, and after the war he had worked for some large newspapers. But over the years the bottle had taken its toll, laying waste to his useful abilities. But that was now irrelevant in our lives.

The night and the packing dragged on. I was almost asleep when I heard another car approaching. I watched as it pulled onto the grass in the front yard and stopped. I will forever remember a big man with short-cropped gray hair stepping from the black Chevy and making his way into the house where he shook hands with some of the policemen. It was obvious that he knew them.

After viewing the scene and shaking his head in disbelief at what had happened, he stepped into the room across the hall with someone, and I could hear them talking. I was alert now, in spite of having been awake most of the night, and I had an urgent desire for answers. What lay ahead for us? Where would we go and live and who would feed us? And what about school? It would be starting soon, and this year Little Mark was supposed to start first grade. My mind was spinning into confusion—too many questions with no answers.

We had already been exposed to a multitude of insecurities, and as hard as our mother had tried to shield us from the things we shouldn't see or know, we all were aware that life was hard. We had seen a lot of fighting and physical abuse, but in spite of that, we still loved Big Mark, so we'd always forgiven his transgressions. Our love for our mother was strong—it was her absence that I feared most. I'm sure my brothers felt the same.

We were orphans now and the tears would tumble down our cheeks for some time, as the anguish of this night was destined to torment all four of us.

The gray-haired man and the policeman stepped into our small room. The waning night hadn't cooled much, so I was still soaked in sweat. We were on the bed and when the gray-haired man approached, the neighbor lady stood and allowed him to sit beside us.

Finally, with a somber face, he looked at Danny and me and said, "Boys, my name is Keith Loveless. I'm so sorry about what's happened here. Right now, though, what concerns me is you little fellows. Because you have nowhere to go, I'll be taking all four of you with me to a new home. We'll take good care of you there, and you'll all be loved and fed, and soon you'll begin a new school year. Your belongings have been packed, and when we get to where we're goin', we'll see that you have everything else you need."

The words did little to convey any sense of comfort, but I sensed that the old man was aware of this. There were no words that could have helped us this night. The air hung heavy with a thick curtain of despair. Try as I may, I felt like I was being swallowed by a dark hole of uncertainty.

# 4. The Trip

HE LOOKED OLD TO ME, BUT Mr. Keith Loveless was a big man with broad shoulders. His gray, almost white, hair was short on the sides and a little longer on top. His eyes were blue and warm. At any other time, a look from him would have made me smile. Although he was dressed in a suit and a loosened tie, I would later discover that he'd been a cattle farmer for most of his life before becoming an ordained minister.

Looking at his round face, I curiously thought that if he'd had longer hair and a white beard that he'd look like Santa Claus. That thought, at that instant and for just a moment in time, helped ease my suffering. He took me by my hand and led me into the bedroom across the hall. He would talk with me because I was the oldest.

"No child should ever experience what you've seen tonight, Charlie, and I know how bad you hurt and how confusing all this must be for you. I promise that I'm going to do all I can to ease your pain. I want you to trust me now."

His confident voice made me believe that he would indeed do what he was saying. This old man would be the one to help us.

I would later learn that this wasn't the first such talk he'd had with children over the years and that this task hadn't grown any easier. He knew that trust might never return to our lives.

We had been waiting for hours now. It had taken most of that time to confirm that my brothers and I were truly alone in the world. Had there been anyone else to care for us, the almost–Santa Claus old man would have returned alone to his home in the small, northwest Georgia town of Cedartown. He knew he'd be returning with us, though—he wouldn't have been called otherwise.

I had the thought that it must be almost as tough for him as it is for us. I would find out later that he'd been taking kids to his home for thirty-some-odd years. There were some orphans, but mostly abandoned or unwanted or starving children who had no place else to go. I guess old Keith Loveless had seen a lot in his days.

I knew it was almost time to leave. As I looked around in the house we had briefly called home, thoughts of my life here with my mother swelled to the surface. She had a tough time trying to raise us. Big Mark had contributed very little. Most of his time was spent struggling with his demons—trying to drown them, it seemed.

I remembered helping Momma cut cardboard to slip into the soles of her shoes to help keep her feet dry as she walked to work, whenever she could find any work within walking distance. When I asked her why she didn't buy new shoes, her reply was always the same—"I will someday," she'd say, smiling. I wondered why that day never came, though. And night after night, for months at a time, we'd sit down to a supper of nothing but cabbage and cornbread, but she always made sure that we had enough. Had we been given the choice though, we would rather have starved beside her than live without her tender love and guidance.

"Charlie, it's time," the old man said as he stood. The neighbor lady was dressing Little Mark and Jeffrey as Danny and I dressed ourselves.

Little Mark and Jeffrey were confused.

"Where'r we goin' now, Charlie?" Little Mark asked while they both clung to my arms. They were still little guys and looked smaller than ever now as I knelt down on one knee and held them both.

"Is Momma goin' too?" Jeffrey asked.

"No, Momma's not goin' with us right now. We're goin' somewhere with this nice man, okay? I've always told you when everything's okay and we're gonna be just fine cause we're all gonna be together. Okay?"

I had no idea what lay ahead for us, but my brothers had always trusted me. I was afraid now and didn't know if I would or could trust anyone ever again, but right now I had no choice but to do as Mr. Loveless asked. I only hoped that what I was telling my brothers was the truth—that somehow our lives would be better one day. But on this night, I doubted that.

As I was leaving our small bedroom for the last time I turned and looked at the cramped space—the small bed Danny and I had shared had been home for maybe a year. There, sitting all by itself on top of the chest of drawers, was something my dad had given me years ago—a small, green figure of Buddha that my father had said he'd found in the pocket of a Japanese soldier he'd killed in the war. He told me that it was carved from jade—"that's where it gets its green color," he'd told me. When I was very small I played with it for hours. I walked over, picked it up, and stuck it into my pocket. I really didn't know why, but the small green Buddha would be making this trip with me tonight.

Our suitcases and boxes were carried out by the group. The old man with the short, white hair led us out the front door and down the steps. The policeman had covered the doorway with a sheet so we couldn't see into the kitchen as we passed by.

The black Chevy the old man had arrived in was the biggest car we'd ever been in, and all four of us climbed into the back seat. Jeffrey promptly laid his head in Danny's lap and fell asleep. After some handshakes and goodbyes, Mr. Loveless sat behind the wheel, started the car, and made a turn on the lawn.

The page had been turned—a new chapter was just beginning. One final glance back at the place we once called home. Two men emerged from the side of the small house and deposited the covered body of one of my parents into the hearse, and then I turned around and slumped down into the seat with my brothers.

The old man began to talk, trying his best to ease our pain.

"Boys, where we're going is a place called Cedartown. We have a home there where you'll be living with a hundred-twenty other kids. You'll be able to make lots of new friends," Mr. Loveless was saying. "The home is called the Harpst Home for Children, and we know it'll take you a little while to adjust, but I promise that you'll have everything that you need."

Keith Loveless was telling me what he could about what was coming in our lives, but nothing would ever replace what we'd lost. There could never be another Momma like ours. Now she was gone forever. The only love I would feel for a long time would be for those sharing this back seat with me tonight on this lonely ride to a small town we'd never heard of before.

I was listening intently at first, but soon I was consumed by exhaustion and slipped into a deep sleep.

My dreams were filled with images of a better time. I could see myself riding in my Dad's lap as he let me steer our old car through the turpentine pine and palmetto thickets down the sandy roads near Tifton, Georgia where we lived when I was younger. We were laughing, and I felt warm and safe and content. And Momma leaned in and held me close, and I smelled her sweet scent and felt the warmth of her soft skin and I was happy. But the dream was fleeting and melted away. Through the haze of my exhaustion, I could hear Mr. Loveless trying to awaken us as the Chevy rumbled over the train tracks near our destination.

"Boys, wake up. We're almost here," the man said. I was startled as I realized that the voice wasn't that of my mom or dad. It had always been their voice that had awakened us before.

Mark and Jeffrey were still sleeping, so I shook them gently.

"Where are we, Charlie?" Jeffrey asked.

"I don't know yet," I said.

We were pressed back into the seat as we traveled up a large hill to the home and turned into a long paved drive that ended in a circle in front of a two-story brick building with tall white columns. Two women awaited our arrival. One of the women opened the rear door of the big Chevy and we all climbed out.

The old man briefly spoke to the women, and it became clear to me that we were soon to be separated. Danny and I were being led away in one direction and Little Mark and Jeffrey in another.

"Just wait a damn minute," I said, tearing my hand from the woman's grip. After years of listening to what my mom described as my dad's "Marine mouth," I was prone to use less than desirable language at times like this.

"What's goin' on? Where'r you taking my brothers?"

The women and Mr. Loveless seemed shocked by my language, but I really didn't care. This arrangement was unacceptable.

"First, young man, we don't allow that sort of talk here," the gray-haired lady who had been holding my hand said. The sadness I had been feeling turned to anger.

"I don't give a damn what you allow. You ain't taking my brothers somewhere else!"

That elicited a rather spirited response from Mr. Loveless. After a good dressing down and being told, in no uncertain terms, that this was the way it was done here, I relented. I was allowed to hug my little brothers before we were separated for the night and then they were led away. Then I was sad again when I heard them crying as they disappeared into the dark, but the spark of anger still burned in my nine-year-old gut.

The anger would soon become a manifestation of my grief. I was confused, and I searched for someone to blame. I wanted to hate someone for making all this happen, but I didn't know whom. This had to be someone's fault: Big Mark or Mr. Loveless or these stern old ladies or maybe even God.

I remember Momma always talking about Jesus and God. And how they would take care of us in times of trouble and how she would make all four of us brothers say our prayers on our knees before getting into bed at night. It seemed that our entire lives and hers, too, had been trouble, so where were you now, God? How could you do this to little kids?

From this night on, my belief in the God Momma had spoken of would begin to diminish. Growing up in our household, I had always thought that the promises from God she had spoken about sounded too good to be true. The message of hope was hard to nurture as I watched her get slapped around. I had witnessed firsthand just how painful this life could be—but I hadn't seen anything yet.

It would become a lot worse. Whatever spiritual connection I'd had would slowly become meaningless. The instinct to survive and protect my brothers became the driving motivational force in my life, and I would soon embrace self-reliance.

After Danny and I watched our brothers disappear, we turned and followed the old woman to the second floor dormitory in the large brick building the car had parked in front of. Danny and I walked up the staircase and collapsed into a trundle bed. The sleep that engulfed us was welcomed.

# 5. The First Morning

I AWOKE TO AN EAR-SPLITTING, BLOOD CURDLING scream. When I jumped up to assess the situation, I could hardly believe my eyes. I had fallen asleep on the top half of the trundle bed with Danny below me, and now, the next morning, I was stunned to witness the scene before me.

The old, gray-haired woman had Danny by the ear in what looked like death grip. He was screaming bloody murder while standing on his tip toes in the bed, flailing away with his arms. One thing Big Mark had taught me was to look after my brothers. Being the son of a Marine, right or wrong, I'd been taught to fight when necessary and this was, sure as hell, necessary.

Instinctively, I dove from a standing position from the top of the trundle bed across Danny and onto the old woman's gray head. All three of us hit the wood floor in a heap, with her on the bottom of the pile, and now she was screaming as loud as Danny was. She was hollering for help, but she was the only grown-up in the dorm, so no help would come. By now, she had relinquished her grip on Danny's ear and was trying to extricate herself from the pile, so I stopped fighting, but I was mad as hell. Danny was sitting on the floor rubbing his ear and crying as I stood up, followed by the old woman. She was trying her best to maintain some dignity, which, by this time was long gone.

Her expression was one of absolute surprise and dismay at what had happened, but she didn't say anything. She stood there trying to fix herself up so she wouldn't look like she'd just been in a fight. I don't know how old a woman she was, but she had gray hair, which she was hurriedly trying to wrap back up into a bun.

I don't know what the hell she'd been thinking, but right now, I didn't care, and I was still madder than hell.

"Just what in the hell are you doing, grabbing a kid by the ear before he's even had a chance to wake up?" I screamed at her, as she stared back at me and continued trying to become presentable once again, adjusting her matronly dress and still trying to restore her hair into a bun.

"Here, at this home, young man," she said with a stern face, "we do not soil our quilts by sleeping on top of them. We pull the quilt and sheet back and sleep under them."

I couldn't believe my ears. Maybe Danny had gone to sleep on top of the quilt, cause it was hotter than hell, but for the life of me, I didn't understand why it was such a big deal, especially considering our circumstances.

"And another thing, Charles. I told you last night, and I'll tell you once more that your language leaves a lot to be desired. If you continue to use such foul language, you'll suffer the consequences. Is that understood?" Nobody had ever called me Charles, in my life and why she did was a mystery. "And my name is Miss Dowdy. You'll address me as such. Is that understood?"

"Yes, ma'am," I growled, in response. Damn, I wanted to punch her again.

The commotion had all the other kids in the dorm crowded around the door to the room, straining to see what was happening. There was another trundle bed in our room, against the opposite wall, and the kids who had been sleeping in that bed had witnessed the entire event. By this time they were out in the hall telling the other kids, in detail, about the fight. There were fourteen boys, including Danny and me, who were all about the same age, and the faces of those I could see were smiling. For a few minutes I was consumed with the problems at hand and hadn't thought about the event that had sent us here. When I thought of the previous night, I wished I hadn't. I wished that it would all go away, never to be thought about again. And that moment, realizing that the pain could be replaced by something else, would stay with me for years. From then on, I would try to find solace in the external world of an orphanage.

***

Miss Dowdy shooed the crowd aside and turned and left, apparently with her dignity still intact, or so it seemed to her, and every last one of the boys busted out laughing. It became clear that what they'd witnessed had never happened before. All the other boys filed into our room, and several introduced themselves by name and the others, who must have been too shy to speak, stood and wondered who these two new kids were.

A bell rang somewhere outside and a boy named Bobby told me that the bell was letting us know it was time to eat. He said that Danny and I could walk to the dining hall with him. We all lined up in the upstairs hall, Danny and I taking our cue from Bobby and we walked, as a group, to the dining hall led by Miss Dowdy. Those kind words from Bobby would always stay with me, and our friendship would flourish over the course of time.

During the short walk to breakfast, I learned that I had achieved minor hero status amongst the other boys on our dorm for having stood up to Miss Sexton. I would learn that all the kids who ever resided on this dorm, and many who didn't, practically dreamed of the day they could even the slate with her. I was still steaming from watching her hurt my little brother. As I glared at her gray head from the rear, I knew the score wasn't yet settled.

We had met some of the other boys now, and a strange kinship seemed to be prevalent, at least among this small group. I wondered about the circumstances that had led all these boys here to "the Home," as this place was called. Could any of their journeys be as traumatic as ours? In the near future, we would find that some of their journeys were much worse than ours.

I realized that first morning that life here was going to be what my brothers and I could make of it. I was almost relieved that I was able to feel this much anger. I was also relieved to see that the other boys were receptive to the fight that had taken place.

I was still scared—hell, real scared—but I concluded that it felt better to be mad. I would begin to embrace anger. I had moments when I was so angry at Big Mark that I would have hurt him if I could—like when he would slap our mom around after a night of drinking. I was unaware of it at the time, but most of the boys I was walking to my first breakfast with felt the same way. After what most of them had experienced, anger was the better alternative. Danny reached over and held my hand as we walked, and I thought that was pretty cool. *What a good kid to have as my brother.*

As we walked, Bobby whispered that it was great what I'd done to Miss Dowdy, and the two of us became fast friends. He said that he'd been here for three years now, so he appointed himself my guide and confidant. Little did I know of the adventure that would come with Bobby as my fearless leader.

The first meal was troubling. The dining hall was a huge place, full of rectangular tables and crowded with boys and girls of all ages. I never dreamed that there were so many kids without parents. What had happened to so many that they ended up here? Something was really wrong in this world for so many to not be at home with their moms and dads. I was overwhelmed.

At each table were either boys or girls, all close to the same age, and their attending "house parents," as they were called. I searched for Mark and Jeffrey. Danny spotted them first and elbowed me in the side and pointed them out to me. When they finally saw us, we all waved, and I couldn't believe my eyes. They were both smiling and looked so happy, like the night before had never happened. This made me feel a hell of a lot better.

They were my first concern. As screwed up as Big Mark was, he'd drummed into me that as the oldest, it would always be my job to take care of my younger brothers, and I wasn't going to let anyone hurt them or let anything happen to them. I'd seen and been through enough and so had they. Seeing them smiling on that first morning, I vowed that we'd all make it, no matter what the circumstances.

# 6. The Talk

"WHERE'S MOMMA, CHARLIE?" JEFFREY ASKED, HIS confusion obvious.

It was a question that had to be answered, and as I looked into the deep blue eyes of my youngest brother—the baby of what was left of our family—I struggled for the right words.

*I'm so afraid now, but I won't allow my brothers to see my fear.* With slow deliberateness, I peered into the eyes of each, and seemingly from nowhere, I replayed a long past conversation with my mother.

"You boys have all been blessed with the prettiest blue eyes," I remember her saying. "Y'all got them from your grandpa. Do you remember him, son?" I did, but he had died when I was very young, and I barely had a wisp of a recollection of him, other than calling him "Papa."

"I wanna go home," Little Mark said, jolting me from my reminiscence.

We had been at the home for three days now. I had asked the old gray-haired woman, Miss Dowdy, if I could see all my brothers together, and she'd agreed. After lunch, I took all three of them into the shade of the tall maple beside the Home's chapel, and they sat in the grass in front of me.

I didn't sit—I stood, the burden of truth weighing on my slight shoulders. Only Danny knew what had happened to our parents. All Little Mark and Jeffrey knew was they were in a different place where a stranger now awakened them in the mornings.

No one had said anything to me about whether I should tell them what had happened to our parents. Maybe those who had brought us here discussed it, or maybe not, but I decided my brothers should know. They both deserved the truth. They would eventually discover what had happened and they were my brothers to tell. As much as I wanted to protect them, I knew that the day had come for the painful truth to be revealed.

"This is gonna be our new home now," I said to Little Mark.

"When is Momma gonna come, Charlie?" Jeffrey again asked.

I looked at Jeffrey, his chestnut-brown hair falling over his forehead. Then at Little Mark, with his short blond crew cut. I took a deep breath, gathering my courage, and then I asked, "Do you remember Momma telling us about Heaven—how she said it was the place where we would go after we died?"

"Yeah," Jeffrey said smiling, excited to be thinking of his mother. "She said if we were good then we would all go there to be with God. But if we were bad then we might go to the other place." He pointed down, frowning at the thought of what might lie below, in "the bad place" as our Mom had described it to us.

My heart was breaking and I fought back tears.

*Jeffrey's so cute sometimes with the faces he makes. He's so little. I want to hold him and make the truth go away. Why must he and Little Mark hear this awful truth? And now I'm about to deliver a promise of hope that even I no longer believe—that the God about whom our mother had spoken, was going to make things okay.*

"Momma always told us that Heaven was a place that we would all love to be when we got there, right?" I asked.

"Yeah, I sure wanna go there someday," Little Mark said.

"Well," I began, "that's where Momma and Big Mark have gone—they've gone to live with God now."

I had seen a lot in my nine years. I had tried to do all that was required of me as their big brother—to deflect the disturbing reality, the everyday drama and violence that had permeated every house in which we'd ever lived. But I'd fallen short of my mark—I was powerless to stop what had happened.

Danny sat there in silence—his head hanging, wincing from the devastating weight of what had really happened that night. When I ventured a glance at him, a single tear was clinging to the end of his nose. I knew we shared our measure of pain as I watched his tear fall into the awaiting grass.

"But if Big Mark and Momma have gone up to be with God, does that mean they can't come see us anymore?" Little Mark asked.

Jeffrey and Little Mark stared as I agonized over the awful truth and the impact it would have on them.

Finally, I told them, "Yes, that's what it means."

To my surprise, neither of them cried. Instead, both had a puzzled look as they tried to decipher what my words really meant.

"So they'll be up there with God forever?" asked Jeffrey. "Won't He ever let 'em come see us again?"

"I don't think that when you go to live with God that He ever lets you come back to visit. I think that He wants you to stay up there with Him," I answered. "But you remember how Momma was always making us say our prayers at night?"

Little Mark and Jeffrey both nodded.

"Well, we can talk to Big Mark and Momma the same way we talk to God. So, if there's anything you wanna tell 'em, they'll be listening to you."

"Anytime, Charlie?" Little Mark asked.

"Sure, anytime," I said. "We can talk to 'em about anything we want, anytime we feel like it."

Jeffrey smiled at the thought of talking to our mother again.

"Listen, this is our home now. This is where we'll be till we grow up, so we gotta make the best of it, okay? Even though we live in different houses, we can still see each other as much as we want."

"Will they let you come over and sleep with us sometime?" Jeffrey asked.

"I don't know, but I'll ask, okay?"

They smiled when I said that, which added to my heartbreak. But there was relief, also—them finally realizing that our mother and father were gone from their lives, never to return.

# 7. The Transition

A FEW YEARS PASSED, AND I HAD come to accept our fate.

I had fought against the hate and anguish till I had succumbed, begrudgingly, to a life that I hadn't chosen. Big Mark had sentenced us to a life that my brothers and I had resolved wouldn't kill us, though there were times of such emotional upheaval that they could have propelled even the strongest of souls into an irretrievable downward spiral.

I was scared for us in the beginning, but scared only lasts so long. We had plenty of what we needed, other than love, and there were even those who tried to fill that hole. But when our mother and father exited our lives in the abrupt and brutal way they did, I wondered if anything other than those two would ever suffice to fill that need.

He had once been not only my father but my hero. Big Mark had impressed many in his Marine Corps dress blues, and exploits with him still occupied a fond place in my young mind, in spite of what had happened.

Before the insanity had struck—before John Barleycorn had wreaked his devastation—we had hunted and fished and shot pistols. Big Mark had begun my introduction to a man's world of outdoor things. He was the quintessential Marine—a man's man who was respected by those whom he had fought with on the beaches of those far away islands with hard to pronounce names like Tarawa and Kwajalein and Guam.

From those horrible places he had returned with a Japanese sword and cigarettes and sandals and the little green Buddha I still had. Those were things that I would marvel at as a young boy—things that I could hold and touch and impress my friends with and take to school to show them what a brave man my father was. My display was always accompanied by the glossy 8-by-10-inch photo of him in his dress blues adorned with the service ribbons and medals he had, by all accounts, earned through his bravery. He was a tall man, six foot three, which further lent to the mystique of a conqueror of those far flung islands.

I had been present many a night when his brothers-in-arms paid visits and they had, over beer and cigarettes, rambled on about their exploits. It was a common sight to me for several of the old warriors to break down and cry when the names of their fallen comrades were remembered. Then the group would fall silent.

I learned at an early age just how terrible that war was. I saw that, even years later, the memories of that horrible episode reduced these mighty warriors to tears. I didn't truly understand, but when I saw my father cry on a few occasions, I wondered about those bloody days about which they reminisced.

My young mind could not comprehend how my father had fallen from his status as a war hero to a feeble-minded drunk. I struggled to understand the transition. He had been everything to me. He was larger than life—David felling mighty Goliath didn't hold a candle to what Big Mark had done. He had been a hero to my brothers and to my mother and had made us all proud.

I remembered how swollen with pride my small chest had become when he sat me on the bar at the officer's club at Dobbins Air Force Base where I would listen to his fellow officers remember just how brave he'd been—facing down the Japs on some bloody beach. Many of them hadn't seen combat and wanted to hear about the fighting as much as I did.

He would stand in a circle of his fellow officers and demonstrate how he'd fought hand-to-hand with the enemy before ending his combatant's life. As they gathered around, they almost fought to see who could buy my Dad the next round of whiskey while I vacillated between pride and despair—I knew what was coming. By the end of Dad's storytelling, he would be stumbling over his words, and someone would have to drive us home. Once there, I'd try to help untangle his tall frame and lead him into the house, with Momma shaking her head at yet another episode and him trying, unsuccessfully, to punch her.

I suppose that if he had taken only his life and left us with just our Mother we might have been able, one day, to forgive him. But for now, my memories of him were infected with hate, and I had nowhere to put that hate—it was a constant companion. What he had taken from my brothers and me was irreplaceable and I tried, unsuccessfully, to banish him from my memory.

Being the oldest of his four sons, I'd grown somewhat accustomed to watching his life spiral into madness. Now nothing but enmity remained—only hatred for what he'd done to my brothers. They were the better part of my world now. I didn't want them to feel as I did, though, so I said nothing about Big Mark in their presence.

I hadn't been able to protect my Mother that night, but I was damned sure going to do my best to protect my brothers. We had all been changed by the events of that night and now had come to accept our fate.

Because I was overwhelmed the first few years at the orphanage, I needed something or someone to fill the cavern that was created by the violence of that night four years ago. I was doing all I could, but I felt more than inadequate most of the time. There exists in a small boy's life a terrible need for love and affection and safety for his soul. My life was deficient in that regard. I wanted so much to suffer the vulnerability of the child that I was.

Gone and forgotten were the tender touches and Mom's soft kisses. I did my best to live in the present, and my conscious memories of her were fading. Only in my dreams did I remember her tossing me into a pile of warm clothes she'd just taken from the clothes line and us both laughing when she'd fall onto the bed with me and I felt safe in her embrace.

I didn't want to be as grown up as events dictated. I wanted to feel like a kid, but now I was afraid to. Then one day in the fall of my fourth year at the orphanage, I crossed paths with Old Luke.

I had grown a few years older, and I was deemed big and healthy enough to help maintain the lawns and shrubbery and aid in the general upkeep of the orphanage. Luke Hinton was the one I'd be working under. All of us, boys and girls, were taught that work was something good for us and that a good work ethic would bode us well later in life. We never admitted that we believed it, though.

Indeed, we had chores assigned at varying levels of difficulty and according to our abilities that kept us busy and out of trouble—most of the time.

I had observed this big man for a few years now—Luke Hinton was a tower of a man, at six-foot-six. I was curious about him from the start, because he looked like a giant.

All I knew about Luke was that his path to the home had been the same as ours—tragedy had brought him here. All the kids knew his story.

He and his wife Louise had a daughter who had died from an unknown illness. In search of peace and to honor the memory of their only child, they had decided that a life of service would help to fill the hole left by her passing.

I was curious as to how others dealt with the loss of loved ones, and I felt a kinship with others who had. Luke and Louise had come to heal their wounds and in doing so had helped many kids heal, too. I knew as much from hearing the other kids talking about this big man.

Luke was old when I met him—at least he looked old to me. Of course I was only twelve, so all grownups looked old. His head was covered by a thick mop of white hair and his dark blue eyes were set in a face that was furrowed and darkened from years in the sun. He always had on a well-worn pair of overalls and a tee shirt that showed off thick, well-muscled arms the color of tanned leather.

If I hadn't heard about what a gentle giant he was, I would have been afraid of his imposing figure. I knew that he'd been a farmer, but he looked like he could have been a cowboy. I imagined him out west somewhere on horseback with a six-shooter on his side. He would have made a good cowboy, I thought, or maybe a buffalo hunter or a prospector looking for gold.

On the other side of Fletcher Street, across from the entrance gate to the Home, stood Luke's shop. It was a tinned-roof, one-story brick building, fronted by a single entry door and a set of very high double doors, which accommodated the larger machinery and tractors from the farm. The Home's property encompassed some two-hundred acres, most of which was pastures and hay fields for the herd of dairy cows which was managed by the older boys.

It was here at Luke's shop that everything, from lawn mowers to tractors, was brought for repair. Luke could fix them all.

When I met him at the shop that first morning, I was welcomed with a bear hug from a man whose arms reached all the way around me. I realized then that some of what I'd been missing might be found here. In a split second, I felt a feeling that had abandoned me years earlier. I can't explain it except to say that for the past four years I hadn't felt it.

"Now come out here and help me, Charlie," Luke said, like we'd known each other forever. He walked around the tractor he had been working on and out the only door in the back wall of the shop. I was surprised that he knew my name.

I wondered if Luke had been waiting for me. Later I would learn that he knew the story of how my brothers and I had come to be here. He knew all the kids' stories. He knew the details of what had happened that terrible night, but he didn't bring up the subject.

I don't know if Luke sensed that he would become important to me, but I felt that he might. He had his way of helping to ease suffering, I'd heard. He had been at the Home long enough to know what most of the kids needed. I couldn't put my finger on it yet, but just being in his presence gave me a measure of relief.

We passed through the back door, and I saw a large dog pen made from hog wire, containing a huge doghouse made from weathered old planks and covered by a single wide sheet of tin. Lying on the tin of the roof of the doghouse was a huge gray-blue dog who greeted us with a deep howl followed by a lingering, non-threatening growl. In the shade beside the doghouse was a smaller red dog, who jumped to her feet when she saw us.

"Charlie, meet my two buddies. This big one is a bluetick hound named Buck and the other one is Susie. She's a redbone. Now, you see that trash can with the lid on it? Reach in there and bring 'em each a scoop of food." I did as he asked. "Now, open the gate and drop it down into their bowls, will you please?"

I obliged, without responding.

"Now, let's get the formalities out of the way. I want you to call me by my name. Luke, that's my name. Not Mr. Luke or any of that formal crap, just Luke. Okay?"

"Yes, sir," I said. I'd already heard from the other boys that he would ask this of me.

"You ever hunted with dogs, Charlie?"

"No, sir"

"Would you like to?"

"What do you hunt with dogs, Luke?" I asked, feeling strange calling this big man by his first name. I had never spoken to any grownup by his first name. Big Mark had seen to that. There had been hell to pay if I was caught talking to a grownup without the required 'mister' in front of their name or I hadn't answered with 'yes, sir', or 'yes, ma'am'.

"Mostly possum and coon. That's what Buck and Susie been trained to track. We hunt 'em at night in the hills 'round here and out the Rome Road and over inta Alabama. Would you like to go along one night?"

"Yes, sir. I'd love to go," I answered without hesitation. I was hoping he'd ask me. I'd heard the other boys talking about his night-time hunting.

"Alright 'en. I'll come by and pick you up, and we'll see if we'cn do any good."

It's as if he magically knew what was missing from my life. Luke's value at the Home had been recognized long ago. He had a gentle way about him, and Mr. Loveless appreciated Luke's way with his charges and even encouraged his hunts with them.

The rest of the first morning I spent with Luke in the shop.

Outside the dining hall was a large cast iron bell that was rung to summon everyone to meals. When it rang, Luke and I walked over for lunch. I sat at the table with my group, and Luke went to sit with his wife and the group of girls she looked after.

The rest of that first day at his shop was filled with Luke teaching me about the internal workings of a tractor engine. I was mesmerized by all the tools and equipment while the smells of kerosene and diesel and hydraulic fluid filled the air.

In the back corner of the shop stood a wood-burning stove around which Coca-Cola crates and upturned five-gallon buckets had been arranged like chairs. There were old, well-worn tools of all descriptions hanging from rusted nails driven into the wooden beams around the large room. Nailed to the wall to the left of the stove was a half sheet of plywood covered in photos and yellowed newspaper clippings.

Two photos seemed to be placed in prominent positions. In the upper left corner was a picture of the new president, John F. Kennedy, and below it was a smaller picture of Luke and Louise and a young girl who was maybe four or five years old. In the yellowed photo the young girl was smiling and had a puppy in her lap.

"She's my daughter, Charlie," Luke said, as he saw me looking at the photo. "Me and Louise lost her a long time back," Luke said, smiling.

Seeing him smile at the memory of his daughter made me wonder if I'd be able to smile about the memory of my parents one day.

Some of the other boys would duck in and out of the shop, and Luke would assign them some other chore and they'd be off, grabbing a sling blade or a set of pruners to carry with them, depending on what Luke wanted them to do.

But it was the way Luke spoke to us that made us want to do what he asked.

"Do you think you could do this for me, or would you mind doing this for me?" was how he'd speak to us. He made us all want to do whatever he asked, without complaining. Most everybody around us was constantly ordering us to do whatever needed doing, which is exactly the best way to piss off a bunch of orphans.

"Well, looks like it's quittin' time, Charlie. Been another long hot day and we've gotten the good out of this 'en. Say, whatchoo think about going to run the dogs with me and a friend of mine Saturday night?" Luke asked. "If you wanna go, I'll make sure it's okay, and I'll come by and gitchoo 'round dark."

I'd heard of Luke's hunting exploits from the others. I didn't understand why, but most of those who'd gone with him didn't want to go again. But I was excited about going. I didn't know what was out there running around in the hills late at night, but I sure wanted to see for myself.

"Yes, sir, you bet I want to go."

"Alright 'en. Just make sure you wear old jeans and yo' work boots, and we'll go have some fun in the woods."

Bobby, my best friend, was hanging up his sling blade.

"Hey, Luke, can Bobby go with us"

"Sure thing, if he wants to."

Bobby and I walked toward the dorm, talking excitedly about our upcoming adventure. My thoughts as I turned in for the night weren't about that terrible night long ago. I was wondering just how in hell you caught a coon and what you would do with him if you did catch him.

I realized that something had changed in me today, and the change had everything to do with meeting Luke. For the first time since coming here, I dared to hope.

# 8. Meeting Buddy

I worked alongside luke for the next few days, meeting at his shop every morning, excited about what the day might bring. I was rediscovering a feeling that I vaguely remembered from when my father was alive—the warm feeling of affection that had slipped away after my parent's passing.

Maybe it had to do with rekindling my hope, or maybe I just didn't want to feel crappy any more. The changes were subtle but recognizable. I felt good again, somewhat. Perhaps Luke had inspired this change, but I had been foundering in a dismal, hopeless sea for years now, and I welcomed the change.

Entering the door to the shop each day, I was hit with the unmistakable odor of oil and grease and diesel fuel and the mildewed smell of the drying grass that was stuck under the lawnmowers. Over the next couple of years it would be an odor I would become very familiar with.

"Good morning, Charlie," Luke would say, as I approached him from behind as he worked on a piece of machinery. "How'd you sleep last night?"

It was the small things like that, that Luke said that made a difference. No one had asked me such a question in years.

"Well, I slept good. How'd you sleep, Luke?"

"Great, Charlie. Thanks for asking. You and Bobby ready to go run the dogs tonight?"

"Yes sir, but I'm still not sure that Bobby's going. He might chicken out."

"Well, if he does, we'll still have a good time."

"Yes sir, I think we will, too," I said. Bobby had told me yesterday, after he'd thought about it some, that he really didn't want to be running around and tripping on snakes in the dark, trying to keep up with a bunch of hound dogs and pulling briars out of his butt after we got back home.

"Well," said Luke, "If he comes, that's fine. I'll come by and pick you up before dark, so be ready and get Bobby ready if he's gonna go."

I wanted to do almost anything that would take me away from here. I needed to see other places without a whole group of us going somewhere together. I had come to accept that living here required supervision, but I had no freedom. All of us hundred-twenty or so orphans were together all the time, and tonight I had the opportunity to leave, if only for a few hours.

After supper I put on my jeans and boots, like Luke said. The day's sweltering heat was beginning to dissipate as the sun ducked behind the trees. Just as he'd promised, Luke pulled his old, faded blue Chevy pickup around the circle and blew his horn.

"No Bobby? Just as well. It's not a place to be unless you're having a good time. Let's stop by the shop and load the dogs," Luke said.

We pulled up to the side of Luke's shop where, under a small shed, stood a wooden box that Luke had built himself for transporting the dogs. It was as wide as the bed of his truck and deeper still, with two large doors in front and some room between the boards for the hounds to get plenty of air and a piece of tin screwed on the top for a roof.

I helped Luke put his dog crate into the back, and Buck and Susie, upon seeing the crate loaded, started howling and tore out for the crate when the gate of their pen was opened. Buck leaped onto the tailgate and bounded to the top of the crate and let out an ear-splitting howl before jumping down and joining Susie in their temporary home. They both knew that when they saw their crate in the truck something good was happening.

"They love to go run, Charlie. It's a good day for 'em when they see their crate loaded and they can get free for a while."

I understood, I thought. I felt like they did—wanting to get away and go adventure, if only for tonight. I sat in front with

Luke and we headed down the hill, the old blue Chevy's well-worn frame rattling over every bump in the street.

The Home was literally on the wrong side of the tracks. Once you crossed the triple set of train tracks that were between our hill and town, the neighborhood changed dramatically, from nice well-kept homes on the town side to run down, unkempt shacks where most of the town's poor folks lived on this side.

Some of them were drunks and ne'er-do-wells whose lives and attitudes were reflected in their trash-strewn yards, but most of those living on our side of the tracks were struggling, hard-working folks trying to better themselves. I'd come to know many of them by name as I'd walked to town. Some of the old ladies would call me by name as I passed by.

Some of those around us had saved enough to outfit their humble dwellings with bars on their windows, trying to protect their meager possessions. But there wasn't much joy in the faces of those we passed as Luke drove through the neighborhood. There were roving bands of boys, sons of those who lived here, who would holler as we rolled past—street urchins that I couldn't help but identify with.

Luke took a right at the bottom of our hill. A few blocks later, we entered the colored neighborhood. Most of the homes here—shacks very similar to those we had just passed—were kept up well in spite of being on this side of the tracks. The houses were small and close to the street and covered with tin roofs. Some were freshly painted different colors, and others were unpainted, left to rust. Flowers grew in yard after small yard, and pots of colorful blooms were on every porch.

Most of the colored folks were out on the porches in their swings, talking to their neighbors from house to house down and up the street in what looked like a half-mile-long, continuous, porch-to-porch conservation. The street was filled with kids running and laughing as they played. It looked as if most of the folks had found some joy in life in spite of their circumstances. We passed a small park that contained a baseball field, and in the dim light of dusk, I could see a game being played by a large group of colored boys about my age, mostly. Those who weren't playing were running and rough-housing and wrestling in the dirt, but all were smiling and having fun.

This was a world of unfamiliarity. With the exception of meeting one colored man Big Mark had fought with in the war and had taken me and my brothers to visit, I had never spoken to a colored person. I had never attended school with a colored boy. Our schools were separate. There was a separate waiting room for them at the bus station off Main Street—even separate water fountains for the colored folks to drink from. One water fountain had a large sign over it proclaiming "Whites Only" lest someone stumble by completely unaware and drink from the wrong fountain and succumb to some incurable disease. Wherever whites and coloreds were forced to mingle, there were similar signs so all the folks would know just what the rules were. I had always wondered, from the time I was a small child, why we had to live in this separated world. I was entering a world that, although different, caused me no worry.

Yet for as long as I can remember, my mother had taught us that white folks and colored folks are no different—that we were all God's children. I felt a measure of pride for having been taught that, and I felt no fear as Luke and I drove into the colored quarters.

Luke stopped his blue truck in front of a small house and killed the engine and stepped out. The tinned-roof house had a small yard surrounded by a picket fence that had been freshly painted white even though the clapboard-sided house was unpainted. Several well-tended gardenia bushes filled the thick, night air with a sweetness I could almost taste. On the edges of the wide, covered front porch were containers of all sorts, even old coffee pots, containing blooming begonias and daisies. It was obvious that whoever lived here cared a great deal for things living and beautiful. At one end of the porch, sitting in a weathered oak porch swing, was an old colored woman. Luke spoke to her.

"Annie Mae, you look absolutely beautiful," he said, enticing a charming, bright smile from the woman.

"Luke, you always know jus' how t'make me feel good, now don'cha?" she replied, and laughed. "Let me fetch a glass of tea 'fo you and Buddy go traipsing off'n 'em hills? Fo' the life of me I don't see how y'all find pleasure chasing 'hind a bunch o' hound dogs out 'ere in'a dark."

"I'd love some tea. Two glasses, if it ain't too much trouble. I got somebody I want you to meet." And to me, still sitting in the truck, Luke said, "Charlie, get out and come meet my friend, Annie Mae."

I had been mesmerized by the welcoming feeling emanating from the small home, and I was intently aware of Luke's interaction with the lady in the swing. I was more curious than surprised when Luke stopped here.

"Sure thing, Luke," I said as I stepped up on the porch.

"Well, bless yo heart, child," Annie Mae said as she saw me. "Come here and let me git a good look at you. Now ain't you one handsome boy." She stroked my hair back.

Annie Mae gave me a hug that almost brought tears to my eyes. She felt warm and soft and smelled like fresh-baked bread. Maybe it was the timing again, but I swear I hadn't been hugged by anyone the way this unknown colored woman embraced me that night. Maybe I was reading a lot into what was happening to me. Who knows, but I felt welcomed.

"Annie Mae, I want you to meet Charlie. Charlie, this is Annie Mae, Buddy's keeper. Where is he anyway?" Luke asked, turning his head, looking for his friend.

"He seen you turnin' the coner and went out to git Blue," Annie Mae said to Luke. "Now let me git 'at tea for you and young Charlie here. I bet he's thirsty," she said before disappearing through the screened door.

Annie Mae had a tender smile—like that of an angel, I imagined. She was a small woman, dressed in a long, dark cotton skirt, over which she wore a bright, flower-print apron. She was thin, with gray hair and black eyes that seemed to dance in her face, but what was interesting to me was how I felt in her presence— much the same as I felt with Luke. She put me at ease quickly.

It wasn't so much what she said but rather the way she said it. Almost like kindness was pouring from her lips as she spoke.

"C'mone, ol' man. Been a long, hot day but if'n you gonna drag me out in 'em woods agin, 'en let's git," a deep voice said from around the side of the house. He quickly appeared.

The voice I heard didn't match the man I saw. Buddy was almost as tall as Luke but skinny, and his overalls appeared to hang from his thin shoulders and didn't touch any other body part on the way to covering a pair of work boots that looked as large as small boats. His hair, too, was graying, and his dark face was weathered and creased.

On the end of a leash, his big hound was excited, pulling him toward the truck.

"You must be Chalie. Luke done tol' me 'boutchoo. Said he hoped you'as goin' wif us. Glad you'cn make it," Buddy said. "Pleased to finly meetcha, son," he said, shaking my hand. "'Is here's Blue, brother to Buck, Luke's dog, and 'ey sho' love huntin' t'getha."

Blue was a thick, tall bluetick hound with huge feet. When he heard the other two dogs in the truck, he almost pulled Buddy off his feet trying to get to them.

"Yes, sir. I've never been hunting before, but I'm excited about going, Mr. Buddy."

"Well, t'night ain't gon' be much. Too hot, but we gon' have fun. Kin you clim' a tree, Chalie?"

"Yes, sir. I love to climb trees," I answered, puzzled at the question.

"Chalie, let me tell ya sompin. Me and Luke bout t'same when it come t'the mister thang. Just call me Buddy, if 'at suits you."

"Yes, sir," I said, and Buddy laughed.

Annie Mae reappeared and instead of two glasses, she presented me with a glass jug of cold sweet tea with wedges of lemon and ice cubes floating in it.

"Charlie, I know 'ese two ain't waitin' fo' you t'drink a glass so's you better take 'is with you'ens and y'all can share. And you best watch out for the two of 'em. When they git ready to run w'those dogs they act like youngens 'emselves," she said, her radiant smile intact.

"Yes, ma'am, and thank you," and with that send-off we loaded ourselves into the truck with me in the middle.

I had a thousand questions to ask. Here I was, sitting between two old men in an ancient pickup with three hound dogs in back, headed to some far away mountain to get lost in the dark, and for the first time in years, I was on top of the world.

Luke headed down the street toward the highway. "Why did you ask me if I was good at climbing trees?" I asked Buddy. His question had been bothering me since he'd asked it.

"Well, Chalie," Buddy said, "here's the problem. Me and Luke done got too damn old to be shinnying up trees, y'see. And when one of 'em dogs gits on'a track o' a coon or a fat possum, the first thang's gonna happen's 'ey going straight up'a tree quick as they can git up it."

Still not understanding just why my presence in the same tree in the dark with a snarling animal was necessary, I asked, "Well, just what in hell am I supposed to do in the tree, then?"

"Don't worry, Charlie," Luke said laughing. "We'll show you, and I promise you'll have fun. Me and Buddy been chasing dogs and climbing trees most of our lives, and we always had fun doing it. You will too—just trust me."

It would be the first time in years that I would trust anyone.

I was sitting in the seat between these two old men, one colored and the other white, going to wherever they wanted to take me, completely without fear. I'd just met one a week ago, and I was just getting to know the other. As I listened to them discuss where we should hunt tonight, my curiosity got the best of me.

"How long have you two been friends?" I asked when there was a break in the conversation. I must have asked something funny because out if the corner of my eye I could see both of them smile at the question.

"All our lifes, young Chalie," Buddy said, chuckling. "And I mean all our lifes. Me and Luke been friends since we was younger'n you. When I's a little-bitty boy, a long time back and times was bad fo' my family, Luke's Daddy gave my Daddy a job on'is farm. Luke's Daddy helped my Paw git back on'is feet and they stayed friends from 'en on out. Reckin how old we was 'en, Luke?"

"I don't rightly 'member. Some'ers 'round four or five," Luke said. "I still got a old picture of us some'ers if I'cn find it. Hell, Buddy, you's skinnier 'en 'an y'are now," Luke said laughing and looking at his friend.

"So me and old Luke here growed up playin' in'a corn'n cotton fields and went and done everthang t'gether, cept go to school. We was just like brothers. We hunted and fished all'a time. Weren't too many youngens stayin' 'round near where we stayed, so most time's it' us, jus' me'n Luke." Buddy continued. "When Luke's Paw or my Paw didn't have us working on sompin we's playin' and climin' trees or swimmin' down'ta the swimmin' hole in'a crick and it didn't take long 'fore we was best friends. Been 'at way ever since. We even joined up in'a army t'getha when we got a lil older."

I was old enough now to know that the state of Georgia and most of the south, if not the entire country, was embroiled in a battle for the civil rights of colored folks. I had been insulated from most of the fight and what little I was aware of came from listening to the news or overhearing grownups. In spite of all the horrible talk and newsreels, I found myself between these two old friends, both of whom were completely unaffected by the storms of deeply held conviction on both sides. They seemed to be ex- empt from the ravages of the hate-filled social diatribe.

As Luke's old pickup made a left at the highway and we head- ed toward the hills, I was aware of what a special night this could be for me. I had found a mentor, possibly two. In spite of the social debate, or maybe because of it, I was being exposed to a re- lationship between these two men that had risen above the color of their skin. I was now proud that my Mother had believed the way she did and had taught my brothers and me to believe that we were capable of rising above discrimination as she had. There came a feeling of accomplishment with this knowledge.

"Did anybody ever get upset that the two of you were such good friends?" I asked them.

"Oh yeah," Luke said. "Ever since we was little, somebody has had something to say about it. Me and Buddy both had our share of scrapes to deal with cause we was friends, but we didn't much give a damn 'bout that, did we, Buddy?"

"Naw," Buddy said, laughing, "butchoo 'member how skeered we was 'at night 'at farmer caught us huntin' on'is place and got so mad when he saw we'as differnt colors 'at I thought he's gon' shoot us bof. He'as madder'n hell at you n'when he seen 'at me'n'you was t'gethea, I knowed sompin bad 'as fixin'ta happ'n."

"What did happen?" I asked.

"Well, he skeered hell outa us is what happ'nd. At old farmer's standin' 'ere shakin', wif 'is shotgun pointed right at us n'me and Luke looking at one'nother, 'en back at 'im and all'a sudden, he lowered 'is gun'n tol' us we better be gettin' hell outa 'ere. He walked off, shakin' his head mutterin' sompin, but we really didn't care much 'bout what he'as saying. I wished you could'a seen us, me and Luke tryin' to set the co'n on fire, headin' tow'd home, fast as our skinny legs'd tote us."

They both laughed so loud about that memory that I found myself laughing along with them.

We had been driving for twenty minutes when Luke said, "Here we are, Charlie." He then turned the truck off the Rome highway onto a small dirt road that immediately shot up into the hills. After a few minutes of Luke negotiating the ruts and potholes of the well-worn logging track, he pulled into a clearing and stopped.

"Awright, Chalie, time fo' me to learn'ya how t'do what we been talkin' 'bout," Buddy said, handing me a large flashlight. "You foller close'hind me and Luke and don' git too fer back. When'a dogs git'a trackin' they'kin be quick. Don' need'ta worry 'bout nuttin' out 'ere 'cept'a snake, but wi'me'n Luke out front, you gon' be okay." Buddy reached into the truck's glove box and pulled out a .22 caliber pistol.

"Jes' in case we come-up-on a rattler," Buddy said. "Oh, by the way, Chalie, this here's the same old .22 I's toting 'at night me and Luke thought we was gon' git shot," and he handed it to me. "Mind tote'n it fer me?" Buddy handed me the beat-up old pistol.

"Yes, sir," I said, swelling up a bit, amazed. If this was the same gun he'd carried that night, then he had kept if for sixty years, at least.

Luke was behind the truck talking to the dogs and said, "Y'all ready?" to which Buddy hollered, "Turn em loose," and all three hounds leaped from the tailgate and tore a path through the dark woods, their noses to the ground, with the three of us in pursuit, following behind in the beams of three powerful flashlights.

The night was dark, with no moon, and for the first few minutes, the hunt was relatively calm and the dogs were easy to follow—then all hell broke loose. All three of the hounds started-ed bellowing at the tops of their lungs, and the pace picked up quickly.

"Keep up with us, Charlie," Luke hollered back at me. Every couple of minutes we'd stop so Luke and Buddy could determine which direction to take and the best way to get to the dogs.

We crossed large gullies and went around and over fallen oaks and through briar patches—as if the two old, experienced hunt-ers had reverted to young men, they deftly leaped and jumped and climbed in front of me, taking care that I could manage behind them.

When the dogs seemed to stop running and the bellowing was coming from one location, Luke and Buddy, breathing hard and sweating, exchanged a determined glance and smiled and Luke said, "They done treed, Buddy." And to me, "Let's go, Charlie."

We followed the sounds of the dogs and in a few minutes came to a small clearing. The dogs were all gathered around a large sourwood tree, standing on their hind legs with their front legs reaching as high up on the tree as possible. It looked like the hounds were going to climb it. They were looking up, alternately jumping down and running in circles around the tree and howling as loud as they could at whatever was above them. I was covered in sweat and my jeans were covered in brambles and briars. Luke and Buddy were in a similar condition but didn't seem to care—this is what they'd come for.

"Shine yo' light up 'ere Chalie, so's we'cn see what we got," Buddy said calmly. I did as he asked. In a minute I spotted the red eyes of a fat raccoon looking down at us.

"Well now, mista' coon, how'ya been doin' 'is evenin'?" Buddy asked the snarling raccoon who was perched precariously on a limb about thirty feet up in the sourwood. We were all gathered around, soaked in sweat and breathing hard with all three lights shining up at the coon. The dogs seemed to be in their glory. They had accomplished what they'd been trained to do and were obviously happy about it. I still had no idea what was gonna happen next, but I was caught up in the sweaty excitement.

"Now Chalie, 'is's whur you cm' in. 'Member me askin' if you'cn climb'a tree?" Buddy asked. "It's put-up o' shut-up time, boy."

"I can climb that tree okay, but what am I supposed to do once I'm up there?"

"Well," Luke said, "I want you to get below the coon and shake the top of the tree till you shake him out and the dogs'll do the rest."

"What do you mean the rest? The rest of what? What's gonna happen then?"

"You fixin'ta see. Now be careful gettin' up 'at tree." Luke gave me a boost to reach the lowest limb, and the climbing was easy from there. I was apprehensive at the prospect of doing what Luke was asking, but I trusted that it was something he'd done himself probably hundreds of times when he was younger. I wasn't about to chicken out now.

As I climbed higher, Buddy and Luke kept one light on the coon and the other on my next choice of limbs to guide me to the hissing beast. What a beautiful animal, I thought, when I approached him from below. But as I closed the distance between us, the coon didn't seem to want me to come any closer. He hissed and spit and scampered even higher.

"Boy, he's a fat'n," I hollered down. Looking down, I was blinded by the beams of the powerful flashlights pointing up. "What do I do now?"

"Stand up on'a limb you on'n see if you'cn shake 'im loose, but hold on tight," Buddy hollered back at me through the howling of the dogs.

"Alright, here we go," I hollered. I was feeling more than a little trepidation as I stood and began shaking the treetop with both arms. As I looked up at the illuminated raccoon, I could see him trying to gain a better hold on a different limb, so I gave the tree one last violent shake and he slipped. He was falling, grabbing at every limb he passed, tumbling so close to me that his ringed tail brushed my face on his way to the ground.

Luke and Buddy had put the leashes on the dogs and from my perch in the tree I could see why. When the coon hit the ground, all three hounds leaped on top of the now furious animal and without control over their dogs, the coon would have been killed quickly—or so I thought. In fact, the opposite was true. I had a bird's eye view of the violent melee below, and as the fur began to fly, it appeared that it was the coon who was getting the upper hand on the dogs.

Luke and Buddy stood off to the side, holding the long leashes, watching the ruckus as I felt my way down the tree to get a better look at what was happening. Down on the ground, I stood close by Luke's side, mesmerized by the sight, respecting the ferocity of the coon. The dogs were whimpering and hollering as the smaller animal bit and clawed in defense of his life.

All three of our lights were shining through the thick cloud of dust the animals had kicked up. The sight and sounds of the violence before us was remarkable. The smaller coon balled up and the dogs were having trouble getting their mouths on him. Just as one of them began to bite the animal, the coon would reach out with his small, sharp claws and draw blood from the dog's nose. The offending dog would retreat and howl in pain before rejoining the battle. After a minute of the violent spectacle, Luke and Buddy began pulling the dogs away, and the fat raccoon tore a hole through the brush and disappeared into the dark woods.

"Wow," was all I could say at first. "I had no idea that a raccoon could fight like that. Do you think the dogs hurt him?" I asked.

"Well," Buddy said, "he ain't no worser off'n the dogs. Whatever bites and scrapes any of 'em got'll heal soon enuf."

Buddy and Luke were checking to see that the dog's eyes hadn't been damaged and in a minute announced that all was well. Their noses were bloodied, but they didn't seem to be bothered by it. Prancing around slinging slobber into the air, they were as excited as ever.

From here we walked back toward the truck—"to git past the scent o' the coon," Luke said. When we crossed the dirt road, the howling started again. The dogs were released, and they soon treed, but this time it was a possum instead of a coon. I climbed the tree, not to shake the animal loose but to get a better look. Buddy said that she might have young'ens around somewhere so they didn't want me to shake her out.

"Wrong time o' year, Chalie. Ole' possum ain't gon' fight like a coon. 'Em dogs'll make quick work outa her. Wait'll it's colder 'en the woods'll be full o' fat possums. So many you ain't gon' be able to tote'm all."

"What do you mean Buddy, by tote'm all?"

"Is winter, when is good'n cold out, we keep 'em possums 'n some coons, too, 'n fatten 'em up and sell 'em fo' folks t'eat. You'cn sell mo' possums 'an we'cn catch. We'll bring tote sacks and fill 'em up and bring 'em back wif us and put 'em in a pen and feed 'em till they good'n fat. Me'n Luke'll show ya when'a time's right. How's 'at sound t'ya?"

"Sounds great," I answered, wondering why someone would want to buy, much less eat, a possum. I had no idea that this would later turn into an enterprise.

With Buck and Susie and Blue on leashes, we made our way back to the truck. The dogs dutifully bounded up and into their crate, and Luke closed them in. We stood at the back of the truck and shared the jug of tea that Annie Mae had fixed for us. Warm sweet tea never tasted so good.

To me, the night had been a satisfying adventure. The experience was more gratifying than I had imagined.

"Well, boy, y'done good. You said you c'climb 'n you sho did a good job. Me and Luke'll take you wif us all'a time, if'n it suits you," Buddy said.

"Yeah, that's alright with me. I want to go whenever you go."

We talked all the way back to town, mostly about Luke's and Buddy's experience of growing up.

Tonight felt like the beginning of something for me. It was after one in the morning, and I was bone tired, bleeding, and sleepy, but I felt like a part of something again. It wasn't like being a part of my family, when my mother and father were alive, but I had a warm feeling of being wanted. These two old friends had welcomed me into their world, and it felt good. I would soon feel that I had been blessed by the presence of their influence and mentoring. It had been a good night, and there would be hundreds of these good nights over the next few years as both these men were destined to impart their wisdom and experience to me.

After we dropped Buddy and Blue back at their house, Luke and I returned to our home on the hill and we stopped and returned Buck and Susie to their pen and unloaded the crate.

"Charlie, I'm glad you went with us."

"Me too, Luke. Thanks for letting me go."

"Come on now, son. I'm gon' leave m'truck here, and I'll walk you t'the dorm," Luke said and we headed across the circle together.

"I'll see you tomorrow," he said as I opened the door to go in, but as he turned, he said, "Oh, by the way Charlie, if you ever need someone to talk to about anything, I'm always around. Okay?"

I don't know why Luke said that to me—it's as if he knew that I had been needing to hear that someone would listen—that I'd been searching for just the right person that I could talk to.

I knew then that one day I would talk to Luke about everything that had happened the night that had sent me here.

My body was sore and tired from running through the woods and climbing trees, and while looking up into the night sky from my bed beneath the window I had Big Mark's small green Buddha in my hand. As I rubbed its smooth surface with my fingers, I hoped that my sleep would be filled with dreams of the future and not my past.

# 9. Luke's First Lesson

"I NEED TO ASK YOU SOMETHING, LUKE," I said as I walked into the shop the next morning. "You remember telling me I could talk to you about anything, right?"

Luke was stooped over a tractor with a wrench in his hand. He turned his head and smiled at me.

"Well, good morning, Charlie. Sure thing, son. Ask away," Luke replied.

"And good morning to you too, Luke," I said.

"Now, about that question."

"Just what is a nigger?" I asked him.

Luke stopped abruptly. He stood and turned to face me, wrench in hand.

"Where did you hear that, Charlie?" Luke asked with a puzzled look on his face.

"I was talking to some of the boys on the dorm, and one of 'em said that colored folks are niggers—all of 'em."

"Have you ever heard that word before?" Luke asked.

"Yes, sir, I've heard it before, but nobody's ever told me what it means. Just what does it mean?" I asked him again.

"Let me ask you something, son. Did your dad or mom ever talk that way?"

"No, sir. Mom always told us that God made us all equal—that it didn't matter what color a man is. My Daddy used to carry us to see friends of his who were colored—men who fought with him in the war, and we'd play with their kids. I never heard either of 'em use that word, but I heard other folks say it before—grown-ups and kids."

"Reach over there and hand me that hammer, if you will," Luke asked.

Luke bent over and banged on something near the tractor's engine, then stood again.

"There we go," he said, his task finished. He wiped the black oil from his hands with a dirty rag and tossed it on the work-bench.

"I thought that some people just always used that word whenever they talked about colored folks."

"Well, Charlie, some of 'em do," Luke said. "Grab us chairs from over'ere in the coner, and let's sit a spell."

The shop's chair selection being rather slim, I drug two old rickety wooden chairs around the tractor and we both sat down. The two chairs, especially Luke's, creaked and popped while de-ciding if they could hold the weight imposed upon their well-worn legs.

Luke pulled a tobacco pouch from the top pocket of his over-alls. After deftly retrieving a three-fingered chaw and placing it in his mouth, he rolled the pouch up and put it back in his pocket and brushed his hands together, wiping them off.

"Son," Luke began, "They's a whole lot wrong in this world."

"Yeah, I already seen some of it," I said.

"And one of the problems is'at folks are just afraid of so much. And the sad part about being so scared is it robs a man of the joy that life has'ta offer."

"What are folks so afraid of?" I asked.

"A whole lot of thangs, Charlie. You 'member telling me how y'all went to the Methodist Church when yo' folks was alive?"

"Yes, sir."

"Here's a good example for you—the Methodists and the Bap-tists don't git along so well sometime, and both of 'em are scared to death of the Catholics, and Lord have mercy if you ever talk about the Jews. Now the only reason these folks don't love one another is because they belong to different chuches. Even though they all worship God, Charlie, they let the differences between how they worship—the thangs they do in their chuches—create an air of fear amongst 'em just 'cause they don't do everythin' alike. Instead'a all of 'em just loving the same God, they think their way is the only way and they criticize the others for not believing just like they do."

As Luke continued, I listened intently, wondering what he was getting to.

"I don't know why, son, but just because something or somebody's different from us, it don't set well with most folks," Luke said. "Now you take something as obvious as the color of a man's skin—for as long as I been here, folks have been afraid of that difference. Le'me ask you something, Charlie—did you have a good time yesterday with me and Buddy?"

"Yes, sir," I said exuberantly. "I had the best time I ever had, probly."

"Did it matter to you that Buddy's a different color than me'r you?"

"No, sir, not one little bit."

"Now, here's what I believe's the biggest part of the problem—most white folks never took the time to get to know any colored folks like Buddy and Annie Mae. Me and Buddy grew up together, son, and played together, and we never knew we was a different color till somebody told us. All we ever knowed was that we was friends. And, to this day, I'd give my life fo' Buddy, and he'd do the same fer me. They ain't no cause, son, to be afraid of another man 'cause he looks different from you or worships different or comes from somewhere different. You understand?"

"Yes, sir, I do," I told Luke.

"Right now, in our country, they's a whole bunch of fear and hate goin' round cause a lot of folks don't want to believe that my friend Buddy and his lovely wife deserve to be treated like me and you, just cause they don't look like us. They didn't let me and Buddy go to school t'gether, and they's still lots of places that Buddy can't go 'at I can, cause he's colored. I know 'at's wrong, Charlie, and so does Buddy. But 'cause I love my friend, I don't go nowhere he's not welcomed either. And that brings us back to your question—just what does the word nigger mean?"

Luke stood and walked over to the workbench and spit in an oil can and brought it back to his chair and sat down again.

"That's a hateful word, son. That word was born out of hate, and it'll always represent hate. It was created by those who live in fear of what's right and long overdue. There ain't never a time to use that word that'll ever be right," Luke said.

"How did it ever git so bad," I asked.

"Most folks don't like change, Charlie. They wanna keep thangs the way they always been, and when it comes to colored folks and the change they deserve, it scares 'em to death. Those are the folks who use that word, son—the ones who are scared to death about the changes they see coming. Now if a man's a Christian and believes in God, it's impossible to hate another man for any reason. Yet they's a whole bunch of so-called Christian folk who don't want colored folks to be equal. Am I making any sense?'

"Yes, sir. But I still don't know why it's so hard for other people to understand."

"Well, son, I don't know why either. It's hard to figger, other than the fear of change. Buddy's people been fighting their battle a long time and some good thangs are gonna happen soon, we hope. But I believe if most white folks would take time to get to know some colored folks then we might hurry the whole thang along."

"I sure do like Buddy," I said. "And I really like Annie Mae. She made me feel good being around her—sorta like I used to feel around my Mom. She sure is a sweet woman. I bet she can cook good, too."

Luke laughed.

"Well, you really took to Annie then. She gonna be proud she made you feel so good. I reckon she liked you too, boy. Now they're your friends, Charlie, and you'll never find anybody that'll love you like they will. They'll be a blessing in your life just like they are in mine. And, yes, she sho can cook good. I bet if you play yo' cards right, she'll treat you to some o' her cooking one day."

"When we goin' huntin' again, Luke?" I asked.

"Won't be long, son, and you gonna go with us ever' time, okay?"

"Thanks, Luke."

I liked the way Luke called me son all the time. I knew that he wasn't my father, but he had become a shelter from the storm. The chaos that reigned around me was quieted in his presence.

I had discovered more than just two friends in Luke and Buddy—I had been drawn into their world—a world of tenderness and compassion that sparked the birth of hope—something I'd become used to living without.

"As a matter o' fact, I need to see Buddy about something. You wanna ride with me?"

"Boy, do I," I said.

"Well, load up then and we'll go pay Buddy and Annie a visit."

I came to realize later that Luke had no business with his friend that day—his only reason to see them was because he knew that I wanted to. It was only one of the thousands of unselfish kindnesses that Luke bestowed upon me. I would learn from watching and listening to him over the years. Slowly, my world became a less hostile and confusing one because of him.

# 10. Moving Up

THEY MOVED US AROUND AS WE grew older. If you lived at the Home long enough, you would live in several different dorms, and this would be the third and final move for me.

I was a teenager now, and the bittersweet day had arrived for me to make my final move. I was headed to the cottage—the last stop for the boys on the hill. I would live here until I graduated from high-school and moved on to a life beyond the Home.

It was bittersweet because I'd be leaving Danny behind, at least for a year. My brother and I had lived in the same dorm since coming here. But the day would come when he, too, would move up with me, and we'd both spend our final few years at the cottage, together. But now, at least for a while, we'd be separated. It was bittersweet, too, because I'd no longer be working for Luke—I'd be put to work on the Home's dairy farm.

But Luke had assured me that we'd still be seeing each other every day and that he and Buddy and I would continue our hunting. I'd grown fond of Luke—he was the only grown-up I trusted.

So it was a different group of boys in a different dorm doing different chores. All wasn't brand new, though. Except for a few of the oldest boys, I'd grown up with most of the fourteen who lived in the cottage. Bobby already lived here, and as luck would have it, I'd be moving into the same room with him. And as he'd done my first morning at the home years ago, he once again appointed himself my new mentor. Having lived in the cottage for all of six months and thus being 'experienced,' he'd show me the ropes.

Homer Gant and his wife, Millie, were the resident house parents. I'd soon discover that Homer ruled his kingdom with an iron fist.

Homer had come from Alabama years ago. He had been hired to manage the dairy farm and herd. Later, he and his wife were offered a position of residential house parents, and the two had been managing the older boys since their arrival. Millie did her best to act as a mother to the boys in the cottage, except for the most serious disciplinary problems—that's where Homer's heavy hand came into play.

Homer was a big man with a big belly. He was maybe six feet tall with dark, graying hair that made him appear older than his forty years. I had been told that no one had ever seen him smile. He was hated and feared by the boys in his charge.

The Home owned two-hundred-sixty acres, most of which—beyond the dorms and administration building on the hill itself—was pasture. The dairy and hay barns were connected to the hill by a gravel road that twisted its quarter-mile length along a ridge, where it ended in a gravel circle at the cluster of barns. It was a working farm with a chicken house and rabbit hutch and several gardens and an orchard, all of which I'd soon become familiar with.

The boys in the cottage were all sizes and shapes—skinny and fat, tall and short—but we acted and lived as a band of brothers, undeniably connected by causes and conditions imposed by someone else.

"Four o'clock comes early," Homer told me. "You goin' to the barn with us in the mornin' to learn how to milk cows. Most o' 'em boys turn in early. I suggest you do the same."

Those were the first and only words he'd said to me, and then he turned and left. Homer Gowans didn't have a warm and fuzzy side.

There was a crew of six boys who milked—always the same group—and I'd been chosen to join them. The kid whose place I'd be taking had turned eighteen and was leaving the home soon.

I was nervous about what the morning would bring. Little did I know, when I turned in, that I had good reason to be.

It was a rude awakening—Homer pounded on and then opened the door, turning on the light.

"Let's go, boys," was all he said before walking out of our room.

I saw Bobby get up and walk into the bathroom. I laid my head down on my pillow and fell back to sleep.

"Whap!" That was the loud sound made by the leather belt impacting my butt beneath the sheet, and I jumped straight up in the bed, screaming in pain.

"What the hell!" I hollered, still groggy.

"When I come back aroun' you better have 'em boots on and yo' feet on the floor." Homer said. "Now git 'em on and les' go—we got cows t'milk."

Bobby re-emerged from the bathroom.

"Yeah, o' Homer's a sumbitch," Bobby said, when I told him what just happened. "Wait till you meet Eustace—he's just as bad."

"Who's he?" I asked, while frantically pulling my boots on.

"Eustace's Homer's brother-in-law from Alabama, and he works at the dairy, too. He's a dumb sumbitch and worse'n Homer."

My first day was leaving a lot to be desired, but the worst hadn't even happened yet. My butt was still smarting as we exited the cottage.

Six of us piled into the back of Homer's pickup and headed down the road past the small ball field, where we intersected the gravel road to the barn. Mike and Clayton, the oldest boys in our group, had been making this same trip every morning for years.

The entire herd of Jersey cows was milked twice daily without fail. And now, unfortunately, I would be one of those doing the milking.

Joe-Bob and Cecil emptied from the back of the truck first, followed by me and Bobby, then Mike and Clayton.

"C'mon, Charlie," Bobby said, "and me and you'll go get the cows up."

The dairy barn was a white, one-story, long cement building with a large, fenced concrete slab corral on one end.

Homer sat in his truck while the other boys disappeared into the dairy, and soon the entire area was ablaze in light from poles positioned around the barns. A huge hay-barn was connected to the dairy barn by a long cement walkway.

Bobby led me down the walk, past the hay-barn to a gate, beyond which stood sixty-eight cows, anxiously waiting to be fed and milked.

"Better move aside, Charlie," Bobby advised as he slung the gate open. The herd orderly filed past in single file, stepping from the dirt onto the concrete, their brass numbered tags hanging from chains around their necks all clinking in unison.

"We gotta count 'em all," Bobby said loudly above the noise of the restless herd. "If'n they don't all come up from the pasture, we gotta go fetch 'em."

The cows were now corralled on the slab outside the dairy barn and a double sliding door opened which allowed eight cows at a time to file in. With military precision, they each turned and placed their heads through metal gates, which closed around their necks and restrained them temporarily while being fed grain in the cement trough in front of where they stood.

I was amazed. I mean how in hell does a cow know how to do all this?

"Let me show you what's next," Joe-Bob said. "The first thing you gotta do is warsh 'em. Grab 'at bucket of soapy water and wash her udder 'fore you put the milkers on'er"

Once the udder was properly washed and the four-pronged milker was attached, the suction did the rest. The white milk was sucked from the cow's udder and was propelled up and through a glass tube, into another room and ended up in a large stain-less-steel vat to be chilled. Rotating in the center of the chilling vat was a large, slow-moving wooden blade that kept the cream from rising.

A large Jersey, with number forty-nine around her neck, walked into the barn through the thick, clear plastic strips that hung in the open double-doorway.

"Hey, Charlie," Mike hollered, getting my attention. "How 'bout washin' her and attaching the milkers," he said, nodding his head toward old forty-nine.

Mike was the largest of all the boys—muscular and tall at six feet. An athlete and a fastball pitcher on our high school baseball team, he was well liked by all of us. His parents were dead, too—he was an orphan like me, so we got along well. I thought nothing about his request.

"Sure thing, Mike," I replied, grabbing the rubber soap bucket and sponge.

I was about to receive my initiation to the world of the dairy barn—I just didn't know it.

I approached forty-nine from the left, moved the bucket close, and squatted beside her. Just as the warm, soapy sponge hit her udder, I noticed her left hoof move backward a few inches. Then, with lightning speed, she thrust her leg forward as far as she could and kicked out and backward, planting her immense hoof squarely in the middle of my shoulder, spinning my entire body backward six feet. I came to rest on my back on the wet, sloping concrete floor, wondering what the hell just happened.

I was lying there looking up at the white ceiling and suddenly became aware that all the boys in the barn were gathered around me, busting a gut laughing.

"Welcome to the dairy, Charlie!" Joe-Bob said through his laughter, grabbing me by the hand and pulling me to my feet. You'd have thought watching forty-nine kick me half way across the room was the funniest thing they'd ever seen.

"Don't get pissed, Charlie. The same thang's happened to all of us, by the same damn cow," Clayton said, laughing.

"Yeah, welcome to the barn," Cecil chimed in, grinning.

"Yeah," Bobby said, "consider it your initiation."

It was still pitch-black outside—not even five yet, and I'd already been blistered with a leather belt and kicked on my ass by old number forty-nine.

It was gonna be a long day.

# 11. Lanny

"How'd everything get so screwed up, Luke?" I asked, looking as always for the answer about why my brothers and I had ended up here. "How come God lets things happen like He does?"

"Well, we'd better sit down for this one," Luke said, motioning me over to the swing that hung from a big limb of the massive white oak that stood outside the shop. The way that the fat limb grew around the rusty chains supporting the weathered swing gave the appearance that the links had sprouted from the big tree.

"Life ain't never been fair, Charlie. I really don' know why the world's in'a fix it's in, but I do know one thing—God, in His infinite wisdom, gave us a privilege He don't even give His angels—that's the power to choose how we gon' live. You'cn do good or you'cn do bad. So, you'cn blame God all you want to, but the truth o'the matter is we mess thangs up, not Him."

He stopped for a minute and peered off into the distance.

A prolonged silence followed by a deep sigh. Finally, he continued.

"Now, some things happen 'at 'ere don't seem to be no answer for. You take my daughter, for instance. Me and Louise spent years wondrin why she had to die so young. We thought we'd been living right. We went to chuch. We prayed and did all we's sposed to. I didn't make 'at choice f'her to die no more'n you chose this life for you and yo' brothers.

"Way I understand it is 'at I gotta choose 'tween believin' God's in charge o' all this mess or He ain't. We cain't have it both ways, son. It's an either-or and 'ere ain't no in between. Either

God is or He ain't. Now here's the tricky part for lots o' folks—you understand what faith is, Charlie?"

"Maybe," I said.

"Well," Luke said, "faith's b'lieving in something you can't see or touch or taste or feel. But in spite of all that, you know it's real. They's a whole bunch of folks who cain't believe in God just because they can't shake His hand and have Him o'er fo' supper. I happen to believe 'at, even though me and you and the rest of the world cain't answer why things have happened in our lives, that He does have the answer."

"Then when do I get an answer to my question? When do I find out why?"

"Now I said it was tricky, din' I? Maybe you don't get an answer at all, least ways not the way you'd like to."

Luke had talked to me about this before. Maybe I was incapable of understanding what he was saying. Nothing had sparked the birth of any faith for me. Not yet.

"I know you mad about what hap'ned that brought you'n yo brothers here, but come one day you gonna b'lieve what I'm sayin'. In yo' own time, and maybe not 'xactly like I'm talking, but sooner or later you gonna git yo' answer. But ain't nobody gonna walk up and tell you why things hap'ned like they did. It ain't 'at simple. But one day you gonna have yo' answer, and I hope I'm still 'ere when it comes fo' you."

Luke turned and looked at me. Beneath his thick, gray hair, his furrowed face broke into a big smile and he said, "I promise you that, okay?"

"Yeah, okay," I said, smiling in return.

"Charlie, there's something else that I want to talk to you about."

"Sure, Luke. What about?"

"You know how tough it is fo' some of you boys when you first git 'ere. You, more than most of the boys I've met in the past sev'ral years, showed up here with a heavy burden yet somehow you managed to deal with it."

I thought, *True, but without your help, I may have not been able to deal with the pain at all.*

"Well, they's a new boy coming to live 'ere in a few days. He had a real hard time, and I want you to try'n hep him some. Maybe knowing what happened to you and yo' brothers will hep him feel better 'bout being 'ere—he lost his daddy, too. Just talk to 'im and if you can, be his friend."

"Sure, I will."

Luke had never asked me to look out for another kid before, and I figured there was a good reason he's asking now. Luke was always looking out for the hard cases—as he'd done for me and was looking to do for this new kid, there must have been hundreds of others he'd done the same for. Although he'd never been trained in any field other than farming and common sense, his gentle, no-nonsense ways had proven valuable.

I didn't ask what circumstances concerned the new boy, and Luke didn't volunteer any information.

The truth was… most of us orphans tried to help the new kids anyway. Every now and then a kid would arrive who was so damaged and angry that he made it hard for anyone to accept him. Sometimes they got over it, sometimes they didn't—or they found some other outlet for their madness.

One day, we had a new arrival named Randy who wouldn't so much as talk to anyone for days. He would stand in a corner by himself and dance. He just stood there and danced in one spot for hours at a time to whatever music he heard playing on the radio. He would dance after the music was turned off, as if he could still hear it in his head. No one could get through to him. And finally, one day, he was gone. We never knew where he'd gone. We were curious for a couple of days, but we'd seen so many kids come and go that we just stopped wondering about them.

The lunch bell rang, and I stood and started for the dining hall.

"You go ahead, Charlie, and I'll be over in a few minutes. Oh, by the way, the new boy's name's Lanny and he's 'bout yo' age, just so's you know."

Another week passed and I'd almost forgotten about the new boy. Then, one afternoon, an official-looking car pulled into the driveway.

Lanny was a tall, skinny kid with long brown hair. When he stepped from the back seat of the car he glared at the two men who'd brought him here. Because the car had an official-looking logo on the doors, all of us wondered where he'd come from.

I walked to the car and introduced myself to the new kid. It was obvious that he trusted no one. Nonetheless, as the two men in suits talked to Homer, I helped carry one of his two suitcases into the house, where he would be rooming with Fuzzy.

"Thanks, Charlie," Lanny said as I was leaving his room, leaving Fuzzy behind with him.

The next few weeks saw Lanny become one of us, and at Luke's urging, I spent as much time with him as I could. He worked at the barn with us, and although we became good friends, I never asked him about the circumstances that had brought him here. All I did was tell him about my journey—how my brothers and I had come to live here and how I still suffered with the hate that had been born that final, terrible night in our house. I shared everything with him, leaving nothing out.

And then, one day, after listening for weeks to my tales of heartache and broken dreams, Lanny finally opened up. We were alone at the hay barn tossing hay bales down to awaiting calves when he suddenly asked, "Why the hell do these things happen... I mean how do things get so screwed up that people just want to hurt other people?"

"I don't know," I said. "I've wondered that myself. Maybe we'll never know and that's just the way it is. Luke told me that there are things that happen to everyone that we just have to accept. I guess he's right. Maybe that's the best we can do. I still hate my Dad for what he did though—maybe I will forever, who knows?"

We made our way down from the loft to the ground where we'd thrown the hay. The mid-morning sun was beating down now. After scattering most of the bales amongst the calves, we pulled the last two into the shade of the barn and sat down on them.

"Do you know why I'm here, Charlie?"

"No, I don't," I said, "and you ain't gotta tell me nothing if you don't want to."

I had been waiting for this moment.

"It's bad—really bad," Lanny said.

"Worse than mine?"

He nodded. "I want you to promise that you ain't gonna tell nobody about this, okay?"

"Yeah, I promise," I answered. "You know what? I've never told anyone except you and Luke why I'm here either. It's never been anybody's business. I just feel like no one needed to know. But when I told Luke about it—well, since then it ain't been such a big deal. He told me that to talk about it would be healing."

Lanny sat there on his bale of hay, seemingly contemplating whether he wanted to even think about what had happened, much less talk about it. Then, he began.

"I came here from the reformatory where I'd been living for a long time. Those were the men who brought me here that day."

"That explains the car," I said. "I'd wondered about the emblems on the doors."

"My dad was a drunk just like your dad, Charlie. But it was worse'n that."

It was a couple of minutes before he spoke again. He had a vacant look in his eyes as he struggled with his demons. I waited for him to speak. I knew how terrible memories could be.

"I wish I could have stopped him, but I couldn't. I wish it had never happened." he said in a whisper. I drew closer so I could hear him.

I waited for a while as he remained silent.

"You wanted to stop him from doing what?" I asked.

"From hurting me, Charlie. He'd been hurting me for a long time—almost as long as I can remember." He finally raised his head and looked at me with tears welling in his eyes. "Do you know what I'm talking about?"

His shame wouldn't allow him to describe the events other than to say that he was hurt. I took it to mean that his Dad had been abusing him sexually in some way—otherwise he would have just told me what the problem had been. I had heard another kid talking about the same thing, describing the terrible things that had happened to him, in the same way.

Lanny stood up and began to pace around in the grass.

"I'm so sorry," I said. "I think I do."

Lanny's vacant stare into the distance returned. He never looked at me. Instead, he whispered, "It started when I was little," he whispered. "He came in drunk and slapped my mom around for a while, then came into my room and held me down while he hurt me."

There was a brief silence, and then he shouted, "He'd grab me by my hair and shove my face down into my pillow. My own fucking Dad did that to his own son; can you believe that shit?" The tears that had been held in check tumbled down his face.

He held his arms out in front of him as if begging for an answer and then screamed, "Can you believe that shit?" The tears flowed unabated now.

I walked over to him and he laid his head on my shoulder and sobbed. I did all I could do which was to hold onto him for a minute. Then he turned away and started pacing again, all the while crying his eyes out.

"He didn't stop, Charlie." His voice was raised again, now. "The son of a bitch didn't stop for years. I told my mom about it, and you know what she did? All she fucking did was tell me that I'd better not tell anybody or he might kill us both. She was as bad as him. She knew about it and didn't do a goddamn thing to stop it."

Lanny stopped pacing and returned to his seat on the hay bale. He put his elbows on his knees and his face in his hands and was quiet. A few minutes passed before he continued.

"I told him that one day he would be sorry that he'd ever touched me, and he was so drunk that he just laughed."

There was another lengthy pause. "I hated that fuckin' bastard."

One of the weaned calves walked over and nudged Lanny's knee with his nose. Lanny pushed the animal away. A dozen other calves came close and stood watching us.

"About a year ago, he stumbled in again and I could hear him beating my mom. She just stayed there and took whatever he dished out. But I wasn't gonna let that bastard hurt me ever again."

Lanny looked at me. His expression had changed. When he stood up again, the pain and anguish on his face had been replaced by intensity and anger. He wiped his face dry with the bottom of his T-shirt.

"When he was done beating my mom that night I heard him coming down the hallway to my room again."

Lanny paused, wringing his hands together. He then pushed his long hair back over his head with both hands, mustering the courage to continue. His face was wet with sweat and tears.

"I picked up my Little League bat I had in the corner, and when he opened the door I swung it as hard as I could and caught him right across his forehead and he collapsed in front of me. I hit him four or five more times in the back of his head before my mom came in and stopped me. I was screaming, and I told her to get the hell away from me or I'd do the same to her."

He sighed and exhaled loudly. He was quiet for several minutes, but he wasn't finished.

"In a minute my mom checked him, then looked up at me."

"She said, 'He'll never hurt you again, son. Your father's dead,' and then she just turned and walked back to her room and closed the door behind her."

Lanny seemed relieved that he'd finally told someone about his demons. He lay back on the bale of hay and looked straight up into the pale sky. The tears were gone now. I understood—my tears had also stopped when I finally reached the refuge of confession. There was silence for a few minutes, and then a large flock of crows found a temporary resting place in top of a nearby, tall, dead oak and cawed loudly.

"What happened after that night?" I asked, stunned by his story.

"The police came and took me to jail at first," he said. "Some men kept taking me into a room, and for days I had to tell them what had been happening in our house—what my Dad had been doing and how my mom had known about it. Oh, she denied it at first. But when they put us together, she finally admitted to them that she knew what he'd been doing. I never saw her again after that day—never even talked to her. I hope I never do. I hate her."

I don't know which is worse when you're a kid—losing your mom and dad the way I did or losing them the way Lanny did. I suppose the result is the same—there are no winners, only losers.

"They told me that they didn't know what should happen to me, so they sent me away to the reformatory for a while," Lanny continued. "I stayed there for almost a year, until somebody convinced some judge I shouldn't be in jail. That's when they sent me here."

As if the flock of crows had listened to enough anguish and despair, they silently took flight. I watched until they were out of sight.

I didn't know what to say to my friend. I was just a kid who'd been through a whole lot of crap like Lanny had. Maybe that's why he shared his story with me, though. We had both suffered in different ways, but the pain is the same. I suppose that after hearing about my suffering, he'd felt that he could trust me with his story. Maybe he'd felt some relief in talking to someone who had suffered as much as he had.

We both lay back on our hay bales and stared up at the clouds and waited until the pain and heartache began its slow retreat to that dark vault where our nightmares and terrible secrets and demons go to be safely stored away. Maybe the best some of us could ever hope for was that we could pile enough joy and happiness and good memories on top of the refuse that it could never rear its ugliness again—never lead us into the dark place that we feared more than anything.

I knew that Lanny's journey would be fraught with the same images of hell that had visited me in the beginning. I was a little sad that all I could do to help was to be his friend.

Our conversation that day was finished. From my own experience I knew that talking about what had occurred that night in his home had made him feel better. I also knew that it was going to be a long time before he talked about it again—if he ever did.

We became true friends that morning. We had shared our measure of pain with each other and promised that our secrets would be kept, and they were. I knew that something special was created when you bared your soul's darkest secrets with someone you trusted. I trusted him, and after that morning, I knew he trusted me.

As we finished our chores and began the walk back to the hill, I told Lanny about Luke and Buddy in the hope that he, too, might be able to discover the hope that I'd found in confiding in my friends.

That never happened for him, though—maybe his demons wouldn't allow it.

We never again talked about the conversation we had that morning.

# 12. The Railroad Yard

THE RAILROAD YARD BEYOND THE BOTTOM of our hill is a place of deep mystery. There were trains coming and going and being swapped out in the side yard by the mammoth, diesel-driven engines that made the yard a magnet for our curiosity.

The heart of the mystery, though, was the strange folks who could be found down at or around the train tracks—folks who could instill fear in the hearts of many an orphan kid who had missed the school bus and had to walk to town.

When we were younger, it was a gauntlet that we feared traversing.

There were days when I had to walk that way by myself and I imagined ugly, mean ogres lying in wait for me as I approached. I'd keep my eyes straight ahead—my step quickened and my heart beat faster until I was long past the tracks.

And there were several good reasons to be afraid. When the trains weren't running, the yard seemed consumed by an eerie, supernatural silence that had to contain more than a few ghosts.

But the train tracks were also the haunt of many a living ogre because that's where the dreaded Bagget boys could be found most of the time. And not only that, but just beyond the far side of the tracks was the haunted-looking house where Joe-Ricky and Pearl Whacker lived.

The Bagget boys were two brothers—well, they were spoken of as brothers but I'd never found any living soul who claimed firsthand knowledge of this. Indeed, I know of no orphan who'd ever had the courage to speak to them. They were never seen apart—where you would find one you'd always find the other, the two of them riding patched-together bicycles like a pair of fiends, and we orphans would travel far around the yard to avoid them.

It was reported that the older brother was named Ben and the younger J.R., but no one knew where this information came from. Maybe some orphan made it all up—the names, I mean, and everybody from then on just believed it because no one could ever really confirm what their true names were. I sure as hell wasn't going to ask them. In fact, I don't believe the Bagget boys could even talk—no one had ever heard them utter anything other than loud grunting noises that scared the crap out of us. So conversation, had one of the orphans even chosen to attempt it, was out of the question.

I believe the boys lived somewhere near the tracks but because they were always mobile, no one had determined just exactly where the pair called home. They were most often spotted at the railroad yard, yet from time to time they were seen down at the crossing on South Main making their way further down the rails before disappearing into a short, spooky tunnel through which the trains traveled.

Ben was tall and skinny with black greasy hair flowing down his neck. He rode a bicycle that must have been made for a kid because it looked too short for him. His knees would almost drag the ground as he pushed himself around on the bike as much as he rode it.

JR was shorter and wore thick glasses that made his strange, red eyes look huge. This only added to his terrifying appearance. The glasses had been broken and repaired with black tape and were secured to his head with a length of baling twine wrapped around his overly large cranium. He sort of resembled a Tootsie Roll Pop, with a huge round head mounted on top of his pencil-thin body. I sometimes wondered why he didn't just fall over from being top-heavy.

When Ben and JR spotted one of us walking across the triple set of train tracks, they would immediately stop what they were doing and the chase would be on. It wasn't a fast chase—I don't believe they were capable of much speed—but it was a chase just the same. They'd both raise their heads in our direction like a wild animal catching the scent of prey. After a few seconds of deliberate contemplation, they would begin a slow roll on their rusty old bicycles toward us, and our pace and heartbeats would quicken. JR was always carrying an empty Coke bottle in his right hand, and theories as to what he might do with it if he caught us were more than enough motivation to hurry the hell up.

Both of their bicycles were adorned with big, deep wire baskets that always contained an odd assortment of junk—coke bottles and hunks of pipes and bricks or any other item that might catch their eye. In the event that we didn't put a good deal of distance between us and them, or if they surprised us by lying in wait behind a caboose or a boxcar, the items at hand would rain down upon us, forcing us to dodge the hunks of debris and scramble to safety toward town or retreat back toward our hill. Only when we were out of sight of the dreaded fiends did we feel safe.

But, the Bagget boys were only the beginning of the gauntlet.

On the far side of the railroad tracks stood an old and large two-story house that at some point in its history must have been a handsome home for a respectable family. It had now fallen into disrepair, its paint hanging on for dear life to the siding planks that were popping loose all over. At first glance, the weather-beaten dwelling seemed uninhabited. All the windows on the second floor had long been boarded up. In the evenings, bats could be seen dropping from under eaves that, for years, had begged for repair. A ghostly ambiance resided here.

Was it a haunted house? Probably, we thought, or most certainly it should have been. Just for good measure we treated it as such. It stood next to Fletcher Street, and when we approached the place on the way to town, we kids crossed to the other side to avoid it.

Its crumbling appearance belied the fact that it was, indeed, occupied and its inhabitants were as threatening as the Bagget boys at the tracks.

Joe-Ricky Whacker had been living in the haunted house with his wife, Pearl, for as long as I'd had the misfortune of having to walk by it. When I was smaller, walking by his house was the most threatening end of the gauntlet. The Bagget boys weren't always around the tracks, but Joe-Ricky or his wife were always lurking somewhere about the eerie place. Even if they weren't there, I still had to pass their pack of mangy, drooling, sharp-toothed dogs, and that was scary enough.

Joe-Ricky must have seen better days at some point—his shoulder-length, greasy gray hair, or what was left of it, swirled around a bald patch, sporting more than a few scabs, and he was the proud owner of a beer gut that would have pleased Buddha. His pockmarked face was adorned with a crooked nose you'd hardly notice if you were close enough to see the three long and pointed teeth that were the highlight of his thin-lipped mouth.

Not to be out-shined, though, was Pearl, the princess of Joe-Ricky's castle. I wouldn't want the job, but with enough money and months of patient work, Pearl's vanished beauty might have been resurrected to the point of manageable unsightliness. Her waist-length rat's nest of graying-blonde hair was frequently entangled with twigs and leaves, leading one to surmise that she likely enjoyed sleeping in the woods or had recently been on a camping trip. She wasn't ugly beyond description yet, but without intervention, she would be soon.

I suppose that if the honest truth was taken into account, the day for her beauty's redemption had long since come and gone, and she was left to guzzle cheap whiskey with her loving husband for her remaining time on earth, which was regretful since she still had most of her teeth. Had she tried, she might have done better than Joe-Ricky.

Joe-Ricky's fearsome reputation preceded him, yet even the warnings I'd received prior to walking this path didn't prepare me for the "Terror of Fletcher Street."

The wide, wrap-around porch of the house had become a home to a collection of seedy, ripped couches and a variety of other tables and chairs in various states of furniture death throes—even an old mattress, whose stuffing was continually torn to shreds by their gang of mongrel dogs while fashioning themselves a comfortable place to spread their fleas.

I don't know if the dogs belonged to Joe-Ricky or not—the growling beasts were often joined on the mangled mattress by Pearl, who—I suppose—found the mattress inviting in spite of her four-legged companions who barely tolerated her presence.

Pearl was so well endowed in front that mention of her name almost always brought comparisons to the heifers we milked at the dairy—she certainly topped the charts of any of our young recollections. It was rumored that if the stars lined up just right and Pearl was fueled by the proper amount of whiskey, she wasn't adverse to displaying her whoppers, pulling up her stained old T-shirt and wowing us with a quick glimpse of her immense, pendulous womanhood.

I need to say, though, that the chemistry involved in such an event must adhere to a very precise set of circumstances, which did not include Joe-Ricky's presence. It was rumored that once upon a time one of the kids tried to get Pearl to display her hefty ta-tas by screaming, "Show 'em to us, Pearl," while a drunk Joe-Ricky was present. A brisk chase ensued and could have ended in disaster had Joe-Ricky not collapsed a hundred yards from his love nest and been carted off in an ambulance, teetering on the brink of a stroke.

To make matters worse, his rear end suffered severe lacerations from the shards of broken glass from the ever-present pint of whiskey he carried in his back pocket, which shattered when he rolled down the sidewalk.

The offending orphan, having been dispatched down Fletcher Street quite a ways by Joe-Ricky's growls and threats of death, never again attempted to entice a nude display from Pearl while Joe-Ricky was anywhere within earshot.

If I'm not mistaken, blood stains from Joe-Ricky's bleeding rear are still visible in the concrete today.

Having survived the initiation of fear and successfully avoiding premature death at the hands of the Bagget boys or Joe-Ricky and Pearl, I was somewhat buoyed by my accomplishment. I had, in a few years, grown large enough to protect myself. After the hundreds of perilous crossings across the feared railroad yard, I could finally walk through a free man.

The Bagget boys still haunt the railroad tracks. Curiously, they appear to have not aged a day since I was much younger. Unfortunately, the same can't be said for Joe-Ricky and Pearl. These days they're most often seen together on their front porch, where they've successfully usurped the dog's home on the mattress and made it their own. They recline there together, against one another's shoulders in loving bliss, while enjoying the foggy, fuzzy reality inspired by the ninety-proof.

# 13. Confiding in Luke

LUKE ASKED IF I WANTED TO go squirrel hunting with him on Saturday. I had grown so trusting of my friend that I would have spent every day with him had he asked. By now, after spending more than two years with him, the relationship felt more like that of a father and son. Maybe he needed that as much as I did, but he'd never said as much.

"I'll bring along a .410 f'you t'use," Luke said, "and I'll come by in the aftanoon to pick ya up," Luke said

"Anyone else going," I asked.

"No," he said. "Just me'n you. 'At okay w' you?"

"Sure is," I said

The November afternoon was accompanied by a chill wind. The pale blue sky was clear and the air was crisp as we headed down the hill in Luke's truck, his .22 and .410 hanging from the gun rack in the back windshield.

"Charlie, I'm gon' take'ya to a patch'a'woods 'at not a lot of folks know 'bout. I been huntin' squirrels here fo' fifty years. Me and Buddy just hapnt to stumble on 'is place, runnin' dogs a long time back, and I never took nobody else out 'ere. It's a special place f'me. When I lost my little girl, a long time back, I used to go out 'ere, sometimes with Buddy and sometimes by myself and just sit. It's a good spot to think and boy was I hurting back 'en. I'd sit out 'ere and wonder how come God allowed my little girl to die, and I'd cry like a baby. I'd be 'ere fer hours walking the woods. When Buddy and me went t'getha, he'd talk t'me 'bout my baby. He'd seen her almost everday of her short life and he loved her almos' as much as me and Louise did. And we'd talk and cry togetha, and I's grateful 'at I had a friend who's willin' t'shoulder m'pain wi'me."

Luke was talking to me about his feelings—something he'd never done before. I wondered why he was doing so now.

We passed through town and out into the county, heading north. The heater in his old Chevy fought a losing battle, but I was unaware of the cold autumn air blowing through the cracks in the old truck. Luke was speaking differently than he ever had so I was paying close attention. About eight miles from town, he turned left down Booger Hollow Road, then onto a narrow, overgrown dirt road which looked as if it hadn't seen any wear for quite some time. Finally, he slowed and came to a stop. The road ended here at a rusted farm gate. Beyond the gate, spread out before us, was a vista beyond belief.

We were sitting on a slight hill and beyond laid a mixture of bright green ryegrass pastures and large stands of hardwood thickets still displaying the remnants of the Georgia autumn's golden maples and the purple of the sweet gums. I understood, at once, why Luke found this to be a special place.

We both sat there in silence, listening to the breeze rustle the dried leaves that still clung stubbornly to their trees, as a red-tailed hawk cruised low over the field before us, trying to spook a rabbit from its hiding place. The spiritual essence of the place was palpable. Several minutes passed—then Luke spoke.

"They's a special beauty 'bout 'is place, Charlie. I feel closer to God here 'an I do anywhere else, even chuch. Maybe it's cause I discovered it soon a'ter I lost my daughter, and it was here, over the course of many months, that I began to heal a bit from my pain. I was mad at God when I first come 'ere, though, and I'd ask Him how he could'a let her die. Over and over again, I'd ask Him."

I was surprised at Luke's words. We were friends and I'd grown to love and trust him, but never before had he shared such intimate information with me. Then Luke turned on the truck's torn leather seat to face me and asked, "You e'er been mad at God, Charlie?"

Luke's question struck me with a force I hadn't felt since that horrible night five years ago. The denial that had protected me for so long vanished in the question he'd asked. Stunned for a minute, all I could do was nod my head. Then, my old friend reached over and squeezed my shoulder. I knew then why my friend had asked me to come here with him. He knew it was time and that I needed to heal, like he had healed. He gave me all the time I needed, and I just sat there with him, in the cab of the old truck, watching the wind blow. My mind filled with the memory that had impacted the lives of me and my brothers forever. What I'd tried so hard to forget, he was now asking me to remember one more time.

Finally, summoning forth what courage I had, I began.

"Yeah, Luke, I'm still mad at God," I said, unable to control my tears. Now I wept openly and unashamed, and I'd said it, finally—something that I'd privately known ever since that night. *I was mad at God.* The battle I'd been fighting with my banished God was still alive.

"It's okay to be mad at God, Charlie," Luke said, softly.

"Since that night, Luke, I've been telling God that if He was gonna let us hurt like we did then He needed to let us alone from now on and that we'd make it fine without Him." I struggled with my words and feelings. "Before my Mom died, she had been taking us to church and teaching us about how much God loved us and how great He was, and maybe He does and maybe He is, but when I saw the sadness in my brothers faces and hurt as much as I did, I became confused. I've thought about this a lot—I live on a hill with a hundred twenty other kids that He's left out in the cold, so tell me just how can a god who's supposed to be so great do that, Luke?"

I turned in the seat to face him, and I was spilling angry tears, not at Luke, but my anger at God was choking me and I could hardly breathe.

I could see the tears welling up in the eyes of my friend. He was hurting with me, much as his friend, Buddy, had hurt with him, decades before. Luke knew that this had been a long time coming, and he was willing to experience this with me. He was driving me to confront the thing that was holding me back, and he wasn't going to allow me to be alone when it happened. He knew pain, but he'd been able to overcome it, and it no longer ruled his life. I knew that about my friend and had, for a long time, wondered how he'd accomplished this. That was the purpose of the trip here today. It occurred to me that the sole reason we were sitting in his truck in this cold beautiful place was that my friend was willing to share my burden. He'd chosen this day for this purpose, and I didn't feel the loneliness that had become my hate's companion. I knew what was happening. In my soul, I knew it was time.

"Charlie, I'm so sorry f'what happened t'you and yo' brothers, and I know that I cain't make the pain go away," Luke said, wiping a tear from his blue eyes and weathered face, "but what I can do is to try to help you to understand some o' what happened."

There had been others who had tried to talk to me about that night, but my anger had only grown over the years. I'd internalized every ounce of the event. Most of the trauma had been pushed downward into the dark recesses of my memory. I still caught hazy glimpses of the carnage I'd witnessed in my dreams from time to time, but over the years I had made a conscious effort to banish that night from my memory. This day, however, would prove to be the day that the memory would gain new life.

"I can see it all, Luke." I had my face in my hands now.

"You can see what, Charlie?"

"I can see Big Mark with the pistol in his mouth, and I remember being confused and just as I asked myself why he was sitting there with the barrel in his mouth, his head exploded, and I remember being hit with pieces of something that hurt, and I WANT TO ASK GOD WHY HE LET MY DAD DO THAT! WHY GOD DAMN IT!" I asked.

We sat there in silence a minute longer.

"Let's get out of the truck, Charlie." Luke said, and we opened the doors and stepped to the front of the truck and leaned on the gate.

"The time's come to ask Him, Charlie," Luke said. He nodded up to the sky and said again, raising his voice this time, "Just ask Him. He's right here, right now, and He's listnin." Luke paused. "You've been wanting to for a long time. Look up to the Heavens and ask God why He let that terrible night happen."

I looked at Luke as I sobbed and realized that it was finally the time to find out.

I braced myself against the cold, rusty gate and looked up at the sky's fast-moving, thin clouds and begged.

"Why the hell did You let it happen? I don't know, and I really need to know, and I hurt so much, God, and my brothers hurt so much, and it makes me madder'n hell what happened to us!" I pleaded to the heavens for an answer as the blue of the sky swam in my vision.

Luke was by my side, and he turned to me and hugged me tightly to his chest and held me, and we wept together. We stood there for a long while, in spite of the cold wind, I felt the warmth of the love from my friend, and for the first time in a long time I felt security. It was the same feeling—almost completely erased from my memory—that I had felt in my Mother's presence. Since that night, everything in life had seemed temporary—everything except the love for my brothers. I had unknowingly allowed loneliness to dominate my world.

We stood there, side by side, Luke with his arm around me for a few minutes, not talking. The hawk made slow circles over the field.

"I asked the same question of God, Charlie, standing in almost this same spot, a long time ago."

"And what did He tell you, Luke?"

"That He didn't want me to hurt no more, Charlie. That He wudden gon' put more on me'n I could handle and 'at I was blessed. From whom much is taken, much will be given,

Charlie, and much has been taken from you and yo' brothers. God never left you. He knowed you'as mad, and He also knew 'at one day, you'd ask Him why, just like He knew I'd pose the same question to Him, long ago. But it was whiskey 'at made yo' daddy do what he done, not God. Fer a while, maybe it heped yo' Dad with his pain from seein' and doin' what he done durin' the war. I've seen liquor kill many a man, Charlie. 'At was a horrible time in his life and the lives of millions of good men and women and many of 'em who fought in 'at war was damaged forever, in differ'nt ways.'

"Why didn't God just stop him from drinking, Luke?" I asked, still crying, with Luke still holding me.

"Because, son, God gave us the greatest gift of all. A gift 'at he don't even give His angels, and that's the gift of choice. We can choose how we want to live or die. We can choose to be happy or sad or mean or nice. We can hate our lives or choose to change what makes us unhappy. It's the greatest gift we e'er been given. We can love, or we can hate. But God is pure love, Charlie, and He wants only the best for all of us. Unfortunately, whatever pain yo' Dad was goin' through, he treated with whiskey and 'at only made things worse. I've been checking on what sort o' fella he was and by all accounts, he was a good man."

I had never heard anyone say that about my Dad before. In the beginning, when we first came to the home, I'd been able to remember the good times with Big Mark before the drinking changed him, but what he had done that night overshadowed all those memories, and finally the resentment began to grow. I had searched for someone to blame, and I needed someone to hate.

Luke released me. He stepped back and held me by my shoulders. He then took a handkerchief from his pocket and wiped my eyes, then his, before putting it back in the top pocket of his overalls.

" C'mone, son, les' tak'a walk," Luke said, as he unlatched the rusty chain and opened the gate.

We stepped into the verdant field. The rye was knee high, and the wind was making waves in the tops so that the whole field waved before us like the back of some slithering reptile. We waded through the field toward a thick grove of hardwoods some three hundred yards away. One hawk was joined by another and the two of them sailed in circles, high above our heads, screaming something to each other, their red tails clearly visible as the sun bore through the feathers. Neither of us spoke until we were halfway across the field.

"Probly the most important thang I ever learned about in life, son, is fergiveness. Only two folks in'a world know 'is 'bout me—my friend Buddy, and my wife, Louise, but I did the same as yo' daddy did after I lost my little girl." Luke and I kept walking toward the grove as he continued. "I was in such pain that I went to a friend o' mine who made some good liquor and I bought me a gallon. I'd find me some place to nurse my wounds and just sit 'ere in my truck drinking till I passed out. Louise would send Buddy out looking fo' me when I didn't come home, and he'd find me down by some river or out in the woods, sommers. Sometimes, he couldn't find me, and I'd be in my truck, passed out, and I wouldn't come to till morning. That went on fer a long time, Charlie. My loss was great, but what the liquor did t'me was worse. There were times, when I's drunk, 'at I thought the world might be a better place without me in it. Those were dark days then.

"When I finally come out' it, with a lot of help from Louise and Buddy, I had to deal with the aftermath. I knew 'at Buddy'd always forgive me, but what I'd done to Louise took a terrible toll. She'd suffered as much or more'n I had, but she hadn't crawled into a jug of liquor like I did. She was forced to sit at home and cry, all alone, and I should'a been with her. Oh, she forgave me, and understood even, she said, but it was a long time 'fore I could forgive myself. The reason that I've never taken another drink is 'cause of what it almost allowed me to do, and would have done if I'd kept on. One day, son, you gon' find forgiveness in your heart for your father, and when you do, it's gon' feel like a burden's been lifted off yo' back. With all I done wrong in my life, God's shown me, through His Grace, that forgiveness is a must and that judgment is His and His alone." Luke paused for a minute and then asked, "You think you'll ever be able to forgive yo' daddy, Charlie?"

We had reached the stand of trees, and stopped. I hadn't answered Luke's question yet, but he said, "Come on, let's find a place to sit fo' awhile.

The grove was mainly large red oaks with a few white oaks and hickories. The level ground was carpeted with a kaleidoscope of colored leaves. The late afternoon sun was shooting beams of light through the dwindling canopy, and we stopped and took a seat in this living cathedral.

"I can almost forgive him for what he's done to me," I said, "but I hurt so bad for my brothers. They sure didn't deserve any of this."

"Nor did you, son, and don't ever forgit 'at. I see you with 'em and I know you try to protect 'em and that you'd make their pain your own if you could, but here's something you may not be aware of: not one of them saw what happened 'at night. They probably ain't been affected like you have. Sure they miss your parents, but I've been on the hill for a long time and I've seen similar circumstances, where brothers remember thangs different. You happened to see the entire event and had to take care o' yo' brothers afterward, and it's you who've suffered the most. I've spent some time with 'em, and they gon' be okay. You got to trust me 'bout 'at."

There was a rustling in the dried leaves, and Luke looked at me with his finger to his lips. "Shhh," he whispered, and pointed in the direction of the noise. I looked and it became apparent that the creatures were squirrels, but they were unlike any I'd ever seen before. They were red and huge. They were as big as housecats and they barked as they chased each other around and up and down the tree they were in.

Luke tapped me on the leg to get my attention.

"Fox squirrels," he whispered.

I'd never heard of a fox squirrel before. *This is what he'd brought me here to see. This is one reason this place is special to him.* We watched as they put on a show for us, then several more appeared and joined in the ruckus. They came close and were right above our heads, and we both lay down on our backs to watch them play in the limbs above us. I was impressed to know that old Luke still had enough boy in him to lie on his back in the woods, like a kid, and enjoy the spectacle. For the first time this afternoon, I had a smile on my face. Just as quickly as they'd appeared, they took off for other trees to play in. With a loud groan, Luke sat up.

"I been watching 'ese old fox squirrels f'years. I never seen em anywheres else in Polk County," Luke said, smiling.

"I'm confused. You said we were going squirrel hunting, but…" then Luke interrupted me.

"Not for these rascals, Charlie. They're too much fun to sit here and watch. You may not believe it, but me and Buddy have come here and watched 'em fer 'ours. I don't tell nobody that, though. Most folks would think it a little crazy, two old men lying on their backs in the woods, watching squirrels play in the trees," and we both laughed.

The sun was nearing the horizon and the sky began to change color.

"Let's head to the truck," Luke said. "But first, see if I got any leaves in my hair," he said laughing, as he turned his back to me. I was laughing too, as I brushed the leaves from his head. "Louise is gon' wonder just what I've been up to if I come home with leaves all o'er me," and he chuckled.

As we walked, Luke pointed to the edge of the pasture. In the twilight stood three does with fawns, which had already lost their spots. We watched them walk into the field in search of dinner.

"After today, son, you'll begin to heal. Remember what I said about making choices?" he asked. "Charlie, you're gonna live a good life if you want to. You can choose to let what happened to you determine who you are, or you'cn choose to forgive yo' dad fer what happnt and move on. 'At don't mean you condone what he did, but it does mean 'at you can live a life free from the bondage of what he did. I had to come to grips with the same issues you're facing, and I found a lot of peace on the right side of fergiveness."

When we reached the gate, we stopped to catch our breath then closed the gate behind us and leaned on the truck. I was overwhelmed by the events of this afternoon with Luke.

"I miss em, Luke. I miss both of them something awful. I wish you could have met my Mom just once. You would have seen why I miss her so much. As much as I hate what my Dad did, I miss him, too. He wasn't always bad, Luke."

"No, he wasn't always bad, Charlie, and I know you'll always miss 'em both. I still miss my baby, but she lives in my heart and mind, and I know 'at one day, I'll have her in my arms once again, just as much as I know 'at you'll see your Mom and Dad again," and we both wiped away one final tear.

"Charlie, I want to tell you one more thing before we head back."

"What's that, Luke?"

"I've come to know you quite well since you come here. I always wanted God to bless me and Louise with a son, but He had other ideas and that's fine. But you've brought blessings t'my life, and if God had given me a son, I'd hope that he'd be just like you, Charlie. You a good boy and you gon' make a fine man. I'm sorry for what sent you here, but I'm glad this is where you ended up."

I just thought that I'd shed the last tear, but this time they were tears of joy. I had just heard the highest praise I would ever hear in my entire life, and it came from a man whom I respected more than ought to be allowed. I had lost one father, but I felt like I had found another.

"Luke," I said, laughing through the tears, "if we could have chosen who our fathers were gonna be, then I would have chosen you, too," I said, as he started the truck and began to turn around. I smiled as I watched him try to dry his face and turn the wheel at the same time.

There was a lot of healing for both of us that day. We witnessed the birth of a trust and a relationship that would flourish for years. Luke had wanted me to ask God why this had all happened, and now, I believe that part of the answer was sitting in the old blue truck with me. I knew in my heart that meeting Luke was the best thing that had ever happened to me.

# 14. The Bees

OLD MAN PICKETT'S FARM HAD BEEN supplying hay for the Home for years. We supplied the labor to harvest his hay, and in return, the Home would take half of it. The long, narrow hayfield was bordered on one side by Cave Spring Road and on the other by Cedar Creek and ran for at least a mile that way.

Sitting in the middle of the hundred-yard wide, flat stretch of good Bermuda hay stood an old home-place where today, like all the other days when we worked in this field, we had stopped for a water break and to escape the blistering sun.

The solid, unpainted, old house under whose porch we now sat had been kept up and used for storage. Old Mr. Pickett had put a new tin roof on the place, and now the rooms were stacked from floor-to-ceiling with sacks of wheat and excess hay bales.

We had been working here since daybreak. Homer had driven six of us down here in the back of his pickup, with Eustace following in the hay truck. The plan was for them to leave us here to work and come back around noon or so. The hay truck would be left for us to load as the bales came off the baler.

The two trucks had parked on the paved road at the field's entrance. As I walked over and opened the gate, Homer and Eustace walked into the field to survey the coming day's work and, I suppose, to make some highly intelligent decisions as to what we were to do after they left. They thought of themselves as Generals and us as their conscripts. It was a sad reality, but we harbored no sympathy for them—we just wanted them to leave.

It was then that Carl decided he had to pee, so he stood right in front of the hay truck and did his business, jumping back into the bed of the large truck when he'd finished.

When Homer and Eustace returned and were giving us our orders, Homer noticed the wet puddle in front of the hay truck where Carl had just relieved himself.

"'At truck run hot comin' down hea'?" he asked Eustace.

"Naw. was running just fine."

"Well, looks as iffn' we got a problem o' sum kind," Homer said as he pointed to the wet pool on the pavement under the front of the big truck.

"Huh," was all Eustace said, grunting and dropping to one knee to examine the wet puddle. "Don't look like it's got no an-nee-freeze in it," he remarked as he bent over. Then he touched the pee with his fingers, rubbing them together under his nose for a smell.

We knew it was too late now to say anything about the situation. We'd be worse than dead if Homer or Eustace knew what was happening. We were looking amongst ourselves, trying not to burst out laughing—then, the unthinkable happened.

"Don't taste like it, neither," he said after he touched his fingers to his tongue.

That was it. That's all it took for the six of us boys in the back of the truck to lose control and start howling as if a huge dam of hilarity had ruptured and spewed forth the funniest flood on earth. We laughed until our sides were aching and we were rolling in the bed of the big truck.

Homer and Eustace stood there looking at us like we were idiots or something worse until finally the painful laughter began to subside.

"Just whatso god-damn funny?" Homer asked, looking at us with a condemning stare.

"Well, nothing but a stupid joke Bobby told us," I replied, sputtering through the remnants of gut-busting laughter.

"Time fo' you boys to stop 'is and git to work. They's a cooler full of wautah 'ere in the truck. You better have all that hay raked and baled and sum o' it loaded, time we get back. Now git to it."

And that was the beginning of a long day in the hayfield. It was better than most beginnings, though.

Buoyed by the humor of the day's beginning, we worked hard for the next several hours. Mike and Clayton were driving the tractors until the hay was raked and baled, then we all pitched in to load the bales into the truck before we stopped to cool off. While we were all sitting in the shade on the porch of the old home place in the middle of the hay field, Bobby decided to explore the inside of the old house. In just a few minutes he returned and poked his head through the front door-way.

"Charlie, com'ere a minute," he said to me.

My best friend, Bobby, was always finding something to show me. More times than not, his discoveries were worth investigating so I followed him inside to a room in the back corner of the house that was half-filled with grain sacks.

"Com'ere," he said, "and listen."

He put his ear to the wall and motioned for me to do the same, and then he knocked on the wall. I quickly jerked my ear away as something inside the wall buzzed loudly.

"What is that?" I asked Bobby.

"It's bees, Charlie. Honeybees, millions of 'em," he said excitedly. "And the whole damn wall's full o' 'em. I saw 'em goin' in and out from the outside, and I knew they had to be in here somewhere. They ain't no telling how much honey they got made in that wall."

"Yeah," I said. "And what about it?"

"Well, we could come back down here and rob 'em somehow."

Now, Bobby didn't know anything about robbing honeybees and I sure didn't either, but lack of knowledge had never stopped him before.

"Listen, Charlie, all we gotta do is smoke 'em somehow. I heard sommers if you put smoke on 'em they calm down and we can take all the honey we want."

I knew that Bobby wouldn't stop now until the bees had given up their honey. He had that crazy look in his eyes—the wide-eyed look that always preceded one of his risky plans. The big picture was already hatched in his head. All that was left to determine were the details.

"Alright, I'm in," I said, wondering, once again, why I'd even entertain the thought of buying into one of his far-flung adventures. These things never turned out good.

We could still hear the bees buzzing in the wall. Maybe they were listening to us hatching the plan for their demise, maybe not, but the buzzing was suddenly louder.

We surveyed the size of the job and determined what tools we'd need and decided that we'd formulate the rest of the plan later. We'd keep it to ourselves; just the two of us would attempt to pull this off.

Later, in our room at the cottage, all Bobby could talk about was this coming Saturday when we planned to rob the bees. He did some research, looking up honeybees in the *Funk and Wagnall's* encyclopedia, and by the end of the week we were ready. I had asked Luke if he knew anything about robbing bees, but all he could tell me was that beekeepers used a device that would squirt smoke where it was needed. We were orphans and didn't have a smoker and didn't know where to get one, but we did have what we thought were the necessary tools, which consisted of a hammer and crowbar and two five-gallon buckets for the honey.

The big deal was the smoke, and Bobby was relatively sure he had solved that problem. His plan, which he described as "foolproof," was simply to use a metal paint bucket and some oily rags. We were now ready, for better or worse.

Saturday arrived and afternoon chores were completed. When we had several hours of free time, we snuck off the hill, tools and buckets in hand, and walked through town trying to be as discreet as possible so none of the townsfolk would call and rat us out. Old man Pickett's farm was just a mile past town, and we made it there and into the old house with plenty of time to spare.

"Okay, what do we do now?" I asked Bobby.

"Let me get a fire going in the can then you can start prying some boards loose. I'll try to keep as much smoke on 'em as I can, and then we'll see how they act. Okay?"

"Sure," I said. I had no idea what we were getting ourselves into, but I was willing to find out.

Bobby quickly had a fire going and a small cloud of smoke began to billow from the smoldering, oily rags. I wedged the crowbar tip under a board and pried until the rusty nail heads were loose and used the hammer to pull them the rest of the way out.

The bees were buzzing louder than ever now, and it was with great trepidation that I made the next move—I grabbed the end of the eight-inch wide plank and pulled it free from the wall. Now the bees in the wall knew what was coming and they were pissed. Huge chunks of honeycomb tore loose, stuck to the board, and the first of thousands of bees followed.

"Smoke 'em, Bobby. Throw the smoke on 'em as much as you can," I hollered.

Bobby was doing all he could as fast as he could with the smoke. He was blowing and puffing at the smoke as it emerged from the can. He looked like he was going to pass out. His whole head was red from blowing the smoke into the wall, but it seemed to be working. We'd both been stung a couple of times, but we had expected to be.

I pulled a few more planks loose, and we were both stunned when confronted by a bee nest as big as the entire wall. I had no idea that honeybees could fill up such a huge space, but here they were—millions of them, and they weren't happy at all. There were so many bees flying inside the room that it was getting hard to see. For some reason they were congregating around our faces, which was something we hadn't planned for, but what the hell did we know about robbing bees?

"START GRABBING THE HONEY, CHARLIE," Bobby shouted, and I reached into the wall and started pulling out whole, long chunks of honeycomb and dropping it into one of the buckets. By now we had already been stung a dozen times but the smoke, until now, had done a good job at keeping the bees calm. Pulling out the heavy sections of comb changed all that.

The ever-growing cloud of bees didn't care if they were in a cloud of smoke or not. They attacked like miniature kamikazes, covering our exposed skin with stings. Even our clothes and hair didn't stop them. They were in our ears and trying to go up our noses. I became afraid to open my mouth to speak after a bee had flown in as I began to say something to Bobby. I spit the bee out and pulled honeycomb out of the wall as quickly as I could until the buckets were mostly full of mangled, dripping, sticky hunks.

I was covered in honey up to my elbows, and Bobby had chunks all over him where I'd slung it while swatting at the stinging horde. Everywhere the honey was, there were thousands of bees covering it—blobs of bees all over us and growing by the second.

We were quickly reaching the point of diminishing returns. If this was a war, then the honeybees were winning. They were letting us have it at a frenzied pace now, stinging faster than we could fend them off.

Bobby was flailing wildly with his paint bucket in one hand, sparks flying everywhere, and swatting over his head with the other, trying, unsuccessfully, to keep the bees at bay.

"HOLY CRAP, CHARLIE, LET'S GET THE HELL OUTA HERE," he screamed. He dropped the paint bucket, grabbing one of the honey buckets and tore out of the room, swatting away as many bees as he could on his way out the front door with a small cloud of the demon bees in pursuit.

Following Bobby's quick exit, I dropped the tools and with the other five-gallon bucket of honey in tow, I scrambled toward the door with a dark, menacing horde following close behind, surely seeking retribution for the wanton destruction of their formerly peaceful home.

As awful as it was, with the bees still following and stinging, I looked at Bobby, fifty yards ahead of me across the field, and I busted out laughing. The buckets of honeycomb were heavy— at least forty pounds each. Bobby was struggling with his as he tried in vain to distance himself from the dark cloud of persistent kamikazes. He was standing in the middle of the hay field, half way to Cedar Creek, jumping with both arms flailing wildly. Had anyone driven by and seen him, they would surely have reported to the authorities that someone had escaped from an insane asylum.

I didn't fare much better. I had no idea how far the bees might follow, but they showed no sign of giving up the chase.

The further from the house we traveled, the fewer the bees we had to deal with, and when we finally reached the creek, only a couple of dozen still attempted to inflict pain. After emerging from the thick fog of bees in the house, we were ecstatic to have to deal with just these few.

Bobby had reached the creek before me and was on his knees in the water trying to alleviate some of the pain from the stings. I dropped my bucket on the bank and quickly joined him, splashing cold water over my head.

It was then that we looked at one another, and both of us busted out laughing. Bobby's head looked like a pumpkin—swollen, with orange and red splotches all over his face, and I couldn't contain myself, although I knew I probably looked the same. I fell over backward in the shallow creek, laughing my butt off. I was still in that position, on my back in the water, when Bobby spoke, in a very serious voice.

"Oh, hell, Charlie," he said.

I thought that maybe he was having trouble with some more bees till he uttered something again in a tone I'd rarely heard him use, so I raised up in the water to look at him.

"Oh, holy shit," he said quietly while he was pointing back at the old house we'd just escaped from.

I slowly turned my head. We were a sight—swollen and red-faced, sitting on our butts in the water in the middle of Cedar Creek, gazing at a sight that neither of us had anticipated, but one that struck horror in our bee-stung hearts.

White smoke was billowing out of every window in the old house. We sat silently in the water a hundred yards away, and there wasn't a damn thing we could do to stop what we both knew was coming.

To make matters worse, the reason the old place had stood as long as it had was because every board in it had been cut from heart pine. When I was pulling the heavy boards off inside, I could see and smell the fatwood, full of pine resin. Every board in the old place was probably the same. The place may as well have been a powder keg.

A minute later the first flames emerged and began to lap at the wooden siding. In only seconds, the entire structure was a gigantic orange fireball with flames leaping thirty feet above the new tin roof.

We stood in the creek, amazed at the conflagration before us, and then we heard fire truck's sirens coming from town. Someone driving by must have spotted the fire—you sure as hell couldn't miss it—and reported it.

"We'd better be getting hell outa here," Bobby said. We grabbed our honey buckets and moved into the woods on the far side of the creek so we could still watch the unfolding scene and not be spotted.

And what a scene it became. The fire truck arrived and, after driving through the gate, positioned itself fifty yards from the house while the inferno was still at its peak. By this time, Cave Spring Road was crowded with cars, and a hundred folks lined the fence to witness what was big news anywhere. As word spread, more cars and people arrived until it seemed like half the county was there to witness the magnificent blaze. Several folks were taking pictures.

I guess that the firemen determined that nothing could be done—they just encircled the house, watching it burn, not even attempting to extinguish the inferno. What seemed like an eternity was probably no more than ten or fifteen minutes, and then the walls collapsed, almost in unison, blowing embers in every direction, which the firemen quickly extinguished. Where the sturdy old homestead once stood, now there was nothing more than a pile of scorched tin and the fieldstone columns that once supported the structure.

That apparently being the climax, most of the folks returned to their cars and departed.

Old man Pickett arrived and drove through the gate. Soon, no one but he and the firemen remained.

"It's really weird, ain't it Charlie?" Bobby said, his eyes glued to the scene across the creek.

"What is?"

"Well, all we come down here fer was a l'tle bit of honey and now this l'tle bit o' honey's allat's left. The whole house is burnt up an all'a bees in it. Seems kinda sad, don't it? I bet that old place didn't know 'is gonna be its last day on earth."

"Bobby, nobody can ever know that we were here," I said, both of us still watching from our vantage point in the woods. "And I mean nobody, ever. This is a secret we gotta take to the grave with us, okay?"

Bobby, still staring at the smoldering ruins replied, "That's sho as hell okay w'me."

We made our way home that afternoon by a very circuitous route. We must have walked for ten miles to avoid going through town, but we finally made it with our bucket loads of honey and comb and hundreds of bees all mixed together. We lied and told everyone that we had robbed a bee tree way off in the pasture and, surprisingly, they all believed us.

A few days later, when the next edition of the *Cedartown Standard* hit the streets, right there on the front page was a large, color photo of the fully-engulfed structure. Under that, a caption read, "Spectacular Fire Levels Historical Home." After we saw the newspaper, Bobby and I swore to one another again that neither of us would ever tell a soul about that day.

As it turns out, the old home place was almost two hundred years old and may have been the oldest structure in the entire county. Who could'a known?

I walked over to Luke's shop the day after the paper came out and found him sitting in his chair looking at the front page.

"Quite a fire, huh, Charlie?" Luke asked, and he lowered the paper a bit and smiled at me.

"Yeah, Luke. I suppose it was," and I couldn't help but smile back.

He cut the photo from the paper and pinned it right below John Kennedy's picture on the bulletin board in the shop. He never asked me anymore about it nor did he ever mention it again.

The picture from the paper would stay there, pinned to Luke's bulletin board, for the next few years and always elicited a smile from Bobby and me, but neither of us ever mentioned that day again. Luke was kind enough to never ask what Bobby and I had been doing at the time of the fire, but I could always tell by his sly smile every time the subject arose that he knew exactly what had happened that day.

# 15. The Rat Killing

WE WERE HEADED OUT TO COLLARD Valley, to the other farm owned by the Home. Five older boys lived there full time with the Stitts, the old couple who ran the place.

Homer had summoned Bobby, me, and my brother, Danny, after we'd finished at the dairy barn. Now we were riding in the back of the flatbed truck, wondering what sort of task he had planned for us.

The Stitt farm, as it was known, was eight miles northeast of town. The land there was gently rolling hills and pastures. The farms were large and separated by a good distance. Most of the farmhouses sat perched on the tops of the small hills, with long gravel drives.

Horace Stitt was never seen without his cowboy hat. We'd joked that he probably even slept with it on at night.

And his wife, Vivian, was a big woman—a hard working country wife with a heart as big as the rest of her. Although they had no children of their own, Horace and Vivian treated the orphans living with them—Billy-Wayne, Timmy, Tommy, B.J., and Curtis—with the same loving care they would have if Vivian had borne them herself.

All the boys who lived here were chosen for their size, it seemed. Timmy and Tommy, two brothers, and BJ and Curtis were all big kids, and living here meant that they had to drive the machinery the farm required. They had been taught to operate the tractors and combines and the corn-picker as skillfully as Horace could. He had instructed them well, and Vivian made sure they were fed well.

As the morning began to heat up, we spotted activity at the massive red barn a hundred yards north of the house. Homer turned off the main driveway and headed there.

We hopped down from the back of the flatbed and were met by all five of the boys. There were grins and handshakes all around as Homer and Horace walked off into the barn to discuss the day's plans.

"Y'all sho nuff gon' have sum fun, t'day," Billy-Wayne said, grinning from ear to ear.

"Homer ain't tol' us yet what we gon' be doing," Bobby said.

"The hell you say," Timmy said, laughing. "I guess he's a wantin' to keep all 'at fun a secret."

"Come on, now. If you know, then tell us," I said nervously, beginning to wonder what lay ahead.

"Alls I know is it has sompin to do wif the old corncrib, and I really don't know what else," said Billy-Wayne. "I just heard Mr. Stitt talking to Homer on the phone, saying sompin 'bout it. 'At's all I know, I swear."

"That damn old crib's a hunnerd years old. What in hell could we be doin tuit?" Bobby questioned.

We'd worked around the old structure for years, never paying much attention to it. With its weathered logs bleached almost white by the sun, the old corn crib showed its age. It was built like a cabin, with notched ends holding the logs tightly in place. It had only spaces between the logs, instead of chinking, so air could blow through and dry the corn. Seeming to defy gravity, it was perched somewhat precariously on field-rock columns. In spite of its decrepit appearance, the old structure had stood its ground for at least a hundred years under its rusty, hail-dented tin roof.

"Well, we'd all hep you'uns if we wudden gonna be plowin," BJ said, "but we all gotta be doin' sompin else."

"Yeah, we'd hep, if we could," Timmy said, grinning as if he knew what we were about to do.

Homer emerged from the barn, driving the Massey-Ferguson tractor, and then threw three hoe handles, minus their hoes, to Danny, Bobby, and me.

"C'mon, boys, and foller me," Homer said, "let's go git this thang started."

We shrugged our shoulders at the other boys, still wondering just what task awaited us, and followed behind the tractor in the direction of the corn crib, two hundred yards away on the edge of a wheat field.

When we arrived, Homer backed the tractor to the front of the structure and dismounted.

"What are we gonna do with these handles, Homer?" I asked.

"You fixing t'find out. Chalie. I want you t' unwrap 'at chain on the back of the tractor and wrap it 'round 'at stack of rocks under the front coner of the crib. You boys fixin' t'see jus what 'em handles are fo'. Chalie, you git in front. Bobby, you get the left and Danny, go over to the right side."

Tightening the chain around the first column of rocks, Homer screamed over the noise of the engine,

"NOW, BOYS, KILL EVERTHANG 'AT COMES OUTA THEAH. DON'T LET NUTTIN GET AWAY."

Bobby looked at me with fear in his eyes and hollered, "WHAT IN HELL'S HE MEAN BY THAT?"

It became obvious that the corn crib was coming down. The rock foundation, which until now had withstood the test of time, began to lean. Homer, now turned around in the tractor's seat, gunned the throttle, and the first stack of stones tumbled from under the hand-hewn sill they supported. The old logs began to creak, whining a mournful plea as if begging us to stop destroying the crib. The old structure shook but didn't fall.

As dust spewed out between the logs, something curious began to happen—the whole inside of the corn crib appeared to be crawling.

Bypassing the middle column, Homer backed the tractor to the opposite corner in front and again, with the chain re-tied, yanked the stones down. A billowing cloud of dust appeared, but the creaking storehouse, unbelievably, didn't give way. The corn crib was still standing, balanced on its middle, supported in front by only the center stack of rocks. The architect from a bygone era would have been proud.

While Homer shifted the tractor and chain to the remaining front stack of rocks, Danny walked over to me and pointed inside.

"Charlie, what's that jumping around inside there?" he said, peering through cracks between the logs, squinting his eyes to get a better look through the thick fog of dust.

With the third and final assault from the tractor's log chain, the remaining front stack tumbled violently as the entire bulk of the ancient structure collapsed, flinging the rocks outward, scattering the front wall of logs toward us like tiddlywinks while belching a thick cloud of corn dust. When the front fell, the back wall tumbled from its supports and collapsed the remainder of the building into a muddled mess of debris.

We instantly understood what Homer had been telling us and realized why he'd scattered us like he had.

The crib had been in use as late as last winter, and the leftover corncobs still contained plump grains. Buried in the massive pile of corncobs were generations of rats—rats whose lineage could probably be traced back a hundred years. Rats the size of cats, and we'd just destroyed the only home they'd ever known. They were now seeking revenge.

"HOLY SHIT," Bobby screamed at the top of his lungs.

"KILL 'EM, BOYS. KILL EVER GODDAMN ONE O' 'EM," Homer screamed from the safety of his perch on the tractor, and immediately we knew why Homer had given us the hoe handles.

We started whacking.

There were hundreds—no, thousands—of fat rats. As soon as we beat down one of the screaming, snarling beasts, another would take its place.

To make matters worse, the grass was deep, and I couldn't tell from which direction they were attacking. Some were so large that one whack wouldn't do the job. He would raise his head again, leaping from his hind legs with blood squirting from between his sharp pointed teeth, more determined than ever to impale us with a wicked vengeance.

"HELP ME," Bobby screamed. I could see he was surrounded by a large number of the leaping, wounded creatures. He was twisting in circles begging for reinforcements.

"KILL EM, BOYS, OR THEY'LL BITE HELL OUTA YOU'NS AND GIVE YOU TYPHOID OR SOMPIN WORSER," Homer hollered.

Homer was now standing on the tractor's seat, grinning and giving the appearance that he thought this was just a hoot.

In fear of the dreaded typhoid, whatever that was, we whacked away.

Danny held his hoe handle like a baseball bat, swinging from side to side in a sweeping motion, mowing 'em down in droves. But still the bloodied rats came, wave after wave, like a never-ending nightmare.

Every dispatched rat squealed a high-pitched, terrible sound that would have been right at home in some low-budget horror movie. When Homer killed the tractor's engine, the hundreds of loud squeals pealed like a soprano chorus straight from hell.

"KILL 'EM ALL, EVEN THE LITTLUNS," Homer hollered again, even though I'd yet to see a 'littlun.'

As ferocious as mad Chihuahuas, they defended their home.

It was a sight to behold. If anyone had driven up and seen this without knowing what was happening, they would have thought we boys had lost our minds, with Homer on his tractor witness to our madness.

Just as I looked at Danny, a fat rat leaped at him. He immediately caught the screeching creature in mid-air with his hoe handle like Mickey Mantle busting a fastball, drilling the miniature monster into the treetops twenty-five yards away.

After twenty minutes, the battle began to wane. The three of us were soaked from head to toe in sweat and breathing hard, but we dared not let our guard down. Some of the bigger rodents seemed to have a second life or were coming to from being knocked out. These rats jumped back into the fight with one last high-pitched, insane squeal.

Finally, the occasional thunking of hoe handles on lifeless carcasses was all that could be heard. We were speechless for five minutes, trying to comprehend what we'd just done.

"Why in hell couldn' you tell us 'at was gon' hapn?" Bobby finally asked, breathing hard and looking up at Homer, who was still standing on the tractor.

"Hell, boys, that would'a taken all'a fun outa it, now wouldn' it?" Homer said, almost falling from the tractor in laughter. "It was worth a hunnerd dollars to watch you'ens jumping roun', beating 'em rats t'death."

He had tears in his eyes from laughing so hard, as if this was the funniest thing he'd ever witnessed in his life.

"Now comes sum ril fun, 'ough," he said, choking back his laughter so he could talk. "I want y'all to pile 'em rats up so's you'cn burn 'em. Go down'ta barn and fetch pitchforks and sum kerosene. Make'ya one big pile and soak it down and light 'em up. Ain't no tellin' what kind of 'seases comes outa 'em rats, so's you gotta burn 'em and I mean burn 'em good. Keep flippin 'em till they ain't nuttin' but charcoal."

We had six bushels of rats when we finally stacked them into a pile. There were rats of all descriptions. Bobby was fascinated by the size of some of them.

"This'n here's big as a damn possum!" he exclaimed. He had laid all the largest to one side, conducting his personal biggest-rat contest before determining a winner and pitch-forking the bloody winner onto the towering pile of his kinfolk.

Then came the burning.

A couple of gallons of kerosene were added to the pile, and the cremation was underway. But then something happened which took us all by surprise—all except Homer, who had moved away twenty yards or so. The plump, corn-fed bodies began to explode. And in less than a minute, the scorching pile was popping like popcorn, which had us jumping in circles, trying our best to avoid exploding flesh and the stinking acrid smoke from the inferno.

Of course, Homer was beside himself—apparently he knew about exploding rats, which is why he had backed away. He laughed so much that it became infectious, and soon we were laughing with him.

"Y'all pour as much fuel as you need to burn 'em good. Don't leave nuttin," Homer said as he drove the tractor toward the barn.

And then, as an afterthought, he hollered, "YOU BOYS JUST 'MEMBER 'AT 'ERE AIN'T NUTTIN NO BETTER'N A GOOD RAT KILLIN!"

# 16. Lydia

OUR FORT LAY DEEP INTO THE ten-acre stand of thick pinewoods. It was hidden from the rest of the world—a secret place known only to a chosen few, where we convened to discuss a world known only to orphans. No grown-ups or town kids would ever understand this life of ours. They couldn't, even if they wanted to, because none of us could begin to explain our world to them.

This was a special place for us, where we talked and sometimes cried. But mostly, it was here where we laughed away our fears.

The fort was a sturdy structure—built upon a foundation of arm-thick dead-poles we'd scavenged from the woods and lashed together with hay twine between precise rows of thirty-foot-tall pines.

The walls were sound. The rows were planted six feet apart, dictating the width of the fort. Not wanting any interruption of the interior space, we built it longer than wide, stopping at the next row of pines. Across the tops of the walls we lay more poles for the roof, covered it with tin we'd swiped from a stack at the barn, thus keeping the inside dry. Finally, to hide our secret, we'd surrounded the entire fort with limbs, rendering the structure almost invisible.

We were proud we'd built well.

Furnished with stolen quilts and old pillows piled atop a thick layer of pine straw, it became our protective cocoon—it was here we did as we wanted, with no interference from prying eyes or questions from those charged with our welfare.

And it was here that the darkest secret any of us had ever been charged with keeping was birthed.

Cecil is our friend. He hadn't lived here as long as most of us, but he was one of us just the same. We didn't know how he'd ended up here, only that he tried hard to fit in.

Thinking back, he seemed scared—as if frightened by a demon's chase from which he was unable to escape. He wore a mask that haunted the faces of other orphans—an expression that eventually changed in some, yet stayed with others for as long as they lived on the hill.

Cecil had that look from the day he first arrived, but we welcomed him as we had everyone else. And he became a member at the fort, especially after he'd proved his worth by swiping a girly magazine from Mike's U-Tote-Em Superette down on the highway.

We were aware of his younger sister—a cute thirteen-year-old with green eyes and long black hair pulled back in a ponytail.

After all, the day had come when girls began to look pretty and kissing and getting a feel was something that swelled our chests.

It was a warm, late-June Saturday afternoon, and we were at the fort, passing around the pictures we'd cut from Cecil's magazine. He surprised us when he walked up with Lydia and, after introductions, took a seat beside her on the pine straw, his arm draped over her shoulder.

We laughed and talked with her—Mike, the oldest, telling her how pretty he thought she was. I, being the youngest, thought she was beautiful, but I was too embarrassed to tell her.

"You guys really wanna see something beautiful?" Cecil said, smiling. Then, surprising the hell out of us, he began to unfasten the buttons on his sister's baby-blue shirt. As if a little kid, he grinned at the prospect of pleasing his friends by sharing something he knew we'd appreciate.

Even more surprising, Lydia was a willing participant, lending a hand in finishing the un-buttoning. She removed her shirt, then, looking at each of us in turn, she leaned forward and unfastened her small white bra.

I was stunned beyond words—we all were.

Other than one of the older girls pulling up her shirt for us from the infirmary window, none of us had ever seen naked breasts for real. And now, right in front of us, this beautiful young girl sat half naked—and smiling about it.

Cecil stood and, without saying a word, led Lydia into the fort, covering the doorway with the old green Army blanket nailed to the fort's front. Never having heard the sounds of sex before, we listened intently to Lydia's soft moaning. When all went silent, we looked at one another, excited—eyes wide—unaware of what would happen next.

Cecil crawled through the doorway, stood, and zipped up his jeans.

"One of you go on in," he said. "It's okay."

And, as if to reassure us, "It's really okay."

Mike, as the oldest, entered the fort next, without saying a word. When he was finished, he was followed by Clayton, and then Lanny.

Finally, it was my turn.

I crawled into the fort and drew the blanket over the doorway. Lydia was lying naked, her back against the pillow with her knees in the air. A single drop of sweat wove its way down her slim neck and between her small breasts, disappearing into her belly-button. My God, she was beautiful—stunning in fact—as my eyes traveled up her unblemished nakedness.

Smiling, beckoning to me with her extended hand, I nervously lay beside her on the quilt and she rubbed me between my legs, unzipping my blue jeans. I responded by gently touching the soft skin of her chest.

"It's okay," she said, as she gently pulled my head closer.

A battle raged within, even as my hand enveloped the soft mound of flesh between her teenage legs. Should I respond to the instinctual urges and take Lydia as my friends had? Why was her brother here? How could this happen?

I could hear the boys laughing outside about what a great friend Cecil was for bringing his sister with him. Indeed, he had accomplished what he had set forth to do—he was now fully accepted into our group. He had traded his sister's affections to insure his place amongst us.

Was this really even happening? Why would this beautiful girl be doing this? Why would any brother and sister be doing this? Can this be right, to screw this girl who'd just lain with her brother?

Faint memories of my mother's moral teachings assaulted my carnal senses. And Luke's lessons in doing the right thing were also prevailing. The battle, in the end, was won before it began. Even as my body responded to Lydia's gentle touches and she continued to stroke my virginity and I kissed her breasts, I knew I wouldn't consummate my first experience with her.

I wanted to talk to her—to ask her why, to know who she was. But not here, not today, not now. Maybe I would never find the courage to speak to her—I didn't know. Damn, there was so much I didn't know.

In the end, the troubled girl, one year my senior, was gracious. "It's okay Charlie," she said. "I won't tell."

She smiled and kissed me and we stroked each other's hair.

My status in the group was secure. My friends wouldn't know I hadn't taken her as they had.

But I slept fitfully that night, questions with no answers spinning through my head.

We'd made a pact amongst ourselves to never tell anyone about that day. And Lydia promised, as she was leaving with her brother, that it wouldn't be the last meeting with us.

Maybe I wouldn't be as strong next time—I didn't know.

I didn't even tell Luke—I couldn't. I felt our orphan's bond was strong and shouldn't be broken.

Little did I know how much I'd regret that decision.

# 17. Breeding Day and Rabbit Killing

WE WERE BOYS WHO THOUGHT OF ourselves as men. If we weren't men, we sure tried to act the part.

Today would be about all things manly. Spring had arrived and the heifers were coming into season. Breeding was an annual chore that demanded attention and one that we found quite fascinating, so I didn't mind when we were summoned to the barn to help.

We were in a jovial mood, talking about the upcoming event while the gang of us from the cottage, and even some of the younger boys who were also summoned to help, walked toward the barn.

"Yeah, we get to see just what that old bull is made of today," Bobby said.

"Yeah, well, at least he'll be gettin' him some, which is more than I can say for the rest of us," Mike replied, which prompted all of the younger boys to snicker.

"You better speak for yourself," Carl said.

"You ain't never, and you know it," Lanny retaliated.

"Yeah," Carl replied, "but it ain't gonna be long."

The rest of us just laughed.

"Yeah, maybe it ain't. But what we fixing to see today'll probably be as close as you get for a long time," Bobby said as he hit Carl in his shoulder, knocking him off balance. The two of them locked horns and roughhoused.

Yeah, we enjoyed talking like experienced, worldly men, but nothing was further from the truth.

Our small gang was almost to the barn when my brother, Danny, came around the side of the rabbit hutch holding a fat rabbit by his hind legs, its long ears brushing the ground.

For years, we'd been eating rabbit at least twice a month. I don't know if all the other kids knew what kind of meat they were eating, but those of us who were charged with raising and killing the rabbits certainly did. Not that being fed rabbit was a secret, but for some reason, I never heard anyone talking much about it. I had never heard of a kid on the Hill who didn't mind eating it. Some of us even looked forward to it.

But that was soon to end.

"Hey, Danny. What're you doing over here?" I said to my younger brother. He wasn't often at the barn. His chores usually kept him around the Hill, cutting grass.

We weren't prepared for what we saw when we turned the corner to the backside of the rabbit hutch.

The rabbits that we'd had been raising to eat were the big, floppy-eared kind—mostly solid white, but some were white and spotted brown or black. And they were huge.

But now we were shocked, because most of them were dead, in one large furry pile on the ground. And I could see that Danny was crying.

"What's goin' on, brother?" I asked when I realized that he was upset.

"Hell, Charlie, I don't really know," he said, with tears running down his cheeks. "They just told me that I had to kill all the rabbits, so that's what's goin on."

"Why?" I asked him.

"I'm not sure, but I remember somebody say that we weren't gonna be eating no more rabbit after these were gone," Danny said. "Something about the ladies at the church thinking that it ain't right for us to be killing these cute bunnies and eatin 'em. They said that these were too pretty—that they ought'a be Easter bunnies or something. Damn I hate doin this, Charlie."

"How you killin 'em?" I asked as I put my arm around him.

"With a damn ball-peen hammer," he said, the tears really flowing now. "And when they're all dead, I gotta skin 'em all. Look at how many there are—it's gonna take all day."

There was half a pickup load of dead rabbits piled on the ground already.

"How many more you gotta kill?"

"There's only a few left."

"Here, let me finish it for you," I said and I took the hammer and the rabbit he was holding. "How did you even know how to do this?"

"Eustace brought me over here and he killed the first one so I'd know how. But if you don't whack 'em right the first time, you gotta keep hittin' 'em till they stop kickin'. It's awful, Charlie."

"Don't even look, Danny," I said, and he turned away as I dispatched the rabbit into bunny heaven with one quick hammer blow to the top of its head. Bobby and Clayton had emptied the other cages and brought me the last of the rabbits. In just a minute the deed was done. With one final blow, we were no longer in the rabbit business.

"Thanks, Charlie," Danny said as he continued to cry for the pile of fat, now deceased rabbits.

"We gotta go help at the barn then I'll come back and help you with the skinning, okay?" I said, giving him a hug.

It's a terrible thing to send a kid to kill a whole hutch-full of rabbits, especially when he'd never killed anything before. Bad enough that he didn't even have a mom or dad. I was fairly pissed that Eustace had sent my brother over here to do the slaughtering.

As I walked to the barn, I couldn't help but wonder if the old ladies from the church ever felt sad for the deaths of the cows or pigs or chickens that were butchered here. Hell, all those critters were cute, too, at some time in their lives.

Funny how a bunch of old church ladies could come up with an idea so dumb.

But that's the way things were done at the farm. I knew that when Danny was old enough to work at the dairy, he'd see lots more killing and would soon get used to it. The sad fact of farm life was that something was always dying.

"It's a shame," Bobby said, after we'd walked away from Danny.

"What is?" I asked.

"I love fried rabbit," he replied. That's Bobby for you. He's really dumb that way.

Mr. Loveless was standing at the bull pen with Homer and Eustace. The pen was formidable, built from thick oak planks supported by cross tie posts set only six feet apart. It was the home of a gigantic beast—a sixteen-hundred-pound, registered, pure bred Jersey bull, known to us as Old Jake. When Old Jake got rambunctious during breeding, which was his one and only purpose for living, his huge mass couldn't and wouldn't be contained by any regular fence.

I suppose he lived a good life—all he had to do was father more dairy calves, which meant that most of his life was spent just eating and sleeping and waiting for the next heifer to come in season.

Yep, Old Jake lived a life that most of us boys envied.

While no one really knew where his name came from, we were always naming the animals. But we quickly learned that names were best reserved for stray cats and dogs that made the farm their home.

New kids made the mistake of naming one of the farm animals, only to be eating the same animal a few months later. From that point on, they stopped naming anything that might end up on the supper table. I had made that mistake myself and found it very difficult to eat Andy, a pig I'd raised myself. It's a dreadful event when you see your friend on a plate and everybody gnawing on him and remarking about how good he tastes.

"Boys," Mr. Loveless said, "it's time to get to work."

The heifers destined to become mothers had been corralled in a paddock apart from Old Jake. A series of fenced lanes connected the paddock to the bull's home. Old Jake could smell the heifer from some distance, so he was stomping and snorting like some old-timey steam engine about to explode. If not for the formidable fence surrounding him, his exuberance would have him crashing his way through to get to the seasoned ladies.

"Bring him one," Homer hollered to us.

We had gathered around the corral containing the cows, and Bobby, Lanny, and I climbed over the fence and herded the first trembling heifer into the chute that would take her to the finest dust-covered suitor she'd ever seen.

Old Jake was backing into his fence with the enthusiasm of a young boy at the prospect of his first kiss. In his zeal he knocked two of the younger boys backwards, away from their perch on the fence's top rail, and they tumbled to the ground.

"You boys stay off 'n 'at fence if you don't want Old Jake to stomp you'ens," Eustace hollered.

Carl opened the gate that separated the chute from Old Jake's pen. The first heifer, who only weighed maybe five or six hundred pounds, slowly made her way into Old Jake's domain, quivering as the huge bull approached.

Most of the boys had never seen what was about to take place, and all eyes were wide with youthful anticipation as Old Jake's well-muscled mountain of bulk trembled. He dwarfed the smaller heifer. Shuddering with excitement, he pawed the dirt and exhaled loudly before giving the heifer's rear end a lick with a tongue as wide as a pie plate.

Just as some of the boys were wondering how such a frail heifer could possibly support Old Jake's tremendous weight, he mounted her. And after a surprisingly quick series of thrusts, his work was finished and we felt the ground beneath our feet shake as his front hooves hit the earth. With a bellowing snort of satisfaction, he blew a cloud of red dust from the dry clay beneath.

The younger boys watched in amazement, most having squatted down to get a better look at the business end of Old Jake's stud service.

"Wow, I never knew that's how it's done," a red-headed boy exclaimed, his face still mystified, as the heifer scrambled out another chute, the gate closing behind her.

"That's just exactly how it's done," Homer said. "Bring up another'n."

The parade of heifers continued until, much to Old Jake's dismay, the day's breeding was finally finished. He was left stomping and snorting, lumbering around his pen in circles while throwing his huge head back, pridefully flinging copious amounts of drool skyward. Yes, sir, Old Jake was proud of his accomplishments, as if he knew he hadn't disappointed this day.

Of course there was always an element to this springtime ritual that made us boys feel like we'd been a part of something special. Granted, it hadn't gotten us any closer to the manhood we so urgently sought, but somehow it felt that way.

We walked back to the cottage on the hill with a spring in our step and our chests inflated in awe of what we'd just witnessed. While the younger boys snickered about the size of old Jake's huge pecker, we older boys were equally amazed—no matter how many time we'd witnessed the bull's performance.

# 18. The Radio

MOST BOYS ARE FASCINATED BY TRAINS, and we were no different. The railroad yard at the bottom of our hill stood between us and town, insuring that we always had a place to satisfy our curiosity about the steaming, clattering, and clanging goings on.

We frequently had to walk to and from school. The trip took us right across the triple set of tracks and the railroad yard where side rails accommodated boxcars and engines that were being interchanged with other trains or awaited maintenance that would be performed by alien looking machines and cranes. It was a place of great amazement and intrigue.

In the afternoons on our way back home from school, we'd sit in the shade of the tall oaks that surrounded the railroad yard and watch as the rail men—dressed in coveralls, holding their blinking lanterns and radios—would signal the engines to back-up or go forward as they dropped their boxcars or added them to a train that was passing through.

Hundreds of times I'd knelt beside a shining rail and pressed my ear to it, just like I'd seen the cowboys in the movies do, to see if I could hear a train approaching. Although I never did hear a train coming, I wasn't deterred from pressing my ear to the polished steel ribbon the next time I passed by. We would have sat there for hours had we been allowed.

Sometimes the yard was deserted, which compelled us to satisfy our curiosity.

I loved the colossal bulk of the engines, and when we found the yard deserted, we'd hop aboard and explore the silent steel behemoths, climbing every ladder we could find until we'd eventually reach our perch on the very top, twenty feet above the rails.

We'd hoot and holler at the folks in their cars as they drove across the highway bridge that spanned the width of the yard, just an arm's length from the top of the engine.

More times than not, though, we'd be discovered by a railroad security man who had gone unnoticed, and he'd holler at us while we scrambled off the engine like a pack of frightened, fat rats with a tomcat in pursuit. We'd scurry between the boxcars with him giving chase, cussing at us while screaming what he'd do if he ever caught us.

But none of us had ever been caught before, and we had no idea what might happen if we were. We figured the risk was worth the reward.

The exploration of the trains was a learned experience. Those orphans who'd come before us had passed down to us their knowledge of the tracks, so by the time we were old enough to walk to school we knew more about the workings of the railroad yard than any of the town kids. We'd been taught not only how to spot the security men but also how to avoid them. We would climb onto a moving train's ladder as it was slowly being tugged back or forth across the yard or we would hop into a moving boxcar's open door—surely things that all young boys needed to know.

There are dares that must be taken, and how much we were willing to get away with depended on the individual orphan.

Joe-Bob had once accepted a dare and jumped into a boxcar, riding the slow-moving freight for a few miles, he claimed, before jumping off as the train began to pick up speed. We didn't know if and when we'd see him again, and he enjoyed his brief status as a hero when he finally returned a couple of hours later—only to discover that half the adults on the Hill were out searching for him. Although Joe-Bob's antics that day kept him grounded for a couple of weeks, no amount of punishment could have tarnished his standing amongst us.

But the biggest draw of all was when a shining red caboose was left at the yard overnight. This was a rare occurrence, so word spread quickly as we speculated as to how long she'd sit there. To us, orphaned railroad enthusiasts, a caboose was a treasure trove of discovery.

They were always locked, but we knew how to get into them. If we didn't discover an unlocked door at either end, there would always be a window left open for ventilation. That would be our way in.

There wasn't a caboose made that didn't contain a case or two of flares. We would occasionally see them burning bright red at night around the tracks, spraying white-hot sparkles and creating an unearthly red ball of light and smoke. It's inside the caboose that they're always stored.

There has never been an orphan that wouldn't risk it all for a case of these pyrotechnic devices. In fact, we'd burned through hundreds of them since I'd come here. A novice orphan had to be careful because the small tubular flamethrowers had scarred more kids than we ever wanted to admit. The sizzling instruments would burn through flesh faster than a red-hot knife through butter. I still carry a few visible scars of my own.

A few of us had managed to create quite a spectacle three years earlier. We'd long since become masters at slipping out at night undetected, after Homer had gone to sleep. This night we had our minds set on a caboose that had been left in the yard. We quietly made our way down the hill, and in short order we were scrambling around the deserted caboose, making our way inside with little effort. After lifting a case of flares, we stealthily climbed our hill again, sweating from the effort, and made our way to our fort in the woods and hid our prized cache.

Retrieving a dozen or so at a time after dark, we'd sneak over past the barns and create our own fireworks show. We'd strip off our shirts and we'd dance ritualistically like natives on some far-away island. With a lighted flare in each hand, we'd toss the red hot, sparkling tubes of fire as high as we could, dodging them as they fell back to earth. Before our exotic ritual was finished, our sweat-soaked bodies reflected the bright red glow and we resembled a tribe of blood-soaked headhunters dancing wildly about while contemplating our next sacrifice to the gods.

But all good things must come to an end. And this one surely did.

Fuzzy, a new kid who hadn't been at the home long, was with us on his virgin flight of fancy. He failed to make sure that one of his flares was disposed of properly. Knowing the flares burned hot, we'd always stick the burned ends into the ground before we left, making sure they were extinguished completely.

But we somehow failed to inform Fuzzy of this procedure. So, making our way back home, Fuzzy informed us that he had left his flares lying on the top of the ground.

"Well, there's nothing we can do about it now," I said, hoping the flares were extinguished when he left them. Never giving it a second thought, we snuck back in and fell fast asleep.

"Charlie, Charlie," Bobby said frantically, shaking me awake. His nose pressed against the screen while peering out the window in the room he and I shared. He'd awakened to go to the bathroom and spotted something strange. "You'd better come look at this."

Good fortune hadn't befallen us this night. There were four rooms on the end of the cottage that faced the barns, which were across the hill. Before long all four windows were crowded with boys straining to see what Bobby was looking at. We silently watched in horror as the faint distant glow from over the hill became brighter. Something was burning, and some of us knew why.

"Listen," I said quietly but urgently. "Everybody go back to your rooms like you've been asleep, and hurry."

I pounded on Homer's door.

"I just woke up to go to the bathroom and looked out my window. You'd better come look," I told Homer, and we both walked out onto the front porch. By now the glow from the distant pasture was lighting up the night sky in a big way.

Homer scrambled back inside, and I heard him frantically shouting at the fireman on the other end of the phone. In ten minutes, the fire engines from town roared up the hill, sirens screaming and bells clanging, as Homer jumped into his truck.

With tires smoking on the pavement and the rear of the truck fish-tailing from side to side, he blazed down the hill toward the barns.

The entire Home—most all the kids from different dorms and their house parents—was awake now, and kids of every size were gathered by the chapel, still in their pajamas, wondering what the hell was going on, while gazing at the red and orange glow in the night sky beyond the barns.

It sounded worse than it was.

The fire engines were at the barn for a few hours, and slowly the fiery glow dissipated, and the fire was extinguished. We were still awake when the procession of vehicles passed in front of the cottage on their way back to town.

The next day we discovered a charred landscape of a couple of acres and maybe a few dozen tree stumps consumed by the fire. The firemen had discovered the remains of the burnt flares and the entire event was blamed on "some n'er do well kids who must a stole 'em damn flares from the trains."

"I wish I could get my hands on those little bastards," Homer said. "I'd show 'em some fire."

Surprisingly, none of us was ever asked if we knew anything about the blaze. Of course had they asked... well, we really didn't know anything—we'd all been in bed asleep. I was even praised for spotting the fire and waking up Homer when I did—praise which I humbly accepted.

"Just doing what any good boy should have done," I told him.

That event had taught the railroad men a lesson. For the next two years the railroad men made sure that every caboose that was side-railed at the bottom of our hill was locked up—almost every one anyway.

We still checked them regularly, soon discovering an unlocked door at one end of a caboose that was still attached to a short string of boxcars. Our plan was hatched to sneak out later and see what treasures lay within. This time, we hit the mother lode.

"Charlie," Bobby said. "You gotta come see this."

In one of the niches in the wall, Bobby found something we'd never seen before—a battery-powered radio, complete with a microphone and antenna. When Bobby turned a knob, the radio lit up and voices could be heard.

"I gotta have this, Charlie," he said, his eyes wide with excitement.

"I don't know, Bobby. What are you gonna do with it?" I asked him.

"Hell, I don't know yet. Talk to people, I guess. But who knows? I can bring it back, but I gotta play with it for a while."

We'd never taken anything except flares before. But try as I might to discourage Bobby, he packed the radio up. And with Fuzzy carrying the microphone and antenna, the radio left with us.

Because it was compact and almost square, the size of a typewriter but not as heavy, Bobby had an easy time transporting the radio to the hay barn, where he stashed it away for the night.

After chores the next morning, Bobby summoned me to where he'd hidden the device behind some hay bales in the loft of the barn.

"I really think you should take it back, Bobby—before they discover it's gone. Flares are one thing. But when they find out their radio is missing, there'll be hell to pay."

But Bobby was determined to have his fun—for a while, at least. He placed the radio on a hay bale, flipped the power switch, and turned knobs until he heard a conversation between two men. He looked at me, eyes wide in anticipation, deciding he needed to be heard by whoever was at the other end. Bobby keyed the microphone.

"Who is this?" he asked.

The men, startled by his interruption, stopped speaking to each other.

"Just who the hell is *this*?" one of the men finally asked.

Bobby, in his glorious anonymity, had found himself the greatest toy of all.

"This is nonya," he replied.

"Nonya?" the man asked.

"Nonya damn business," Bobby said, almost falling off the bale of hay as he roared in laughter.

"How did you get on this channel? This is a Southern Railway engineer on an authorized frequency of the Southern Railroad. I don't know how you've accessed this frequency, but I suggest you switch to another channel."

"Well, may I suggest that you just kiss—my—ass. Now, what do you think about that?"

"Listen, whoever you are—if this isn't an emergency then you are in violation of the law."

"Well, I'm the damn law 'round here," Bobby told him and then he looked at me with a big grin. I've heard it described before as "resentment of authority." Most of us orphans, including me, shared it—today, Bobby was enjoying it.

He was terrorizing the airwaves and having a ball doing it. Wielding the microphone like a pro, Bobby paced back and forth, insulting and angering anyone and everyone whose frequency he happened upon. Before long, we heard conversations on different frequencies wondering whom this phantom voice belonged to and the steps that might be taken to silence him.

Bored with one channel, Bobby spun the knob until he happened upon another innocent victim. And then he'd start again with whatever rude insults he could think of. He called them fat and stupid and used a vulgarity that would make even a hardened orphan blush. He continued his electronic terrorism for the next hour, skipping from one channel to the next, before finally becoming bored and turning the radio off.

Even I understood the degree of orphaned teenage satisfaction that came from being able to say whatever you wanted—anonymously—to anyone you happened upon. But what neither of us knew was that whatever was said over the radio was never truly anonymous—the folks who had created the radio had ways of discovering who was using it.

When I walked into the barn the next day, Bobby was already on the radio again.

"Yeah, I wish you were here and I'd tear *you* a new asshole, too, buddy. Now what do you think about that?"

"Hey, Bobby. You're still at it, huh?" I said, interrupting the high-browed discussion.

"Yeah, Charlie, ain't it great?"

"Well, you know you can't keep it forever. You best be returning it."

"Yeah, I know. I'll probably take it back tomorrow."

But Bobby just couldn't part with his new toy. Three days later he was still insulting the electronic masses.

We finished our chores and were in the back of Homer's pickup on the way back to the cottage—all of us except Bobby. He told Homer that he'd walk back and most of us knew why— he had finally decided to return the radio and was probably, at this very minute, unleashing one final vulgar diatribe on the unsuspecting ears of his innocent victims before bringing himself to part with his toy.

Just as we reached the cottage and turned into the driveway, a black van—followed by a police car—topped the hill ever so slowly and continued toward the barn. I knew then that Bobby should have returned the radio at least one day sooner. Homer ordered us out of the truck. He backed out and followed the two vehicles heading right for the barn.

I wish I could have warned Bobby, but I knew I couldn't make it back to the barn in time. His goose was cooked.

As sad as it was for all of us who knew what was about to happen, the surprise which Bobby was about to experience would surely be worse.

As if on cue, the black van appeared, followed by Homer's truck with the police car following slowly in the rear of the procession. Homer turned into the driveway, but the black van and the police car continued down the hill toward town. In the back seat of the police car, poor Bobby's head could be seen, drooping low, his chin on his chest, as if heading toward a date with the hangman.

Homer walked in with an angry look on his face.

"Did any of you boys know that Bobby had taken a radio from one of the trains and was talking on it from the barn?" he asked, glaring at us.

Of course, we all shook our heads and said, "No, sir, what radio?"

We lamented the loss of our friend and speculated for hours about what might happen to Bobby.

Later in the day, Joe-Bob could be heard screaming, "The cops are back!"

Sure enough, the police car turned into the driveway.

"Maybe they're coming to pick up his clothes before they take him to the reformatory," Clayton said.

We followed Homer out to the driveway. The policeman opened the rear door and Bobby stepped out, looking somewhat disheveled and rather forlorn—but back on familiar ground, at least.

After a long discussion, Homer shook hands with the policeman and led Bobby to his room. Later that night we heard the whole story.

"Did you know that they can find any radio as long as it's turned on? I sure as hell didn't," Bobby said. "Thank my lucky stars, all they really wanted, after scaring me to death and telling me how I could be in the penitentiary, was their radio back. They even showed me some of the prisoners behind bars and told me that I was gonna be where they were if I didn't change my ways."

In bed that night, with the lights out, I thought about how many times Bobby's grand ideas really didn't turn out the way they were planned, which was most of the time. But most of the time we sure did have a lot of fun in the process, in spite of the failures.

"Charlie," Bobby said as we lay there in the dark.

"Yeah," I said.

"I'll probly be twenty years old 'fore I git off restriction, but I sure did have fun talking on that radio."

"You'll be lucky if you're not on restriction till you're thirty," I said.

We didn't have anything else to say, but I started laughing and so did Bobby. It was only one night of many when I laughed myself to sleep.

# 19. The Klan

It was December 15, 1964, and we were trying to squeeze in one more hunting trip before Christmas.

Luke, Buddy, and I had been over the state line into Alabama and were taking our time getting back home. The night was cold but we'd been sweating as we raced after the dogs into the black Alabama night in pursuit of the biggest possums we'd come across in years.

As possum hunts around here go, we'd been very successful—we had eight of the plump critters in the two burlap sacks in the bed of the truck.

"Whatchoo got'n pin, Chalie?" Buddy asked.

"Well, including these eight, there'll be twenty-two," I said.

"Bout time to sell 'em, ain't it?"

"Yeah, but shouldn't we fatten these up, too?"

"Well," Buddy said, "Gonna be Chrismas soon. Lotsa folks gon' be wantin' to put a fat possum on'a table, so git busy feedin' 'em. Whatchoo say, Luke?" Buddy asked.

"Well, you right, Buddy," and then to me, "Charlie, you ain't gon' ha' time to feed these out. We loadin' 'ese up next week and sellin' 'em. Gon' take all day to clean 'at many and sell 'em, too. You gon' ha'to git Bobby or sumbody else to hep you as it is. Anyway, we gonna git it done so's you'cn make'ya some Chrismas money."

I had planned to use the money I'd make to buy my brothers a Christmas gift—I'd already picked out gifts I was gonna buy for Luke and Buddy. I had found each a hunting knife that I thought they'd like. The old knives they both carried when we went hunting looked as old as they were, and if knives could talk, then I'd love to hear the tales their two old rusty blades could tell.

I couldn't ask them what they would like, knowing they would be quite upset if either of them thought I was gonna spend my money on a gift for them. But if I gave them both a new knife, then they wouldn't be rude enough to refuse, and that I knew.

We had come through Piedmont, Alabama, on our way back and were just about to the Georgia line.

Off in the distance, from what looked like about two miles away, a bright reddish-orange glow reached into the sky and was reflecting off the low-lying clouds.

"Whatchoo reckon 'at is?" asked Buddy.

"Might be somebody's house on fire. Best go see if we can help," Luke replied, and he gunned the engine, heading toward the bright glow.

Luke turned the truck onto a dirt road when we neared the source of the light. Coming over the next rise, he slammed on the brakes and skidded to a stop in the middle of the narrow road so suddenly that Buddy and I were thrown forward in the seat. We both threw our arms out and braced ourselves to keep from hitting the truck's metal dash-board.

Before us, in an unfenced, flat field on the left side of the road was an astonishing and frightening sight—a disturbing event that until now, I'd only seen in newspapers and on television.

There were three large circular rows of men, maybe a hundred and fifty in number, gathered there, holding flaming torches, dressed in the white robes and hoods of the Ku Klux Klan. In the middle of the three circles stood the source of the light—a huge wooden cross, maybe thirty feet tall. Flames leaped from the top of the structure like they were born from hell. Astonishingly, a dozen small children in little white hoods and robes milled around outside the circles of men while their mothers looked on.

Buddy was visibly shaken, the orange glow of the flames reflecting off the sweat on his dark skin. Luke, both hands flexing on the steering wheel, stared intently at a sight that represented the reviled opposite of his beliefs. The leaping flames of hatred from the burning cross danced in his eyes.

As I sat there between my two friends, I realized what a struggle these two men had faced because of their friendship. Now, right in front of us was a tangible example of the hate that these two had grown up with and battled all their lives. Luke's anger and Buddy's fear were suddenly palpable in the small confines of the truck cab.

"I don' know, but I'm thinking we ought be gettin' hell outa here." Buddy said quietly, not turning his eyes from the spectacle.

"Yeah, let's go," was all Luke said. He did not avert his eyes either.

Looking over his shoulder, he began backing the truck into the field on the other side of the road so we could turn around and make it back to the highway. He had just begun to pull away when a red pickup slid to a stop in front of our truck, blocking our exit and the view from the cross-burning side of the road.

Two men were in the truck. The passenger flung his door open and stepped out, carrying a shotgun.

Buddy quickly opened the glove box in the truck's dash and pulled out the .22 caliber pistol that Luke and he always carried for shooting snakes. He then placed the pistol in my lap, and Luke, without looking, reached over and slid the pistol over into his lap and put his hand around the grip.

I was about to crap in my britches. I tried not to move, and as cold as it was, I broke into a sweat.

The man was tall and heavyset and appeared to be in his thirties. He was dressed in overalls and a denim coat. A thick beard surrounded his angry face. Silhouetted in the fire from the cross, his eyes were like two black holes.

He just stood there in front of our truck for a minute, holding his shotgun. Then he made his way around to Luke's side, his gun cradled in his left arm. He looked in past Luke and me and straight at Buddy.

"Whatchoo doin' wi' 'at 'ere nigga in yo' truck, boy?" the man asked in a deep, threatening voice.

*So this is what the real struggle is about.* From this man's perspective, all he can see is that we're different colors and we're in the same truck and that shouldn't be. I wondered how Buddy must be feeling—I felt terrible that he had heard this man describe him as a nigger.

Even though Luke and me are white, just being in the same truck with Buddy is reason enough for this man and those like him to inflict harm upon, if not kill, all three of us for such a horrible display. He doesn't know us. He doesn't know what we think or how we feel, but that doesn't matter to his kind. He only cares that our skin color is different and that we're in this truck together. That one fact is fueling his hatred.

Luke just sat there, not answering the man.

"I JUST AST YOU SOMPIN, BOY," the heavyset man shouted, after Luke didn't answer.

Luke turned his head to look at the man.

"Well, son, here's the way I see it," Luke said, calmly.

"I AIN'T YO' GOD DAMN SON," the bearded man shouted. "Now," the man said, moving close, putting his hand on Luke's door handle and beginning to pull the door open, "you git yo' ass out 'at truck, boy."

The man pulled the door open with his right hand while holding the shotgun with his left. He looked in at Buddy and me and grinned. He had dark tobacco juice running down from his mouth, disappearing into his beard. Luke stepped from the truck and sorta shuffled his way around the door.

I was still staring into the man's face when the tobacco-stained grin instantly evaporated and his face turned pale. I suppose that happens when a man sticks a pistol in your ear.

Luke had made his way to the edge of the driver's side door, keeping the pistol down by his leg and hidden from view. When the man leaned in to glare at Buddy and me, Luke slowly brought the twenty-two up and stuck it into the man's right ear without the man ever having seen it. Then the man heard Luke cock the hammer back.

"Heh, heh, heh—well now, ain't this jes' sompin," Buddy said, as he grinned at the man whose face was now contorted in terror.

"Easy now," Luke told the man, while stepping behind him, snatching the shotgun from the man's arm.

This was the first indication to the driver in the red truck that anything was wrong, and he opened his truck door and stepped out. When the man walked around the front of the truck and got within ten feet of Luke, apparently unaware of what was taking place, Luke pushed the first man out of his way and leveled the pistol at the second man.

"Just hold it right there, son," Luke told the second man, and the man abruptly threw his arms into the air and stood as stiff as a statue.

"Don't shoot mister, please don't shoot," the second man pleaded.

While keeping his eyes on the two men, Luke spoke. "Buddy, come out 'ere fo' a minute if 'in you don' mind." Luke said.

"Come on 'round here son, wi' yo' friend," and Luke motioned the second man around the front of his truck with the pistol and had the two men standing together.

"Now, Buddy, pull their truck up so's we'cn git out of 'ere and take yo' knife and stick a couple o' 'em tires, please."

Buddy started the red truck and pulled it to the side of the road. Then he bent down and plunged his old hunting knife into the sidewalls of two tires on this side. I could hear air hissing as it escaped. Walking back toward us, he threw the keys to the red truck into the pine thicket behind us.

With the red truck now moved, the spectacle from a hundred yards across the road was in full view. Black smoke and cinders were billowing upward from an inferno roaring up the center pole and onto the arms. Even though the fire was in the shape of a cross, the scene was a perversion of anything Holy—there was nothing divine being represented here tonight.

I didn't know much about the struggle that Buddy's people had been fighting—I just knew that he was a good man and he was my friend, and if these two men and the people in the robes

hated him, then I didn't know why. I didn't understand how anyone could hate someone they didn't know.

"You okay?" Buddy asked Luke.

Buddy knew that we were dangerously exposed to the crowd
across the road and he kept looking over his shoulder toward
them.

"Yeah, I'm awright, thanks fo' asking, old timer," and Luke
chuckled. "If you don't mind, hold this shotgun fer me," Luke
said, passing the long gun to Buddy.

I was in awe of Luke's courage—he was calm and deliberate.

"Now, boys, they's two thangs I need to straighten out that
you so impolitely stated. First—I ain't been called a boy in a long
time. I'm a man—an old man, as you so rudely pointed out. Second—you didn't see no nigger in my truck. You saw my friend
in my truck—actually, my two friends. We didn't come'ere looking fo' trouble. All we was lookin' to do was't hep somebody,"
Luke paused, and with a big sigh, continued, "Now, I want bof
o' you to step over 'ere and apologize to my friend for calling him
'at bad name and to my young friend here fo' scaring him like
you'ens did. Ain't no call fer that."

The men took the few steps over to the truck with Luke still
talking to 'em.

"Now, I sure hope you boys walk a different path. Maybe git
busy in a good chuch sommers. Do sompin to make yo' mamas
proud. I know 'ey can't be happy 'bout you running with 'is
bunch." Luke nodded in the direction of the robed circus across
the road.

The two men were stunned. Maybe they thought they were
going to get shot, but what they didn't expect was Luke's reaction
to their behavior. They both did as Luke asked and apologized
to Buddy and me. They even told Luke they were sorry. All the
while, Luke kept the pistol trained at the big man's head.

The crowd across the road was now loudly chanting in unison—all I could make out was the word "glory" being shouted as
the men raised their arms, some with guns in hand, toward the
burning cross.

The three circles of robed men began to rotate—the inner circle and outer circle one direction, and the middle circle, the opposite direction, and I was mesmerized by the entire coordinated dance—the white robes appearing the color of the wicked flames now, like three circles of evil serpents slithering around a common prey.

The man who seemed to be directing the malevolent pageant stood on the tailgate of a pickup. He alone was dressed in a red robe, as if he'd been doused in blood.

Buddy, noticing that a few of the spectators from across the road had spotted something unusual and were now pointing in our direction, grabbed Luke by his arm.

"Bout time we ought be gettin' hell outa 'ere," Buddy told Luke, the seriousness of the situation appearing in his tone.

Luke got back in the truck and started to pull away then stopped.

"Sorry about yo' tires," Luke said. "Here's some money so's you can get 'em fixed," and Luke dropped a five-dollar bill on the ground. "You'cn git two tubes fo' that. I'll drop yo' shotgun by the road a hundred yards from 'ere."

The two men looked at him with their mouths open, not believing what they were hearing. I didn't understand what Luke was doing. They glanced at one another then back at Luke then each other again, confused by what they'd heard. I was madder than hell at the two men, and I didn't understand why Luke and Buddy weren't.

We sped away, leaving the men frozen in their tracks in a cloud of red dust. I was absolutely speechless about what had happened in the last ten minutes of my life. Cold beads of sweat ran down my face. In a few seconds, Luke instructed Buddy to throw the man's shotgun from the truck.

"Whatchoo think 'em boys'll do, Luke?" Buddy was the first to speak.

"Hard t'say. I know what I hope e'll do. I know what I hope 'is whole world should do, but we ain't in charge o' that, are we, Buddy?"

"Ain't 'at the truth," and Buddy chuckled.

"Charlie, I hope 'em boys didn't scare you too awful bad. At ain't the first time me and Buddy run inta 'em spooks," Luke said.

"Y'all don't even get scared anymore?" I asked, bewildered.

"They's thangs you need t'understand bout 'is world, son," Luke said. "They's a lot o' hate out 'ere. Hate that we'cn fight the way they do, with violence, but in the end, 'at ain't gon' git us nowheres."

"So that's why you treated them like you did? I mean, paying for their tires and all?" I asked, incredulously.

"Well, 'em boys didn't mean us no harm or we wouldn't be here now. They would'na been talking—they would'a been a' shootin'!"

I was amazed at the courage that both of these men had. Their friendship and love for one another had weathered the storm of violent racism.

"Don't it make you mad, though?" I asked Buddy.

"Sho nuff makes me mad. For any man to put his-self above any man fo' any reason ain't right. The question is how we gon' change 'is mess. Luke coulda shot 'em two boys—wouldna changed nuttin' tho. We gotta keep tryin' to change thangs, but they's no need to go 'roun killin' folks. They's lotta folks out 'ere everday on the front lines of 'is battle."

Buddy continued, reaching over and squeezing my shoulder.

"That's what Dr. King's out 'ere doin'. 'Magine getting to' up by dogs'n gittin' hit wi' billy clubs and knocked down by fire hoses—takes a whole lotta strenth t'not go git a gun and kill 'em folks 'at's treatin' you like 'at. Yeah, Chalie, I git mad 'bout it, but bein' like 'em ain't the way, son."

"And what about those little kids? I mean, who would take their kids to something like that?" I asked.

"WELCOME TO GEORGIA," the sign said, as we hurtled past it, headed toward home.

"Charlie, me and Buddy won't be alive t'see it, but one day, good Lord willin', you will—the hate being passed along to chi'ren like 'ose you saw out there'll stop. Gon' take a whole lotta hard work and educatin', though," Luke said, as he drove through the dark.

All the way back, I became aware of the dark cloud of injustice. Until that night I had lived largely unaware of Buddy's struggle. I knew then that I'd do whatever I could to help my friend's cause, as Luke had been doing all his life—fighting for justice for his brother.

The three of us riding together in the truck that night were just that—friends, who loved and respected one another. We weren't different colors, just friends.

# 20. Selling Possums

THE DAY I'D BEEN WAITING FOR had finally arrived. With Luke and Buddy's help today, I'd cart all the fattened-up possums down the hill and try to sell 'em.

Saturday morning was cold, with a promise of warmth in a rising sun.

For the last two months I'd been toting two five-gallon buckets of dining-hall leftovers to Luke's shop where the possum pen was located to feed my small herd of snarling creatures. They'd hiss and spit and bare their evil-looking teeth when they saw me approach, but they'd forget I was even there as soon as I poured the steaming fresh slop into the wooden feeders I'd built. The long feeding troughs were nothing fancy—just three rough boards nailed together with caps on the ends, but the fat marsupials didn't seem to care.

The slop, which was a mishmash of leftover meals we'd eaten only a few hours before, would be smokin' as it hit the feeders and the possums would jump into the middle of the swill and rare up on their hind legs and fight ferociously for position, gorging themselves till the boards were licked clean. Not a speck of slop would remain. It was quite a spectacle.

Then the slick-tailed creatures would hiss their way back into the crates located around the pen and sleep until mealtime came around again. They didn't know it, but they'd been living on death row, and this morning's meal would be their last. Soon, these plump, well-fed critters would be roasted, handsome centerpieces on someone's Christmas dinner table.

I had never partaken of possum meat, but those who had—namely Luke and Buddy, who happened to be the only ones I'd ever talked to who had eaten it—deemed it quite delectable.

Though I have to be honest—after two months of watching the creatures eat like they did and because of their close resemblance to giant rats, I would probably live out my entire life without ever dining on possum. That's not to say that those who enjoyed eating them had less than gourmet palates, but for me, all the beasts represented was a payday.

I was the master of my own possum enterprise, and today I'd reap the benefits of my capitalist endeavors.

My first order of business would be challenging—I had to corral the herd into burlap tote sacks for transport. I hired Bobby and Fuzzy to assist. Their payment was to be based on the day's receipts, and they were happy just knowing they'd receive something—it was a learning adventure for them and an opportunity to leave the Hill. At the day's end there would be enough for an RC Cola and a couple of Moon Pies; that's all Bobby had expressed an interest in anyway.

Fuzzy was a short, plump kid around my age and had long ago been saddled with his nickname because his sandy colored hair never seemed to want to lay down on his head. So, according to him, his dad started saying how he always looked fuzzy and the name stuck. He didn't mind being called Fuzzy—as a matter of fact, he liked it. Unfortunately, his dad had been put in the penitentiary for some crime he'd committed years earlier, and his mom didn't want him anymore. Like all the sad stories in an orphanage, he wound up on the Hill with the rest of us. But he seemed determined to make the best of it. Fuzzy sported a round face and fat pink cheeks that gave him the look of a Christmas elf.

He'd be glad to accept my offer, he'd said, but admitted that he, as of yet, had no experience in possum wrangling. In fact, he said he'd never touched a possum, but he was willing. What a heart, I thought, so I enthusiastically welcomed him into my employ.

Under Luke's direction and specifications, I'd built a formidable possum enclosure out of chicken wire and scrap lumber and old fence posts, out of sight from the dog's pen in back of the shop. Because possums are good climbers, even the top of the pen had to be covered in chicken wire. When Buddy inspected the pen, he described it as a "sound possum enclosure," and sure enough, we never had a possum escape.

"Bad enuf 'at Buck and Susie'll be able to smell 'em but they sho can't see 'em or they'll tear down any fence to git t'em," Luke had said when he advised me as to where to locate the pen. So, we had built it as far from the shop as possible.

"How we sposed to catch 'em?" Bobby asked, hands through the wire staring at the possums.

"Well, if you hadn't chickened out on goin' huntin' with us you'd see how easy they are to handle," I told him. "After you mess with 'em for a minute they'll just lay down and play possum on you and then all we gotta do is grab 'em by the tail and put 'em in the sacks. As fat as they are, we'll put only four in each sack then I'll tie the top so they can't get out and when we're done we'll go sell 'em."

"Sounds pretty easy," Fuzzy said after a moment of serious contemplation.

Then without hesitation, he opened the pen door and we walked in—each carrying a burlap sack—and got busy catching the possums. They hissed and scrambled around some, but when we finished we had six squirming sacks full of Christmas dinners. The dirty burlap sacks seemed to have a life of their own and rolled around the pen crashing into one another. The beasts voiced their displeasure at each collision.

"You boys ready?" Luke hollered from out front.

"Yes, sir."

"Well bring 'em on and load 'em up. Better put 'em on the flatbed so's they's enough room."

Luke drove us down the hill, with Bobby, Fuzzy, and me perched on the flatbed of the truck with the six sacks of possums. All three of us were outfitted in stocking caps pulled down on our necks and gloves to ward off the cold December wind. In a few minutes, we stopped to pick up Buddy at his house.

"Chalie," Buddy said, "now reach in 'ere and pick me out a fat'n, will you?" Buddy said. "I'm gonna be the first sale of the day."

"Sure thing," I said smiling, "but you ain't gotta pay for him."

"Naw, naw, naw, now," he said. "That ain't way it's gon' be. Those are yo' possums now. You been feedin' 'em, so take this dolla' bill and put it in yo' pocket. Chrismas right around the coner and you gon' be needin' it. If you don't mind, take 'im on'n put him in the lil' pen out back fo' me."

When I returned, Buddy had some advice to offer.

"Now Luke's gon' go real slow, up'n down the street and you boys gonna ha't holla real loud fo' folks to hear you'ens. You gotta holler 'bout 'ese possums been fed out and they gon fetch a better price than a fresh caught'n."

"Reckon what they oughta bring?" I asked Buddy.

"Well, what'e oughta brang and whatchoo gon' gits two diffent thangs. But I 'spect a dolla' a head's a fair price. But if folks is offerin' mo', 'en take they money okay?"

With Buddy's advice we jumped back onto the flatbed and Luke drove slowly down the street.

I jumped sky-high and almost fell off the truck when Bobby, screaming at the top of his lungs, began his sales pitch.

"GITCHO FAT POSSUMS RIGHT HERE," he shouted, with his hands cupped around his mouth. "THESE HERE'S THE FATTEST POSSUMS YOU EVER SEEN," and he'd turn from side to side so he could be heard in the houses on both sides of the street. Fuzzy and I started laughing and joined in and now all three of us were hollering.

I could see people looking out their windows and folks started coming out on their porches and walking down to meet the truck.

"You been feedin' 'em out, boy?" an old colored man asked.

"Yes, sir, for two months now," I said.

"How much you askin fer 'em?"

"Dollar apiece."

"Well reach in and pick me out two fatten's 'en—I wan'ta fattest uns in the bag now, since I'm gittin' two."

"Yessir," I said while Fuzzy was searching through the sack. He finally came up with a big one by the tail and passed it to Bobby before diving in for the second.

I couldn't believe what I was seeing—people standing in the street beyond, waiting for us to come by. A crowd of little kids had gathered around the truck, wanting to see inside the sacks. We decided that the best way to do this was for Bobby to stay on the truck and keep yelling while Fuzzy and I walked beside the truck to help customers.

"Whatchoo got in 'em sacks, mister?" the little colored kids hollered at Bobby.

"Why, you wanna see?" he asked then said, "gimme yo hand." And he'd lift a kid onto the truck. After doing this once, they all wanted to climb on. In a minute the whole back of the truck was crowded with little colored boys and the possum sacks and Bobby still hollering at the top of his lungs.

"All you young'ens gon ha' to si'down now, "Buddy hollered out his window, "or you gon ha'to git down."

Some of the smallest boys chimed in with Bobby and cupped their little hands around their mouths and started hollering that *they* had possums for sale. Boy was that funny. Even Luke and Buddy started laughing when they heard the squeaky voices of the neighborhood kids.

Up and down the streets of Buddy's neighborhood we traveled with the same results. I forgot about the wind and cold and soon we were down to our last sack when I noticed a really old lady on the porch of a run-down shack, waving her handkerchief at us. While Bobby was helping someone else, I walked ahead to the lady's house and up to the top step so I could hear what she was saying. Completely covered in a multi-colored blanket and a frayed, white shawl wrapped over her head, she spoke so softly that I had to turn my head and put my ear to her face.

"I sho wud like t'ha one o' 'em possums, young man," she said, gently grabbing my arm and giving it a squeeze.

She appeared as if in miniature—so small and frail that I wondered how she managed to walk from her door to the porch. Her eyes were coated milky-white, and I knew she must have a hard time seeing. Her face and tiny hands were as black as the night itself and wrinkled, but in spite of her appearance, she put me at ease with her sweet smile.

"Yes, ma'am. I believe we got one for you," I said.

"Wudju clean it fo' me? I jes' ain't got no strenth no mo'."

I scrambled down the wooden steps and back to the truck, all the while thinking about killing and cleaning a possum—something I'd never done, and didn't know how to do. I'd killed other animals before, but never a possum.

"She wants me to clean it for her, Luke," I said.

"Then let me show you how," Luke said, stepping from the truck, handing me his old bone-handled hunting knife with its six-inch blade.

Luke, seeing the fear in my face, reassured me.

"It's okay, Charlie. This is just part o' the deal. They all gon' be kilt sooner or later," Luke said.

"That lil old woman's name's Addy," Buddy said. "A hunred-five-year-old she is. Been by herself fo' most o' it. They say her daddy's a slave got set free a'ter the war."

With my last possum and Luke's sharp knife in hand, I looked to Luke for instruction. Bobby and Fuzzy watched as I lay the possum on one of the empty sacks on the ground behind the truck.

"Now hold 'im strong 'hind 'is head wi' yo left hand and let 'im settle a bit." I did as Luke instructed, feeling the possum wriggling in my grip, before settling down as if he knew what was about to happen. "Now, Charlie, take the knife'n stick 'im in his throat'n push the knife till you cut alla way through," Luke said.

The sharp knife easily slid through the possum's throat, meeting little resistance. The animal stiffened briefly then went limp. I was surprised there was so little blood. Only the soft hiss of air escaping the animal's lungs indicated change—the eyes remained open as if it was still alive. Buddy, looking on, further instructed me in the art of gutting and skinning. He explained how to carefully push the knife between two vertebrae, separating the head from the body. The result was unlike any cut of meat I'd ever seen. The carcass was surprisingly small without its head and fur.

Quickly and silently, the beast gave his life. I was aware that all the possums we were selling would meet this same fate and that I was a willing participant. That was the way of the world—I accepted my part in it.

Bobby held open one of the empty burlap sacks, and I placed the entrails and skin and head inside and threw the sack onto the bed of the truck.

Holding the animal by its tail, I made my way back to Addy's porch and laid the bright pink meat in an old, dented enameled dishpan that she held. I held open the screen door and she went inside. I turned and made my way back to the truck.

"She tryin' to git yo 'tention," Buddy said and motioned to me.

Addy had returned to her porch. She was holding on to the rickety rail for support, waving a dollar bill in the air with her other hand.

She had taken the last possum I had for sale that day. I had a pocket full of dollars—more money than I'd ever had in my life. I felt warm knowing Miss Addy was able to have the last one.

"MERRY CHRISTMAS TO YOU, MISS ADDY," I hollered so she could hear me.

As the truck pulled away, she stood on her porch waving her handkerchief until we were out of sight.

"That's a nice thang you done, son," Buddy said from the window of the moving truck. "Most folks 'round here try t'look a'ter her. She ain't n'er gon' forgit it. Rest o' folks 'round here won't, neitha. You done a good thang, Chalie."

I knew that any kindness I'd shown Miss Addy was because of Luke and Buddy and the lessons I'd learned from them. They had spent time and money dragging me along hunting and doing other things, and all they wanted in return was for me to do good. I no longer had any parents, but I did have these two. And I would be proud to call either of them my father.

Luke stopped the truck after he turned the corner.

"Alright son, what's the tally?" Luke asked.

I emptied my pockets onto the flat bed of the truck and counted thirty-four dollars.

"That's a right smart pocket o' money," Buddy said, "whatchoo gonna do wi' all 'at?"

"Well, if Luke will stop at the store I'm buying everybody a drink and a candy bar."

"I want a Moon Pie," Bobby said.

"Well, a Moon Pie it'll be then," and I suppose I swelled up a bit when the clerk added up our bill and I paid for everything.

What I had left was a fortune, even after I gave Bobby and Fuzzy two dollars each. I still had twenty-eight dollars in my pocket—the most money I'd ever had, and all I could think about was catching more possums. I had enough to buy Christmas presents for my brothers and Luke and Buddy and maybe something for me.

"Charlie, when they take you huntin' agin, me and Fuzzy wanna go, too," Bobby said.

"Well, I don't know, Bobby. We'll just have to see," I said, feigning a serious look. "You chickened out before."

"Well, I ain't never gon' chicken out agin, I swear," he said, pleading, and I burst out laughing.

# 21. Cecil and Lydia

I AWOKE TO A LOUD BANGING. HOMER was hollering for everyone to get up, his fist methodically hammering on all the bedroom doors. Judging by the tenor of his voice, it was obvious that something out of the ordinary had occurred.

Glancing at my clock as I exited the bedroom I shared with Bobby, I noticed it was three-thirty—thirty minutes before we usually had to get up to go milking. Yes, most definitely, something was wrong.

Fourteen boys lived in our cottage, but when everyone gathered there were only thirteen heads to be counted—Cecil was missing. This had to be the reason for our rude awakening.

"When was the last time any of you saw or talked to Cecil?" Homer asked.

Half the boys were still rubbing their eyes and yawning, especially the ones who weren't on the milking crew and didn't usually get up this early.

"Joe-Bob, you're his roommate. He didn' say nuttin' to you 'fore y'all went to bed?"

"No, sir. 'Fore I fell asleep, he was in his bed. I didn't say much to him and he didn't say nuthin' to me. Funny thing, though—I thought I heard him crying or something. I asked if he was okay, but he didn't say nuthin', so I went to sleep."

"Well, he's gone missin'," Homer said. "Mr. Loveless called me a few minutes ago. His sister's gone, too. Now, I wan' all you boys t'thank real hard. If Cecil said anythang 'bout leavin' 'en I need to know, and I mean now."

Runaways happened here. Not often, but sometimes a kid just decided to see what the rest of the world was doing or maybe thought they could do better on their own.

But there were a thousand reasons why any of us wouldn't want to be here. Those of us with siblings seemed to have a better chance of adapting, but Cecil's sister, Lydia, lived here, too, so the mystery deepened.

True to our word, none of us who knew of the meetings with Lydia at our fort in the woods had revealed a word to anyone. But now, with both Cecil and Lydia missing, I began to wonder if I had done the right thing keeping quiet.

Anyway, our 'us versus them' mentality was strong. In that regard we were a close band of brothers. We fought, but a cohesive force kept us together, reinforced by the knowledge that we all had our own personal demons.

So it seemed to me and the other boys that whatever was going on between Cecil and Lydia and the rest of us should be handled internally.

As far as I know, they never shared with any one of us what their home life had been like. Some kids, like Lanny, did, but for many the memories remained untouched. We didn't wind up here because life had been good to us. Many never wanted to relive the pain brought by remembering.

I consoled myself with the knowledge that this crap just happens. Some kids run away without ever letting anyone know why. But they're eventually found, with one exception.

Years before my brothers and I arrived, one of the older boys ran away and was never heard from again. Luke told me that there was a search for him all over the country, but he was never found. It was suspected that the boy must have been kidnapped or killed somewhere. I liked to think, as did most of us, that the boy made it to wherever he wanted to go and is having a helluva lot of fun there.

Who knows for sure? Maybe the story was created to scare some kid out of running away. Or maybe it really happened just like they think it did.

Our morning discussion with Homer finally ended. No one could offer any information as to where Cecil and Lydia might have gone.

"Come on, Bobby," I said. "We have to be at the barn in a few minutes, anyway. Let's get our boots on and walk over. We ain't going back to bed now."

With the others still grumbling about their rude awakening, Bobby and I headed toward the barn. In spite of the hour, it was a warm morning. The security light attached to the top of a telephone pole at the ball field revealed thick dew glistening on the grass below. All the low areas were shrouded in fog.

"Where in hell do you think they've gone?" Bobby asked as we walked together through the dark, the gravel in the road crunching beneath our boots.

"You ever thought about leaving, Charlie?"

"Yeah, I guess I thought about it. I think we all have. I mean, who the hell really wants to be *here*? I have my brothers to look after though. The only way I'd ever leave is if we could all go together. But I'm not old enough yet to get a job and take care of them and me. But maybe one day. What about you, Bobby? You ever wanted to leave?"

"Yeah, I did leave once."

"You did? When?" I asked, surprised because he'd never talked about it before.

"Before you got here. I was just a lil' kid, and I missed my mom so bad that I took off down the hill. I didn't even take no clothes or nuthin'. I just wanted t'go home."

"What happened?"

"Well, when I got to the tracks, I musta spooked this giant-lookin', mean-ass dog, and he ran me right back up the hill. Scared the hell out of me. That's the last time I even thought about leaving. Damn, he was the biggest dog I ever seen."

We both laughed our way through the foggy darkness.

Bobby had been here a few years when his mom died. He'd taken it really hard. Now all he had was his family on the Hill—that's how it was for most of us.

Sometimes, though, some kid's dream came true and they got to leave and go back home or were adopted by some family. And sometimes a kid would go back home only to return to the Hill, because nothing had changed, and that only made things worse. They still got slapped around by some drunk dad or mom, and they would have been better off if they'd never gone.

I was almost glad that my brothers and I had nowhere else to go. Somehow, knowing that this was as good as it was going to get made things easier. I could get on with my life instead of hoping that things at home would improve.

The security light at the barn was glowing softly, illuminating a ball in the fog as we passed under it and made our way into the milking barn. I felt for the light switch and turned it on. A barn rat spooked us, and we jumped as the fat critter scampered between Bobby's feet. Laughing, we made our way through the milk barn and opened the sliding door at the far end.

"Let's go see if all the cows are up," Bobby said.

Dairy cows operated on a strict schedule. They knew when they needed to be milked, and twice a day they would convene in front of the gate that gave them access to the holding pen where they would wait their turn to be milked. Like clockwork, they showed up on time every day, without fail. That always amazed me.

We walked through the barn door and down the concrete raceway, flipping on the lights as we made our way toward the gate and the heifers.

"Somebody left the light on in the tack room," Bobby said.

"Turn it off while I go let the cows up."

"No, wait on me. I don't want 'em damn cows runnin' me over."

I paused by the pens and started rubbing one of the new-born calves on her head as she tried to wrap her long tongue around my fingers.

*It's so quiet here.* I could hear the cows breathing beyond the gate. And then I heard what sounded like Bobby sobbing.

"Bobby, you all right?"

He didn't answer. I made my way back toward the open tack room door and Bobby. He stood motionless in the doorway, silhouetted in the light from inside the room. I walked up beside him and saw tears streaming down his cheeks. He didn't turn to look at me—he stared straight at whatever he was focused on inside the room. I felt a shiver of fear move through me as I slowly turned my head in the direction of his stare.

My knees gave way, and I collapsed.

Before us, suspended from a rafter, were Cecil and Lydia. Their bodies, so close they were touching, were hanging by thick ropes.

"NO, GOD DAMN IT!" I screamed, as I jumped back to my feet. "Bobby, hurry—help me. We gotta get 'em down."

But Bobby was frozen in place.

*I don't want this to be real. I want so badly to run from this place and time.*

"Look, you gotta help me now, Bobby. Maybe they're still alive, god damn it." I screamed. I took him by his shoulders and shook him violently. He made eye contact and nodded yes and then turned away and vomited down the back of the dark-green wood door.

"Look, grab Lydia and hold her up so I can undo the rope. Hurry." Then I also got sick as Bobby grabbed around her thighs and lifted her up and released the tension. I climbed onto a fifty-five-gallon fuel drum to reach the ropes that were attached to the wall around a large metal eyebolt. The knot came loose easily and Bobby collapsed under her body onto the dusty concrete beneath.

"Now Cecil," I said, frantically, as Bobby wiggled out from under Lydia and lifted her brother. When I untied the second knot, Bobby was slammed to the floor under Cecil's heavier body. I jumped down and quickly began untying the rope around Lydia's neck.

That's when I realized that there was nothing that could be done for either of them. The life had drained from their young bodies. Lydia's face was cold to my touch. Without touching him, I knew Cecil was cold, too.

*Please, God, make this okay. If you can and will, please make it okay.*

Bobby sat there beside Cecil, staring, crying silently. I crawled across the damp floor to Cecil and untied the rope from his neck and cradled his head in my hands as I peered into his distorted face. The faces of brother and sister were ashen, their eyes protruding and half open.

"Bobby, hear me now—you must run and find Homer or Luke or anybody and tell them what's happened."

Bobby, his head hung low, was moaning and unresponsive.

"Bobby," I screamed. I took his face in my hands and pleaded, "You have to go and get help."

Finally, his senses returned. He quickly disappeared through the door. I heard gravel scattering as he ran through the darkness.

All was silent again. I strained to hear any sounds—maybe they would breathe and all would be forgiven and they would be whole again.

*"Oh god, why?"*

But there would be no answer forthcoming. Confusion reigned within. I placed my friends together, side-by-side, and closed their half-open eyes. Then I sat on the dusty floor beside their stiff teenage bodies, leaned back against the oil-stained, concrete-block wall, placed my face in my hands, and wept.

For a moment there was nothing but darkness. Then, into my mind came the gunshot explosion that had rocked my life as a child. The memory of the night of my parent's deaths blasted its way through its protecting cocoon of denial, searing my insides, wracking my soul. I hadn't thought about that awful night for years. I wanted to blame God again for that night and for this.

*"God doesn't punish us, Charlie. We do that to ourselves, well enough." Had Luke really said that? I'm so confused.*

I became that helpless child from long ago, searching in vain for someone to wrap their arms around me—to make it all go away—to keep the demons from my door. Once again—so very helpless. I thought that I would never feel this way again—that my years on the hill had given me strength and calloused my heart, and there was little I would fear any longer. *I had been through enough and passed the test, hadn't I? Would God help me this time? He hadn't before, or had He? Were Luke's words true?* The madness flew through my mind at a blistering pace until I was lost again. The insulation from my pain provided by time's passing was stripped away—the hurt was bared again, in all its painful intensity. *This is going to be more than I can handle.* A distant siren crested the hilltop, interrupting the silence. More than one vehicle skidded to a stop in the gravel parking lot. Car doors slammed shut.

Luke and Mr. Loveless were the first to enter, followed by Homer. Mr. Loveless closed Cecil's then Lydia's eyes with a gentle motion of his hand and began to pray over them. Luke walked to where I was sitting on the floor and helped me to my feet. He embraced me tightly, his big hand gently stroking my hair.

I felt the same comfort from his embrace I'd felt that horrible night long ago when the policeman picked me up, and I cried on his shoulder. Still, it was only a small measure of the comfort I sought.

"Come on, son. You've done all you can do here."

Luke led me away—out of the barn and into the fog.

# 22. The Next Day

THE TRAGEDY OF CECIL AND LYDIA had abruptly altered my life again, reminding me that pain always has a presence on the Hill.

All the children, except the very youngest, were aware of what had happened at the barn yesterday. We now gathered under the tall white steeple of the Home's chapel to remember and pray for Cecil and Lydia. We all took our seats in the pews wherever we wished, not with our own groups like we usually did. Brothers and sisters sat together and held hands—formalities would be dispensed with today—everyone here was hurting.

I had found my three brothers and we sat together, close to the front of the chapel. Bobby sat beside me and beside him were most of the rest of the boys from the cottage.

Danny, Mark, and Jeff had all asked me the question that no one could answer. It was the one-word, answerless question that had haunted me for most of my life—why?

Luke sat in the pew in front of us. He had taken Bobby and me with him yesterday after what had happened. Mr. Loveless had requested that Luke stay with us, but he didn't need to be asked. Luke knew that the horrible scene that Bobby and I now carried wouldn't be dealt with easily.

I hadn't even bothered to ask the unanswerable question yet. Maybe I would soon—probably not, though. After all these years, I knew that *the answer* wouldn't be forthcoming—*the answer* was nowhere and nothing—it didn't exist. And because *the answer* had always remained elusive, I'd grown weary of searching. *Why* was the question that wouldn't be satisfied.

The chapel was beautiful, with sunlight splashing color from stained-glass windows onto the cream-colored walls. Because news of what happened had circulated, many townsfolk and church members were here, and several had brought flowers that now radiated their beauty in the colored sunshine, filling the bright space with a sweet scent. The beauty stood in contrast to the air of total disbelief and grief.

I was heartbroken, but the blistering heat of anger burned through my gut. The anger that had saved me when we first arrived here was a protective wall that I'd sought refuge behind—a wall that had eased the burden of distress because of that elusive answer that could never be found. Yes, my anger had kept me alive before and would again.

I wished that Cecil and Lydia could have discovered my refuge. Maybe if they had, they would still be here. Maybe anger would have saved them, also.

I was, once again, wondering just who should be the recipient of that anger. I would, for years, blame Cecil and Lydia's mom and dad. I didn't even know if they were alive, but surely they must bear some responsibility, whether alive or not.

For years now, I'd listened to Luke teach me about life being about choices—how God leaves all that to us. But I couldn't help but believe that we, as kids, shouldn't have to choose so much. I just wish that grown-ups could do what they're supposed to. We should be loved and fed and taken care of—none of us should have to wonder if life is too painful to bear—whether we should live or die. Why is that too much to ask of grown-ups? Those who are charged with our wellbeing?

*Why?* There's the unanswerable again.

So we all embraced, and Mr. Loveless proclaimed that Cecil and Lydia were in God's hands now, but I thought they'd rather be happy and still be here. I cried and squeezed my brother's hands, and like that night from long ago, I was grateful that my three brothers hadn't witnessed any of what happened to Cecil and his sister.

After the service, Luke asked Bobby and me to spend the rest of the day with him, and we agreed.

When he arrived at the front of the cottage, he had four fishing poles in the back of the truck.

"Let's go see if we can catch a fish," Luke said, trying his best to smile.

Without offering an explanation for his plans, we drove down the hill to Buddy's house and stopped. Annie-Mae offered sweet tea.

"Hey, boys," Buddy said. "Sorry 'bout what happent. Luke done told you we goin' fishin'. Ain't nobody gonna talk 'bout it iffen you don' want'ta, but iffen you do, 'at's okay, too."

We didn't—Luke and Buddy tried to make small talk, but I hardly heard what was being said.

After hugs from Annie, we departed.

We were all silent as Luke's old truck purred its way south, past Cedartown's city limits toward Bremen, where an old friend of Buddy's owned a farm with a large lake.

After twenty minutes, Luke turned off the highway onto a dirt road then through a wooden gate and stopped near the edge of a pond about ten acres in size. It was a beautiful place, with pastures of thick fescue leading all the way to the edge of the water on two sides. The dam and far side had large pines lining the shore.

"They's crickets fo' catchin' bream, or sum o' my homemade catfish bait in a jar back'ere too," Buddy said as we were exiting the truck.

We stayed together and headed to the pond's dam where we sat back against some trees in the shade and baited our hooks and tossed the lines into the water. Soon, Luke's line was playing out into the water, and he promptly reeled in a small catfish, which he threw back.

"You gon' ha' to do better'n 'at, now," Buddy said to Luke.

All at once, our lines started moving, and we all had fish on the hook. At a frantic pace, for the next two hours, we pulled in catfish after catfish and kept only the big ones, until we had filled the stringer. Soon, we started back toward town.

"Life sho's hard sometimes, ain't it boys?" Buddy wanted to know, shattering the silence in the truck.

"Yeah, it sure is," Bobby replied.

"But the one good thang is, it ain't always 'at way. They's a whole lotta good happen to folks, too. But, good folks die sometimes," Buddy said, turning to look at Bobby and me. "Jes' don't seem fair now, do it?" Buddy asked. "Don't seem to be no rhyme nor reason tu'it."

That's all that was said concerning what had happened. No amount of talking would have eased what Bobby and I felt that day. But Luke and Buddy knew that. They had both wrestled with the question themselves during their long lives. They had experienced immense loss and pain, but through their faith, hope had prevailed. So they hadn't spent time offering an explanation or trying to answer the unanswerable question for us that afternoon.

Trying to ease our pain, they simply took us fishing.

# 23. The Church

WE WERE TAUGHT THAT A GOOD Sunday morning soul-saving message from the preacher was what was needed if we orphans were to have any shot at a decent life—not that any of us thought that after the orphanage a normal life would ever be possible. Just what the hell was normal supposed to mean, anyway? We didn't give it much thought, though. My life was filled from can-to-can't with thoughts of eking out as much fun as possible and making the most out of what was a less-than-desirable way to grow up.

But we lived in an orphanage founded and supported by the church, so the Holy Gospel was ordained to be our foremost guiding principle.

We attended Sunday school and the eleven o'clock worship service in the sanctuary and Wednesday prayer meetings and every revival that blew through town and set up their holy-circus tents in some benevolent farmer's pasture. Most of the revival preachers could spew fire and brimstone until they had the orphans wailing and shaking. And the grand finale was always a stampeding altar call during which all the sinners rejected the hideous evil that dwelled within—Lordy, it was a sight to behold.

All of us were so eager for deliverance from our daily lives that we would promise God anything, directly through His messenger on the raised plywood platform down front. While we all hoped our message and promises would be dutifully delivered through this holy man, we had our doubts. After attending probably twenty such spectacles in the last few years, nothing had changed, but I continued holding on to a thread of hope. *Why not?*

We were outfitted with a Sunday suit and shoes—attire that was so important that it was to be worn strictly for Holy events and always to Sunday morning worship service. Once dutifully attired, we boarded the orphanage's green school buses and headed down the hill to the Methodist Church to receive our sanctification.

Usually the most exciting thing about Sunday service was to make it through the sermon without falling asleep, but this particular Sunday would prove to be a red letter day in the lives of at least us fourteen older boys living in the cottage. Most of us would remember it forever—those in charge of us wanted to forget it as soon as possible.

The trip to the church was uneventful. Each bus carried a chaperone, and ours was none other than Mildred Dowdy, whose ear-pulling wrath Danny and I had experienced the very first morning at the Home, years earlier.

Granted, I'd aged a few years and moved out from under her stern tutelage, but her wicked demeanor hadn't changed much, apparently. She still possessed that evil eye, like some mythical beast to be feared. Stiff-postured with her gray hair pulled back severely in a tight bun, she gave the impression that she'd never enjoyed a single day of her existence. She could always be found in a tight-fitting gray suit, looking like a Nazi guard at some internment camp. All she lacked was a pair of knee-high black boots and a whip, or at least that's how I imagined her.

I had vowed to repay her for what she'd done to my little brother—the desire for revenge had been festering for a long time.

So today, here Mildred stood in the front of the bus just hoping she could catch one of us hooligans doing something wrong. She had a sharp eye for such things, and in fact, it was hard to put much past her. That was why she was chaperoning us, the oldest group of boys, to church and back.

Shortly before eleven o'clock on that memorable Sunday, we entered through the front double doors of the Methodist Church. After politely exchanging "good mornings" and handshakes with the fine townspeople, Mildred assumed her Gestapo demeanor and herded us one-by-one into an oak pew that was long enough to accommodate our entire motley crew. Mildred was on one end, and Bobby and I were on the other.

The organ began playing, the opening hymn was sung, and the congregation comprised of local townsfolk and all of us from the Hill recited the usual Methodist ritual and then settled in for a good dose of Divine guidance.

As was the case every Sunday, all six of us on the four a.m. milking crew were having a good deal of trouble staying awake. Mildred, with her eagle eye, would send elbow jabs by proxy down the entire length of the pew until she was confident her message was received.

Having twice been so castigated, and now fully awake, I noticed that Bobby was becoming restless, fidgeting back and forth. He continued for several minutes, rocking from one side of his butt to the other.

When I turned to ask him what was wrong, his face was contorted as if he was in great pain. And then he raised high up on the butt cheek opposite where I was sitting—or maybe his butt cheek raised him. The moment was frozen in time as I realized what was about to occur and that there wasn't a thing I could do to stop it.

The preacher had just reached a Divine crescendo. And at the exact moment he chose to pause to allow his flock to absorb the religious fervor, it happened.

In the heavenly quiet, at that precise moment, Bobby let out a blast that shook the stained glass windows and the good souls of all those in attendance. His butt cracked like someone was splitting a sweet-gum log, and the bare oak pew vibrated from one end to the other. And to make matters worse, the thunder from his butt seemed to go on for eternity. I know it didn't last that long, but to hear it spoken about later, it might have been longer than that.

Bobby's face stayed contorted in pain the entire time and stayed that way until the thundering finally stopped.

The injury was complete, but the insult was just beginning.

To complicate matters further, accompanying the awful noise was an invisible cloud of vile-smelling methane. The congregation was stunned into silence while they collectively contemplated what response, if any, should be forthcoming.

Seconds agonizingly ticked by as the cloud of noxious gas dispersed up and down the pews and across the aisle so the orphans, of course, were the first to voice our disgust when the stink overwhelmed us.

Some practically undressed themselves as they sought to pull their undershirts out from their belts and cover their noses. Others were making gurgling noises as they tried to keep the gas at bay. And just to cap things off, when the noxious cloud enveloped Joe-Bob, he hollered, "HOLY CRAP, BOBBY!"

Not a worshipping soul knew how to react. The congregation's older members frantically waved their wooden-handled paper fans—the ones with Jesus' picture printed on one side—in front of their faces. The stunned preacher braced against his pulpit, his jaw dropping as he contemplated his next move. This was turning into quite an event.

Mildred, a church deaconess, looked as if she might have a stroke at any second. Her face was fire-engine red, and some of the boys would later swear they actually saw smoke coming from out of her ears. She sat there in abject disbelief, trying to melt away into the oak pew, I'm sure.

Try as we might, we just couldn't help it, and finally, the snickering started and quickly turned into uncontrollable laughter. There was nothing else to do—the damage had been done. Let the chips fall where they may, but this event brought out the best in this cynical, confused, rowdy group of orphans.

When most of the town kids began laughing, their parents whisked them to safety down the center aisle and through the flung-open double doors. Of course, the laughter was infectious, and even some of the grown-ups from town joined in.

Finally, Mildred stood. Trying to maintain whatever dignity she had left, she motioned her charges to exit the pew and she escorted us, in single file, toward the doors. When I turned to look back toward the congregation, I could see that some people were horrified. But most seemed to be doing their best to stifle their laughter and some of the town kids were so loud that their parents, feigning embarrassment while fighting back smiles of their own, pummeled their kids with the paper Jesus fans.

It was a spectacle of such magnitude that it could never be forgotten. In the annals of orphan life, Bobby became a mythical hero that morning, to be remembered for a long time to come.

Later attempts to describe the event fell way short of the mark. If it could have been written about in the local newspaper it would have made front-page headlines. Maybe with a full-color photo of Bobby with his round, pink face all contorted.

Mildred became depressed and felt as if she had let her congregation, and possibly even God, down, but not before she made sure that Bobby, in spite of his argument that it couldn't have been helped, volunteered to clean the bathrooms at the church for at least the next six months.

As for the rest of us, we got off easily. We already worked like dogs every day, so any manual labor that was tacked on was worth it. Most folks live their entire lives never having experienced such an event. I, for one, was glad I was there for it.

# 24. Luke and Eustace

"HE'S A NIGGER, NOTHING BUT A black-assed nigger," Eustace bellowed to the boys in the barn.

The loft of the barn was large enough to store the thousands of bales needed to feed the dairy herd through the winter. Eustace was in the hay loft with a captive audience of some of the younger boys, including my three brothers, doing chores. He was off to the side, sitting on one of the bales, issuing orders as the boys restacked the hay that had fallen, making room for a second cutting of hay that was about to take place. On the east end of the barn were two large doors through which the hay was hoisted then stacked. Today, the doors were opened, allowing a breeze to blow through and cool the loft while the boys worked.

I had walked up below the doors, and when I heard Eustace's loud voice spewing his brand of ignorance, I stopped to listen.

"I don' care what nobody says, you jes' can't trust a nigger. You boys jes' wait'n see, but I know what I'm talkin' 'bout. They mite thank 'at nigger's 'ere friend, but ain't nuttin but bad gon' come outa it."

I listened a few minutes more, and then it became apparent that Eustace was referring to me and Luke and our hunting exploits with Buddy. I could hardly believe that he was talking like that to the younger boys. I'd heard enough. I walked into the bottom of the barn and climbed the wooden ladder up into the loft.

"Well," Eustace said, when he saw me coming up the ladder. "'Ere's 'at lil' nigga lova, now," he said when he saw me, followed by a demonic laugh.

The boys with him in the loft were all young. I was angry that Danny, Mark, and Jeffrey had to listen to Eustace's insanity. The boys had been asked to clean up the loft while the rest of us dealt with the rest of the farm chores. Most of them had never even talked to Eustace before. He displayed his ignorance daily, so we older boys who worked at the farm disregarded him. We had heard every vile and hateful thing he'd ever said before learning not to listen to him at all. He was our boss sometimes—when we milked or hauled hay—and being Homer's brother-in-law, we had to do what he said. It had evolved to a point where we stayed out of his way, and he stayed out of ours, but his presence was hard to tolerate. We would play every trick we could think of to make his life miserable, so for the most part, he stayed away from us, too.

"You know what, Eustace," I said. "It's a sad day for these boys when they have to work here. But the worst part about being here is listening to your big, stupid ass spew your hate."

His laughter faded as he looked at me with snarling contempt. The boys stopped stacking bales and were staring at Eustace to see how he'd react to what I'd said, but I wasn't through.

"These boys don't need to hear what you've got to say. It'd be a big step up for you to be half the man Buddy is."

I don't know if any of the boys even knew what we were talking about. They were all about eleven or twelve and were probably only vaguely aware of Buddy and Luke and me hunting. What I'd just said to Eustace was the straw that broke the camel's back, though. He shot off his hay bale and started toward me with blood in his eyes, and I turned and jumped down the ladder.

"I'll show you a man, you little shithead," he screamed down the ladder as I hit the ground running.

Eustace was a big man, but I knew he couldn't move as quickly as I could. He'd been chasing us around for years, mostly unsuccessfully. But he did catch one boy, once, and beat the hell out of him. I knew what the point of no return was with him, so I never let myself get caught. I believed that he was so stupid that in just a couple of hours, he would forget what had happened, and it would be safe to be around him again.

He was leaning out of the loft door, still shouting as I walked away.

"You better run, you lil' bastard. You gon' be sorry when I get my hands on you."

Then I heard the boys in the loft laughing.

"Get back to stacking them bales, you snotty-nosed punks," I heard him say. I felt sorry that they had to work around him at all. No one deserved that kind of punishment, especially a bunch of kids who weren't immune to his contempt.

Eustace was a fixture there, though. I'd heard that Homer had gotten him a job at the Home when he had come from Alabama where no one would hire him.. *Unfortunately,* I thought, *he'll probably still be here long after I leave, and there'll be many more boys who'll have to deal with his crap.*

It was a few days later, after lunch, that I bumped into Luke outside the dining hall. We talked for a few minutes, catching up on things, and I remembered the incident at the barn and told Luke about it.

"Charlie, you 'member the first time you went hunting w'me and Buddy and you ast if Buddy'n me ever had problems with those who didn't like it cause we was friends?"

"Yes, sir, I do remember."

"Well, son, there are a whole lot of ignorant folks in this worl', and old Eustace just hap'ns to be one o' many. Some might change and some ne'er will, and he's in the last category. The bes' we'cn hope for is that they don't spread their venom 'mongst the young folk. They sho don' deserve 'at. So, don't worry 'bout Eustace. Maybe I'll have a talk with 'im, okay?"

"Yes, sir," I said, and that was the end of it, I thought.

Later that afternoon, with nothing left but the evening milking, Bobby and I were bored and decided to walk over to the barn early. In a few minutes we were there and found Luke's truck in the gravel lot beside the dairy barn. Curious, and not seeing Luke anywhere close, we headed down the chute and under the hay barn. Before we reached the storeroom door, we heard a loud noise followed by a grunt. We stopped suddenly, wondering what was happening. Then we heard the unmistakable sound of violence—the slapping sound of flesh impacting flesh. We crept forward until we reached the door and peered through the opening between the edge of the door and the jamb. A stunning sight lay before us.

In the back corner of the room, Luke and Eustace were engaged in the heat of battle. Eustace was drawing back to punch Luke, but before his fist moved, Luke caught him right between the eyes with a massive blow from his huge right fist that buckled Eustace's knees. With his left hand, Luke caught Eustace by his neck before he crumpled to the floor and stood him straight up against the concrete wall. We could hear Eustace choking as Luke pummeled him across his jaw with a last wicked blow that brought blood spurting from Eustace's nose and mouth. Luke then loosened his grip, and Eustace slowly slid down the wall to the floor and crumpled into a pile, sputtering and blowing blood from his nose. Luke backed off and stood there, waiting to see if there was any fight left in his foe. Every time Eustace blew blood from his nose, a small cloud of dust erupted from the filthy floor.

Bobby and I looked at each other with eyes wide and open mouths and then turned back so we wouldn't miss anything.

Apparently, Eustace had had enough. He didn't move at all. Luke removed the handkerchief from his pocket and threw it to the dirty floor in front of Eustace.

"I'm only gon' say 'is one time," Luke said, breathing hard. "Are you listenin' t'me?" he asked Eustace, who didn't speak, but nodded, as the blood continued to flow from his nose and lips, accumulating in a bright red pool in the dust.

Eustace didn't look up at Luke.

"If I eva' hear o' you callin' my frien' a *nigger* agin," Luke told Eustace, "is ain't gon' be the end of it. I'll come find you and I'll beat yo' dumb ass a thousand times if I ha' to. I may be old boy, but I promise you 'at. And if I ever hear o' you layin' a hand on any one'a 'ese boys, fo' any reason, 'en you gon' tote a ass whuppin' fer 'at, too. And while we at it, I don't wanna hear o' you ever sayin' the word *nigger* on 'is hill, ever agin. You understan' what I'm tellin' you?" Luke towered above Eustace.

After a lengthy moment of silence, Eustace mouthed a feeble, "Yes, sir," as he lifted his head and set it back against the wall.

"What did you say?" Luke asked Eustace. "I can't heah you."

"I said yes, sir, goddammit, yes, sir."

Luke wiped the sweat from his face with the back of his hand, and then said, "This'll be the end of it, 'en. Clean youself up. The boys'll be here shortly."

Luke turned to leave then stopped and turned to face Eustace again.

"I ain't neva gon' say a word 'bout what happened 'ere, and I spect you t'do the same."

Bobby and me looked at each other then turned and left quickly, as quietly as we had come. When we reached the outside of the dairy, we started milling about, as if we'd just arrived at the barn. Then Luke walked out.

"Hey, Luke. We were just gonna come looking for you. What you doing over here?" I asked.

"Hey, boys. I just came over to tell Eustace something that I've been meaning to tell 'im fo' a long time," and he sat in his truck. He hollered, "See you at supper," and drove away.

This was too good to be true. We couldn't go anywhere now. I wanted to be here when Eustace finally emerged, and in fifteen minutes he walked out. He was noticeably shaken up. He had blood on his overalls and was sporting a black eye and a big red splotch on the side of his face. I just couldn't resist.

"Damn, Eustace, you look all shook up. You okay? Anything we can do?" I said, trying my best not to laugh. Bobby couldn't help himself, though, and almost fell over laughing so hard.

"None o'yur goddamn bidness what hap'nt t' me, boy," he growled. He looked like a wild animal, his teeth still covered in blood as he spoke.

"Ya'll just stay hell away fm' me."

It was always a good day in the life of an orphan when justice prevailed. I didn't get to see it often, certainly not often enough. I knew that Bobby and I had witnessed a great event, and I would forever remember how Luke taught Eustace a lesson that afternoon, one that I doubt Eustace'll ever forget.

That night, we shared what we'd seen with the others and stayed up late, telling and retelling the details, until we fell asleep. True to his word, I never heard Luke say anything about what had happened at the barn that afternoon, nor did I ever hear of Eustace speaking of it, either.

That day was destined to be included in the folklore of the orphanage, to be passed down for years to come. Before long, the telling reached mythical proportions, like a knight slaying a fire-breathing dragon. One result of that day was certain: Luke had gained the status of hero to every kid on the Hill, and I was more proud than ever to call him my friend.

# 25. April 4, 1968

"C'MONE, SON, AND GIT IN—WE GOT'TA go he'p our friend," Luke said to me. I was on my way back from the dining hall when he pulled up beside me in his truck. He had a serious and solemn expression on his face that I'd seen only once before in the years I'd known him.

"I dun tol' Homer 'at you goin' wi'me."

I did as Luke asked and walked around the front of his truck and hopped in, knowing that if Luke had a friend in trouble he'd do all he could to help. But he had said "our friend," meaning that I had a part in whatever we were about to do.

We headed down the hill, but Luke's expression kept me from asking where we were going. Finally, after a minute of silence, he said, "We goin'ta Buddy's house, son. Sompin's happened and I reckon he's gon' be needin' his friends now."

I didn't ask what had happened—Luke would have told me if he'd wanted to. I privately wondered if Buddy's wife, Annie Mae, had passed and Buddy needed consoling. That was the only event I could imagine that would cause Luke the enormous sadness now portrayed in his face.

The trip to Buddy's house took only a few minutes. When we entered the colored neighborhood a change was apparent—there wasn't a single kid romping around at the dusty ball field on the corner, and all the porches were empty. Whatever had happened had affected the whole neighborhood.

Luke pulled to the curb in front of Buddy's house, killed the engine, and turned to face me.

"Charlie, this evenin', somebody shot and kill't Martin Luther King. He was in Memphis, and 'at's 'bout all I know. It just been comin' on the news. As much as Buddy and Annie Mae love 'at man, I know they gotta be tore up, so's I thought we better come do whatever we can. That alright w'you?"

The news Luke had just delivered was incomprehensible—as stunning a blow to my senses as when President Kennedy had been shot back in '63. I couldn't speak while I processed Luke's words.

"You okay, son?" Luke asked.

"Oh, yeah. Yeah, I'm okay Luke," I said, suddenly jolted back to the present.

Buddy had been in my life for the past seven years—and ever since Luke had first brought me to Buddy and Annie Mae's home when I was ten, Buddy and his wife had welcomed me as part of their family. They had become as much a part of my life as Luke. I didn't know what I could do for them, but I was glad Luke had brought me with him.

Above the unpainted mantle in their house hung two pictures—one of Jesus on the cross and the other a print of an oil painting of Martin Luther King, Jr. Both pictures had hung there as long as I'd known Buddy. Over the years, as he and Luke and I had hunted and fished together and discussed the good and evil of the world, we'd spent hours talking about Dr. King, as Buddy referred to him. The more I learned of this great man from Buddy and Luke, the more I understood why his picture was displayed alongside that of Jesus.

Buddy and Luke had been my best source of knowledge regarding the racial strife in the South. I had learned very little about the true struggle of the colored folks in my school. The information I'd been exposed to almost always cast the colored community in a bad light, not to mention the remarks about the "upstart niggers" I frequently heard around town.

These two friends of mine had tenderly and gently taught me that the world—although full of hope should one seek it—contained elements of evil that I must be aware of. The evil of which they had spoken, the same evil that had cost John Kennedy his life, had once again reared its ugly head and lain waste to another great man.

"Let's go see how they doin' inside," Luke said, exiting the truck. I followed.

Pausing for a moment on the wooden steps, I heard the forlorn sounds of someone weeping and moaning from a couple of houses away. Like a lonely siren song of death, the cries wafted through the windows, delivering distress to any ear upon which they fell. It was the only sound I could hear. It seemed as if the entire world had come to a stop. The joy of this vibrant community had been sucked away. While every physical component was the same—Annie Mae's flowers and the quaint, unpainted houses with their tidy yards—it now seemed that the entire neighborhood was devoid of the hope that usually dwelled here. An unwanted malevolence had taken hold of everyone at once.

Luke didn't knock on the door—there was no need, for he and Buddy were as much brothers as if they'd been born of the same womb—such formalities had been dispensed with, so Luke opened the door and stepped inside. I followed closely behind.

The room was dark. Only the dim yellow glow from an oil lamp and the flashing gray haze from the screen of the old black-and-white Zenith console television illuminated the small room. Before I closed the door, the light from the setting sun illuminated sparkles of tears on Buddy's dark face.

He didn't acknowledge our presence, but he knew that we were there with him. It was as if he had expected us all along. He didn't stand—he sat there in his old, homemade rocking chair. Luke walked over to him, placed his big, rough hand on Buddy's skinny shoulder, and squeezed.

"I'm sorry, old friend," Luke said in a soft voice that conveyed compassion unlike anything I'd heard in my seventeen years. I watched as Luke unselfishly accepted some of his friend's pain and made it his own.

While taking his handkerchief from the top pocket of his overalls, Buddy finally turned to look up at Luke. He removed his wire-rimmed glasses, laying them on the small table that held the oil lamp, and used the handkerchief to wipe his face and blow his nose.

"They finally kilt 'im, Luke. God damn 'em t' hell," Buddy said, his voice a mixture of anger and confusion and fear. Shaking his head slowly from side to side, he began to weep openly.

Luke took a seat on the threadbare dark green sofa beside Buddy's rocker and took both of his dear friend's weathered hands in his. Leaning close to Buddy's face, Luke said, "I wan' you t'listen t'me, old friend—me'n' you been thu' a whole lot t'gether—we fought in a war that showed us both just how terrible thangs can be. We both saw some mighty good men die down 'fore their time. You and me—we know 'bout evil—hell we seen it t'gether, walkin' the same streets me 'n you walk. But we know the fight we been fightin's been just. God's on our side in this'un. We both know that, but we gotta keep fightin' a while longer, old friend. Martin died fighting the same fight we both been fightin'. But we can't stop now. This is my fight, too." Luke paused.

I'd never heard Luke refer to Dr. King as "Martin" before.

"I ain't never give a damn what color you are, Buddy. Me'n you never even talked about it—all I know is you's the best man I ever met and I'm standin' w'you for as long as God gives us a breath. I'm proud to call you my friend. We'll git thu 'is t'gether, Okay?"

Luke didn't move a muscle. The dim yellow light revealed a trail of tears on his cheeks as he wept with the old colored man whose hands he held. Buddy blew his nose again, and for a moment, he looked at Luke and shook his head up and down, acknowledging the words. Then Buddy turned to me and said, "I know young Chalie come wi'ya. Come oer'ere son and s'down wi'me,"

Pushing his pain aside momentarily and welcoming me to sit beside him, Buddy took me by my hand, gave it a gentle squeeze, and then guided me to a seat on the frayed ottoman beside his chair. He didn't release my hand.

And then I felt the power of the bond shared by these two men. It surged through me as if I'd been touched by God Himself, cleansing my mind of anything other than this moment. I was witness to a slice of purity—a giving and receiving of love in its most unadulterated state. And with the feeling of being accepted into their circle, I began to weep with the two old men who had shown me grace since I had arrived here, nine years before.

Although that April evening had started with horrible news, it had turned into something more. Luke hadn't been compelled to visit his friend because Dr. King had been killed, but rather because he knew how the news would affect Buddy. He had gone to Buddy's side to do what was needed—to help fill the hole caused by despair with all the love he had—to help comfort the soul of a friend who was in pain.

By Luke's reckoning, it was simply the right thing to do. I believe that's why Luke took me with him—so I would begin to believe that I had something to give—that simply by my presence, I, too, could help comfort a friend. And in the act of doing that, I would discover I had worth.

That night I was taught a lesson about the value of what most of us overlook, that our true worth isn't about who we are or what we have, but rather how much of ourselves we're willing to give to others.

I eventually fell asleep on the sofa, awakened by Annie Mae's gentle prodding. Walter Cronkite was still on the dimly lit television dissecting what had happened earlier. It was late and everyone had grown tired, so we left Buddy and Annie Mae's. Tomorrow would begin a new day with different news.

The colored kids in the neighborhood below our hill would once again be playing in the streets and kicking up dust on the ball field at the corner. And Buddy's neighbors up and down the street would resume their porch-to-porch evening conversations, though for a while, without joy.

A smile would eventually reappear on the faces of Luke and Buddy. But I couldn't help feeling the loss of another small piece of the waning innocence I had left.

# 26. The Swamp

It was a Saturday. We had milked the herd that morning and returned to the hill for lunch and our house chores. After that, we were headed back to the barn for the afternoon, and we bitched all the way.

We all hopped onto the flatbed truck, and Homer slowly headed down the hill and onto the gravel stretch that all too soon ended at the dairy barn.

Homer reeled off a list of chores that any one of us could have recited by heart, because we'd done the same chores on hundreds of other Saturdays. After telling us that he'd be back to pick us up at suppertime, Homer hopped into his pickup that he'd left at the barn and drove toward the hill.

"I hate that son of a bitch," Carl said as he watched Homer's truck until it rounded a bend in the road. "Him *and* his damn mama," he said, enticing laughter from the rest of us.

"Well," Mike chimed in, "let's get some of this crap done then we'll have some fun till he gets back."

There were two pickups remaining in the small gravel turnaround that doubled as the dairy's parking lot. One belonged to Eustace. The other truck, a beat-up rusty Dodge, belonged to a carpenter named Earl, who worked on the Hill whenever his skills were needed.

We addressed him as Earl, not Mr. Earl. We had long since dispensed with calling anyone around the farm "sir" or "mister." Maybe it was because of the nature of the work but none of the grownups seemed to require that title here at the barn. But away from the farm, we knew that if we didn't say "sir" and "ma'am" to any of the adults, we would pay the price. The protocol was to be respectful to any adult, even if we had no respect for the person.

Before beginning our chores, we decided to pay homage to our old friend. We found Earl in the cavernous underbelly of the main hay barn, which contained the multitude of stalls housing newborn calves. Working under light from bare bulbs, he was busy replacing plank fencing that formed the individual calf stalls.

Earl always had an old metal cooler full of RC Colas—it was really the reason we liked him so much.

"You boys hep' yo'self to a RC," he said, smiling at us while waving his hand toward his rusty cooler.

I had never seen Earl wear anything but a set of light blue, pinstriped overalls with a white T-shirt underneath, his trusty wooden carpenter's rule poking above the lip of his upper, middle-chest pocket. He wore thin metal bifocals pushed down toward the tip of his nose, and above his tanned, deeply creased face was a crew cut of white hair. I thought he must be a nice, old granddad to some kid, somewhere, but I never asked him if he was.

One of our chores was to carry the oak planks Earl was using from the bed of his truck to where he had his ancient table saw set up under the barn. The space under the barn was like a basement—the concrete walls on the sides supported the foundation of the huge hay barn above.

We paired up, and before long, soaked in sweat, we'd delivered a large pile of the heavy lumber. The oak was green lumber—"straight from the sawmill," Earl said. It had a pungent odor that, mixed with the smell of the runny crap from the twenty-or-so calves, made for syrupy air that was almost unbreathable.

"Air's s'damn thick down 'ere I can't breathe," Earl complained. "One o' you'ens rustle up a fan som'ers, will you?"

As we moved calves from pen to pen to help facilitate Earl's repairs, we could hear a tractor chugging uphill from below the barn. Eustace was driving the tractor, heading toward the double sliding metal doors in the wall, opposite the calf pens where we were. The floor of the pens was a cement slab that extended outward past the doors and ended abruptly at what we affectionately referred to as "the swamp."

Cows crap a lot, and I mean more than anyone might ever believe. I probably wouldn't have believed it before I had to clean it all up. Twice a day, three hundred sixty-five days a year, the entire, one hundred twenty strong dairy herd was contained in their holding pen outside the milking barn, and all they had to do while waiting to be milked was stand there and eat and crap. And all that crap had to be squeegeed up, shoveled into a wheelbarrow, rolled down the concrete ramp, and dumped into what was a veritable swimming pool of cow shit.

The swamp wasn't deep though—maybe a couple of feet—but over the years it had grown into a small, fly-infested crap pond of at least a quarter acre. Every week, Eustace would use a blade pulled behind one of the tractors to spread the wet manure onto the hill below so it could dry in the sun, to later be scraped up and loaded onto a truck and spread on the farm's pastures for fertilizer. There were days when the smell could be overpowering, but we'd mostly gotten used to it.

Earl, like us, had never cared for Eustace very much. He just stood there watching him approach the swamp on his tractor.

"I want you to look at 'at big, dumb sumbitch," he said. "I believe he's the stupidest thang whatever come out'a Alabama."

That made us stop and listen for what he was going to say next. Earl was looking in Eustace's direction, his eyes squinted in a devious stare. Yep, something was cookin' in Earl's carpenter brain.

"I'd love t'see somebody jerk his dumb ass off 'at tractor and dunk his head in 'at pool of shit," Earl muttered to no-one in particular.

Then, with eyebrows raised, he turned to us with a big grin, and it slowly became apparent to all five of us just what he had in mind. He cocked his head sideways and sort of squinted.

"Yessiree, I'd give four bits apiece t'see you boys do it and I believe, by God, you can. Hell, I know you can," he said, as excited as a mischievous kid.

We were momentarily stunned, but the idea raced around in our heads. To be sure, nothing would make us happier. We all hated Eustace. He had whipped and chased us around for years and all of us, at some point, had imagined him dying some long, slow, painful death. If we couldn't kill him, then at least maybe we could hurt him some.

"I know we could," Mike said. "But we'd be in damn big trouble if we did."

"You le'me handle 'at part," Earl said, as he spat on the concrete floor.

Eustace was backing the bladed tractor into the swamp to begin spreading manure and Earl waved his arms to get Eustace's attention. Earl made a slicing motion across his throat and Eustace killed the tractor's engine.

"Whatchoo want, old man? I got work to do," Eustace hollered.

"I got a proposition for you," Earl said, throwing his head back and looking down his nose at Eustace.

"Yeah, whas 'at?"

The grin on Earl's face hadn't waned a bit and we could tell he was getting a charge out of taunting an old nemesis. He spoke slowly and deliberately.

"I bet 'ese boys 'ere could jerk yo' dumb ass off 'at 'ere John Deere and dunk yo' head in 'at dung you spreadin'." Earl let the thought penetrate Eustace's thick head. "Now what in hell you got t'say 'bout it?"

We, too, had begun to think about what Earl was proposing. There were five of us—Bobby and I were the smallest, Carl was a bit bigger, and Mike and Clayton were almost grown-man size. The thought of dunking Eustace's head in the "Swamp" was catching on in a big way. We didn't have to discuss it—we all knew we wanted the opportunity to inflict pain upon this ogre who'd been a thorn in all our butts for years.

But Eustace was formidable, well over six feet and weighing close to two hundred fifty pounds. He was probably in his mid-twenties and farm-strong, so the battle wouldn't be an easy one.

"You ain't serious, are you?" Clayton asked Earl, wondering if this was just some of Earl's nonsense. It wasn't out of place for the old carpenter.

"Hell, yeah, I'm serious. Eustace ain't nuthin' but a big, stupid farm-hand, but big he is. Now, I believe you boys can take 'im, but if you don' think you up to the job then don' take it."

Earl was challenging us, but he knew it was a challenge we'd accept.

"What does he have to say about it?" Mike said, nodding his head toward Eustace, who had yet to utter a word in response.

Earl raised his arms to Eustace, as if to say, "what about it." Eustace adjusted his posture in the tractor seat, then spoke. "'Ere ain't *ten* o'you snotty nosed orphans c'n take me off 'is tractor, much less five o'you little bastards, so brang it."

Challenge delivered and accepted by all parties. With tempered excitement we all looked at one another and grinned. We were born to do this.

"Alrigh'ten, let t'fun begin," Earl said. "But listen 'ere. Eustace—no matter how 'is turns out, 'is never leaves the barn or 'ese boys could git in big trouble. No fists either or somebody might git hurt. Agreed? Them's the rules."

"Well, I reckon 'ey ain't wantin' to be tellin' nobody how bad they got 'ere lil' asses stomped, so's I wan' be tellin' it neither," Eustace barked from atop the green and yellow John-Deere.

We didn't give a damn about rules—we never had. We derived a great deal of joy from breaking every rule we could—it was our way of life here. We knew, all five of us, that we were going to inflict as much pain as possible, and we knew Eustace would, too. Years of anger would be our cohesive catalyst. The time for payback had arrived.

"You punks ain't got a sno'ball's chance'n hell'a takin' me off 'is tractuh. If you had half a brain you'd know it. Hell, boys, whatchoo waiting on?" he taunted.

That's all we needed. We stripped off our shirts and threw them over the railing behind Earl. We grinned and exchanged looks. One-by-one, in nothing but jeans and rubber barn-boots, we stepped off the concrete and into the Swamp. The huge tractor was dead center of the small pond, facing sideways to the back of the barn.

The afternoon had turned out to be a scorcher and the sun was high in the sky. Even the millions of resident green flies were still until we disturbed them. Puffs of steam drifted up from every step we took as we trudged forward through the sludge.

We hadn't verbalized any strategy, but we'd grown up together and worked side-by-side for years. Discussion wasn't necessary—we'd use our orphan's intuition to slay our common foe.

Eustace had the advantage of being on top of the tractor, and the first task-at-hand was to dislodge him from his perch without getting hurt. Our sweat-slick bodies glistened under the sun as heat rose from the dark green stew below. Like a pack of young wolves surrounding our prey, we began circling the tractor. We were almost knee-deep in the morass now, our rubber boots filled to the top with the hot manure. We all began to make eye contact as we took our places, our unspoken strategy beginning to unfold.

"Ya'll think 'is is really gon' hap'n, don't you'ens?" Eustace said, as he stood atop the tractor, twisting from side-to-side while trying to ascertain our positions.

His taunts were bolstering our fierce determination. The tractor was surrounded now, and Mike and Clayton were making a frontal assault on the tractor's left side—the side from which a driver would mount the tractor.

"C'mone you bunch a' lil' punks," Eustace hollered, gripping the steering wheel to maintain his balance while kicking at Mike, who was now right below him. Carl had climbed onto the blade at the back of the tractor and was balanced there with both his arms on the rear fenders and didn't see it coming until it was too late. Eustace had been watching him mount the blade out of the corner of his eye and planted a backhand across Carl's face, and he disappeared, on his back, into the crap below, propelling a geyser of smoking manure skyward into a slow-moving cloud of fat, green flies.

Mike and Clayton continued their frontal assault, and Eustace hurled insults while kicking with his brogans. Bobby and I, apparently not being considered much of a threat because we were the smallest, began a slow crawl up the rear tires. I had made it almost to the top—Bobby was already atop the opposite tire, crouched down on the rear fender, holding on with both hands for balance. Eustace was looking forward, fiercely engaging Mike and Clayton.

The stated rules, which neither side had ever really seriously considered, had long been abandoned. Eustace was delivering blows with his fists and boots and was landing more than a few brutal punches. He was thrashing and pummeling with all he had and still screaming for us to "bring it on." Mike and Clayton's heroic effort of a frontal assault seemed in vain.

Sheets of sweat were pouring from Eustace's face. With veins in his head and neck bulging and a demonic grin stretched across his face, he bellowed like some underworld beast when he drew blood from Clayton's mouth.

Then it seemed that he suddenly remembered Bobby and me and began to search frantically for us. He was still standing atop the tractor. To turn to locate us, he had to relinquish his grip on the steering wheel with one hand and grab it with the other. This proved to be his undoing.

Bobby, from his perch on the fender, had been watching and waiting. At precisely the moment Eustace had both hands off the wheel, Bobby—short and squat little Bobby—sprang like a fat-legged bullfrog and hit Eustace at shoulder height. In mid-air, Bobby screamed, *Banzzzaaiiii,* which he must have remembered from all the war movies we'd seen. It was beautiful to hear.

Bobby's momentum carried the two of them—as if in slow motion—toward the putrid cesspool below. From a standing position on the tractor, this was a good seven or eight-foot drop.

Mike and Clayton retreated quickly when they saw Bobby spring, but when Eustace's colossal mass hit the swamp, a tidal wave of steaming, superheated cow shit erupted and overwhelmed us all. I swear I could feel the earth move.

With Eustace dislodged from the safety of his perch, the battle intensified—it was now hand-to-hand combat. He had landed on his back, but with a cat's quickness, he jumped to his feet and was swinging his fists at anybody within punching distance. Mike took a few good shots to the jaw and when he backed off from the pain, Clayton stepped in. About all Bobby and I could do was jump onto Eustace's back and try to get our arms around his throat, but Eustace easily dispatched us into the awaiting fog of flies below.

From our perspective, there was doubt as to the outcome. Even as big Eustace's strength began to wane, I knew we couldn't win this as long as Eustace was standing and able to throw punches. He had already bloodied the two biggest of us, and Carl was wincing in pain from his nose, which appeared to have turned sideways on his face.

Then Bobby, remembering a prank played on the Hill on many an unsuspecting orphan, jumped down directly behind Eustace, on his hands and knees, with the crap reaching to his chin. Mike, understanding what Bobby was doing, dove at Eustace and they both tumbled backward over Bobby. This left Eustace off his feet and at our mercy, or so we thought. Bobby was left sputtering and clawing his way to the surface from his position underneath both of them.

Everyone was close to exhaustion, trying to breathe through nostrils caked in manure and see through mere slits of eyes. But Eustace managed to roll over onto his knees and kicked backward like a bull, in spite of being pummeled all over his body. We sensed the end was near, and we wanted the coup-de-grace but Eustace wouldn't go down any further. We had reached an impasse.

Mike, now standing and kicking Eustace in his side, shouted at me as I was on my knees beside Eustace and had him in a headlock.

"GO AHEAD AND GIVE IT TO HIM, CHARLIE!"

With my right hand I scooped up as much crap as I could and with an upward motion slammed it into Eustace's face. He started coughing and sputtering and when he had spit most of the liquid manure out of his mouth he hollered.

"Enough, god-damn it, I give!" His capitulation was final.

That was it. It was over, finally, and we relaxed our grips.

The scene was something to behold. Mike was the only one standing, covered from head-to-toe in steaming dung, a cloud of the green flies buzzing lazily overhead as if they'd just been invited to a buffet. The rest of us were sitting on our butts, completely soaked in the vile, steaming, soupy manure.

Mike extended a hand and pulled us, one-by-one, to our feet. And even offered to pull Eustace up. But Eustace just told Mike to get the hell on and he'd get up by himself.

We were a sight—our white teeth in big grins and the whites of our eyes shining through the smelly coating. There wasn't a square inch on any of us that wasn't dripping with sludge as we slogged toward the barn to collect our four bits.

"Boys," Earl said as we approached, "I've seen a lot in my days but I ain't ne'er seen nuthin 'at would top 'at. That was the most enjoyable spectacle I ever witnessed, bar none. I knowed you boys could win and by golly you prevailed."

We were exhausted but proud, and when we stepped out of the swamp and onto the concrete, Earl was there to greet us. True to his word, he dropped two quarters into each of our hands.

"Damn, boys that was quite a bargain. The best fighting I ever seen, and it only cost me two-fifty."

I looked back and Eustace was just now beginning to stand up. He was a big, two-hundred-fifty-pound shit-covered mess with a halo of big, noisy green flies. I wondered how long it was

going to take him to flush all the crap out of all those pockets in
his overalls.

We were overcome with the pure joy of having succeeded at
such a daunting task while walking up the concrete raceway to
the dairy to clean up.

When we reached the holding pen, we all stripped down and
scrubbed with soap and bleach from inside the barn. We jumped
around in the holding pen, butt-naked, laughing our heads off.
Good had triumphed over evil this day. Well, maybe not, but at
least we'd gotten some pay back and it felt good.

Somebody mentioned that we hadn't done the chores we were
supposed to do, but they wouldn't get done today. We just didn't
give a damn.

Eustace never mentioned what had transpired at the barn
that afternoon but not because he was an honorable man and
wanted to keep his word—he just didn't want anyone to know
that a bunch of snotty-nosed orphans had whipped his butt. We
weren't honorable either—by suppertime, every orphan on the
Hill knew what had happened.

# 27. The Potato Fight

IT WAS LATE IN THE AFTERNOON. The milking was finished, and we were on our way to the Stitt farm in Collard Valley to do something most of us hated to do: harvesting the potato crop. None of us was a stranger to hard work, but this is the one thing, other than catching chickens, that we really despised doing.

We all realized the importance of potatoes. After all, we sure ate enough of them. We ate them for breakfast, lunch, and dinner. Every way a potato had ever been cooked, I'd eaten. We had not only eaten them—we'd planted them, fertilized them, sprayed them, dug them, and hauled them. All different types of potatoes, not just the normal kind—Irish potatoes, baking potatoes, sweet potatoes, red potatoes, and some weird potatoes that were blue (I swear). You name them and I'd had something to do with them.

I had once thought that if I somehow survived the orphanage, I'd probably never again in my life eat another potato.

We felt very unfortunate today, because Eustace was heading up the harvest and the combination of the two—the potatoes and Eustace—would border on torture.

The temperature was in the low nineties, normal for an early September afternoon. Ordinarily we'd be enjoying it in spite of any chore, but potato digging took all the fun out of it.

By the time the truck reached the farm and Eustace was hollering for us to unload, we were already wondering just who needed to be hurt and when we could do it. Every now and then comes a day when all of us orphans, all at the same time, are ready to fight. And today our hostility at the world was fixing to bust wide open.

"Y'all stay put and I'll fetch the tractor and the forks," Eustace said as he walked toward the barn.

"I hope that sumbitch trips and breaks a damn leg," Clayton said, sitting in the shade, leaning against the rear wheel of the flatbed truck.

"Well, even if he does, we still got a whole field o' taters to dig," Bobby said.

"Yeah, well, at least that creep wouldn't be here. I don't know why he's here anyway. We can drive the tractor and get this done by ourselves." Clayton was tall—almost as tall as Mike, and skinny, with short, sandy hair. Most of the time he didn't have much to say. But he didn't like having to work around Eustace today.

Eustace pulled up on the Ford tractor towing a trailer that was loaded down with the forks and bushel baskets.

"Now, you boys all getchoo a tater fork and the spuds the tractor don't get up then dig 'em out," Eustace told us. "We need ever tater we can get."

A potato fork is a shortened version of a pitchfork and has dull, square tines, so it does less damage to the potato as they're dug from the ground.

"What the hell you talkin bout, Eustace?" Carl said. "You ain't even gonna eat these damn taters, so why the hell do you care?"

Eustace rarely ate with us at the dining hall. He preferred a hamburger joint down on the highway for most of his meals, mainly so he could gawk at the two hefty waitresses who worked there.

"Just dig 'em damn taters up like I'm tellin' you'ens to. You got 'tat?"

No one answered. Eustace drove to the end of the field and dropped off the trailer with the bushel baskets that would hold the potatoes and the stubby potato forks. Then he drove back to the barn to attach a plow that was specifically made for lifting the potatoes from the ground. Upon his return, he positioned the tractor over the first row of the withering potato vines and looked back at the truck where we were still standing.

"Get y'alls asses over here, god damn it and I mean now," he hollered at us.

We slowly trudged toward where he sat on the old blue tractor, and with every step, we felt like we had sand bags tied to our legs. We all knew today wouldn't be an easy one.

The two-acre garden was flat and the ten rows had been set apart just the right distance from each other, allowing the tractor to drive between them and lift the spuds from the ground. The three-hundred-foot rows appeared daunting as the red earth shimmered in the heat.

Eustace plunged the turning plow into the soft earth and the tractor began its slow journey down the first row, exposing and lifting the potatoes to the surface. The dreaded task was now upon us. The plow was positioned in the earth below the level where the potatoes grew and dug a deep furrow. It created a hill on the surface, and the potatoes rolled into the lanes between the rows. Our job was to fill the bushel baskets before the tractor began to plow the next row. We had to use the potato forks to dig and uncover the potatoes that were hidden under the loose dirt. This was always the worse part. It was backbreaking work, and we'd remain bent over most of the afternoon.

When Eustace reached the end of the first row, he turned the tractor around and positioned it over the second row and killed the engine.

"Don't you'ens throw no cut'uns in 'em baskets—they gon' rot the rest of 'em," he hollered from his seat atop the tractor. Eustace was referring to the potatoes that were damaged by the plow, which we were supposed to separate from the undamaged potatoes.

"You know what," Mike hollered back at Eustace, "it's hotter'n hell out here and we been pickin' up taters longer'n your dumb ass has even been here, so why don't you just shut the hell up and leave us to what we're doin'. You just drive the god-damn tractor."

Mike was almost as big as Eustace and the oldest of the eight of us. He'd had enough of Eustace's mouth. After his bold resistance, the rest of us chimed in and voiced our disapproval. It wasn't that we minded the back-breaking work—we'd picked up taters for years. But it didn't sit well with us to be hollered at by anyone, much less Eustace.

Much to our chagrin, it had been a very good year for taters. The tractor was unearthing twice as many as last year's crop, and the ground was covered in spuds. We filled the baskets as quickly as we could, working in silence. Finally reaching the end of the first row, we looked back and counted over fifteen bushels filled.

"Damn at the taters," Bobby said. "I aint never seen so many. Ain't but one row down and nine to go. Kinda depressin', ain't it?"

There are days when I can tell that something bad is looming on the horizon, and today was one of those days. We were all soaked to our underwear in sweat and dirt. The mixture had us covered in mud up to our elbows, and our faces were dripping as we wiped the sweat from our brows with our muddy hands. We'd stripped off our shirts and before the end of the afternoon we'd resemble the clay people from the *Flash Gordon* show on TV.

Agitation hung in the air.

Eustace had already passed us and moved on to plow the second row. That was when it happened.

Jim, who'd just moved over to the cottage to live with us older boys, accidently threw some dirt into Carl's face with his tater fork. Before Jim could apologize, Carl was on top of him and fists were flying. Then, in the heat of the battle, Carl pushed Jim backwards into Lanny, which was enough spark to cause the cauldron of agitation to explode. In an instant, all eight of us were punching and kicking, and blood was flying from busted lips and bleeding noses. Oddly enough, in the heat of the melee, I thought that some of the faces resembled clowns as the blood and mud mixed together. I was smiling about that image until I was coldcocked in the side of the head.

Anarchy reigned now, and it was every man for himself. Eustace dismounted the tractor.

"HEY," he shouted, walking closer to us, "CUT THE CRAP AND GIT BACK TO WORK."

That was exactly the wrong way to stifle this mutiny. We had always fought and probably always would. Our pent-up anger had to be relieved in some fashion, and fighting was inevitable. But afterward, our differences were settled and the offending parties moved on and reconciled. It was a vital and unavoidable aspect of living and working together. We all understood and accepted it.

But we weren't going to tolerate Eustace jumping into the middle of our fight.

When we saw that Eustace was walking toward us, those of us who weren't actively engaged in throwing punches reached down and selected the fattest potatoes we could get our hands on and came up firing.

Bobby, who had picked up a spud that must have weighed a pound, caught Eustace square in his chest, slamming him to the ground like he taken a direct hit from a cannon ball. Just as fast as he hit the plowed ground, Eustace jumped back to his feet and scrambled to the relative safety of the tractor.

"YOU BOYS BETTER CUT THAT SHIT OUT," he screamed, "OR THEY'S GONNA BE HELL TO PAY."

Eustace's screaming begged for a response in the form of a hail of hefty spuds flying in his direction. When he saw the deluge, he crawled under the tractor just as potatoes were banged off the Ford's hood and fenders. Eustace was no longer making himself a viable target, so we turned on ourselves with the potatoes, flinging the spuds as accurately as we could to inflict as much pain as possible.

With nothing else available for protection, we all picked up the bushel baskets and used them as shields as we each retreated to separate positions in the garden. Screaming battle cries, we hurled the missiles through the air, and then squatted to search the ground for more ammunition.

Chaos reigned and everyone was the enemy.

Eustace must have felt safe, because he emerged from the safety of the tractor and once more began to scream. That was a big mistake.

Mike, who was a really good pitcher for the Cedartown High baseball team, hurled a spud fastball and caught Eustace right in the forehead, knocking him down instantly. He must have a real hard head, I thought, because he came up fast.

No longer satisfied with sitting this one out, he engaged in the battle with us, flinging the small missiles in our direction as he stumbled back toward the tractor. He connected a few times, which obviously made him happy as he, too, grinned and shouted obscenities just like he was one of the orphan kids.

I suppose he gained some respect from us by inserting himself into the fight instead of acting like a sissy and hiding. But after a minute of seeking some revenge he reverted back to adulthood.

"ALL RIGHT, BOYS. THIS HAS GOT WAY OUT OF HAND NOW AND IT'S TIME TO QUIT," he shouted and with that, the potatoes rained down upon him again. The intense battle had a life of its own and wouldn't be stifled in the least, especially by Eustace's shouting.

The heat and mud and blood had been forgotten, and the battle raged on. But after thirty or so minutes of hurling and dodging spuds and ducking for cover, the sun and fatigue couldn't be ignored any longer. Those who had even an ounce of energy left feebly flung one last tater at the least defended victim. Just like major league pitchers after nine innings of fastballs, our arms were wrecked.

It was a phenomenon of sorts, for just as quickly as the potato war had begun, it waned and was finally finished. We threw our basket shields aside and lay down on the soft, hot ground, catching our breath as the sun squeezed the sweat from our over-heated bodies. We were bruised and battered, muddy and bloody, but we were no longer angry. It was always amazing to me how that happened.

Jim was the first to finally stand and holler, "You can come out now, Eustace—the coast is clear." And Eustace slowly emerged from behind the tractor.

Jim and Carl, whose fight had started the whole thing, stood and shook hands. Then we all began laughing when someone noticed that Jim was missing one of his front teeth. We all looked pretty rough. But Jim, a short fellow with long black hair, appeared to have taken most of the punishment. He was still smiling though, now sporting a bloody gap where his tooth had been.

"I better not see one more god-damn potato come my way," Eustace said, walking toward us. "Ain't nuttin gonna be said about what happened, but it'd better be over with."

And it was. But the downside was we still had the rest of the potato crop to dig. And on top of that we had to find and pick up all the ones we'd thrown.

Was it worth it? Hell yeah it was, so we got back to work as if it had never happened.

We picked up and loaded potatoes until it was almost dark. Just as we were loading the last bushel in the truck, Homer drove up in his pickup, wondering what was taking us so long.

"What in hell happened to you?" Homer asked his brother-in-law. By now, Eustace was sporting a large red goose egg right in the middle of his forehead where Mike had beaned him.

Eustace sorta glanced at us, then said, "I was under the tractor checking on a noise I heard and raised up and almost cracked my head open."

"Looks bad. You'd better get that looked at."

"It ain't nuttin. I'll be okay."

Eustace wasn't gonna let on that anything had happened because he'd be in trouble for his part in the fight, and we knew that.

"And just what the hell happened to you?" Homer asked Jim when he saw that he was missing a front tooth.

"Bobby hit me in the mouth with his tater fork," Jim replied. "It was an accident."

At that, Homer just shook his head.

"Looks like tater diggin' is getting to be pretty dangerous," Homer said, noticing the blood on our jeans and shirts. He knew that more had occurred than we were letting on, but he didn't probe any further.

Eustace reattached the trailer and after a few trips all the bushel baskets of potatoes were hauled and stacked into a shed. Our day was finally finished.

To our amusement, old Eustace would sport that goose egg for another week. It drew a laugh every time one of us looked at him.

Yeah, I'd have to say, the day had been worth it.

# 28. The Pond

THE WORKING CENTER OF THE FARM—THE large hay barn and smaller dairy barn and chicken house—sat high on a hill, overlooking level fields that fanned out far below. From the loft of the cavernous barn, the flat forty-acre hayfield, pasture, and almost all the farm pond could be seen to the south, connected to the barns atop the hill by a steep, gravel-covered dirt track cut deep with furrows.

There were many days when we cottage boys would sit in the hay loft and daydream about being cowboys out west, with trusty horses and rifles, living off the land and sleeping under stars.

Day after day we'd discuss testing our wits against the world. Having been here at the orphanage for years now, we were relatively sure that we had enough sense and ability to make it anywhere on our own. Surviving what we'd already survived and having grown up in this most challenging of circumstances, we had a teenager's unrelenting confidence—confidence that was enlarged when we were amongst our orphaned brothers.

This life on the hill had forced us to know more about many things normal kids would never know, and although we didn't realize it now, we would be grateful for these lessons later in life.

We were a band of brothers, always together. And when confronted with the boredom brought by idle time, someone always proposed an adventure.

This particular summer day, the afternoon milking finished, the holding pen cleaned, and the dairy barn washed down, we had several hours to kill. The six of us—Bobby and me, Mike, Lanny, Joe-Bob and Clayton—decided that we'd go fishing down at the farm pond.

The pond was a place of intrigue. We'd caught snakes of different colors there and seen wading birds of various kinds—herons and cranes, mostly, and kingfishers—and watched as deer and foxes came to drink. I'd caught a giant snapping turtle there once. He'd entertained us, snapping branches in two with his sharp beak of a mouth until we tired of the game and set him free.

But the biggest draw was the fishing.

It was a large pond as farm ponds go—probably close to three acres, as best I could determine, and at least eight feet deep at the dam end. We'd measured its depth before because we were curious, or at least we made an educated guess. I stuck one of our long cane poles in at the dam and we made the collective guess of eight feet, give or take an inch or two.

There was a creek nearby, but the pond's source of water was runoff from surrounding hills, keeping the pond full except during droughts.

Contained by an earthen dam some thirty yards across, the pond was longer than wide and shaded on the north side and at the shallow end by maples and pines growing close to the bank. The dam end and south side baked perpetually in the hot Georgia sun, with the bank on that side gently sloping into the surrounding pasture.

I suppose it was an old pond. Those who had come before us had said as much. It looked old, anyway. If the size of some of the fish I'd caught were any indication, the pond had been here forever. I'd caught some whoppers and I'd heard tales of twenty-pound catfish being dragged out. Of course, we all wanted to believe the monster fish stories. But when a bunch of orphans start telling fishing tales, there's no telling what the hell is true or not.

Some days were better than others. On a good afternoon, we'd all catch fish, but there were also days when nothing would bite. I imagine Luke would find a way to include a life-lesson in that.

The boys usually declared what they were after—Bobby said he was going to catch a big cat, and Mike and Clayton were always after bass. I didn't much care. I just hoped that anything would bite.

It was only around four-thirty and the sun was still high in the summer sky. It was hot enough that the pond's surface shimmered from the heat. The shallow end was muddied from the cows drinking and wading up to their bellies to escape the biting flies they constantly chased with their tails. The cows watched collectively as we approached, unafraid of our presence, no doubt wondering why we were going to interrupt their peaceful afternoon. Dairy cows are like that. They knew us well, since we'd milked them twice daily for years. We had to run them out of the water when they didn't want to leave, but no one felt any pity for them—they were standing between us and the monsters lurking just below the surface.

Through the woods by the creek stood a large, wild cane patch from which we cut our fishing poles. I had made my selection three years ago from a fourteen-foot skinny, but thick at the bottom, piece of cane that I knew would take me to the Promised Land beyond the bank.

But one must be wise in choosing a pole. I had learned the art of pole selection from several orphan anglers who had grown up and moved on to lives somewhere down the road, but I valued their judgment—the pole must be as straight as possible and formidable enough to handle a big one, but light enough to feel even the slightest tug on the line.

After a long search, I'd stumbled upon the perfect pole and cut it. Then I waited a month to see how it would dry out. Some canes would bend or split but when mine didn't, I knew I'd found a keeper.

We all prized our canes. At day's end, we'd lay them up on limbs in nearby trees, safe from the curious cows that would gnaw them to pieces or trample them if they were left on the ground. Many a novice orphan had returned to the pond to discover that his prized pole was in pieces. That would be the last time he'd fail to lay up his pole.

Hidden in the cane patch in a hollowed-out stump, an old blue Mason jar housed our treasured collection of fishing line and hooks and sinkers that we had purchased with our hard-earned money. Whoever had spending money would pitch in a few pennies to re-stock our cache.

Our money was spent only for line and hooks. We never had any store-bought corks, which were an avoidable extravagance. I could always find something that would float well enough for a bobber. When the bream were on the bed I'd employ a dried pinecone that worked well until it became waterlogged. Those of us who wanted a catfish fished on the bottom anyway. Store bought sinkers, the kind that slipped over your line and mashed shut, were great, but a rusty nut from Luke's shop worked just as well.

We fanned out around the banks of the pond, each of us with our tin cans full of fat worms we'd dug from up at the barn. Mike and Bobby and Joe-Bob were on the dam, fishing in the deeper end, believing that the big fish would stay in deep water. Lanny and I were in the shade, and Clayton was on the far side, by himself, hollering about how it was so quiet over there that he was guaranteed to pull in the biggest catch.

There's something about pond fishing with a cane pole that makes you pay close attention. While you concentrate on your line and float, the rest of the world disappears. But when fish didn't seem to respond to my healthy worms, even as they wiggled their fat bodies to pieces and became martyrs to our cause, I began to accept that today, like so many others, might see us lose and the fish win.

It was too hot. Too early, too, maybe, but we'd slayed them here before on afternoons just like this. We had been spread out around the pond for at least an hour, and Mike and Joe-Bob had moved into the shade near Lanny and me.

"I wish they was sompin we c'do t'make 'em bite," Joe-Bob said, sitting against the trunk of a pine, sliding his ball-cap down over his eyes, his cane pole stuck down between his legs.

"And I wish 'ese damn flies'd go sommers else," he added, frustrated, swatting at the thick cloud of gnats hovering around his face.

Bobby was sitting alone on the dam and could hear us talking. Being unusually quiet since we started fishing, he chimed in, "I know how we can catch 'em."

"Yeah, genius, and how's 'at?" Mike challenged.

"Well, it's simple," Bobby said, as he lifted his cane pole, struggling to replace his drowned worm with one that obviously had no intention of being impaled by a rusty fish hook. When he finally had the worm on the hook, he tossed his line back into the water. We were all waiting to hear his big plan.

"Down here—he pointed straight down—the water's almos' alla'way t'the top o' the dam. If'n we dig a ditch and let out some water—jes' a few feet, I figger—the fish'll be thick and we'cn wade right in and grab what we want. Hell, we know they's a bunch o' fish in 'ere. Then, all we gotta do's fill'a ditch back up, pack it down and'e next big rain'll fill the pond back up. Nobody but us'll ever know whut happn't."

No one said a word.

Bobby was notorious for having ideas that, more often than not, landed us all in trouble. But Joe-Bob, still with his hat pulled low over his eyes, thought for thirty seconds, tossed a pebble into the pond and said, "Hell, it just might work."

"I'm tellin' you'ens, it'll work," Bobby said, now encouraged by Joe-Bob's somewhat positive response.

"Well 'en," Mike said, "since you so damn excited 'bout it, march yo' short ass up't the barn and fetch some tools and we'll see if it'll work. You'd better haul ass though, cause the sun ain't gonna give us but a couple'o hours."

We never *intentionally* planned on anything going wrong—and went to great lengths to avoid getting caught if something *did*. We'd gotten pretty good at the latter, because most of the time events didn't unfold as we imagined they would. Then again, we reasoned, if we did get caught, what could they really do to us? By now, we'd all been punished by the best of 'em and lived through it. We knew that if we tried to get permission for most of our endeavors, we'd be told no. So we usually just didn't bother asking anyone. We broke the rules and nobody knew it, and that made for a good day.

Bobby made quick work of obtaining the needed tools. He returned, breathing hard and sweating heavy, and nearly collapsed on the dam where we'd all convened.

"Damn, 'at's a hike," he said, barely able to breathe. Still, he believed in the viability of his plan so much that he immediately took the well-worn pick by the handle and scratched out a line in the top of the dam at the lowest point—which happened to be where we were standing.

Clayton grabbed the shovel and began to peel the fescue grass back over the scratch Bobby had made. "If we replace the grass ater patchin' up the ditch, nobody'll ever know what happ'nt," he said with optimism.

We took turns at the trench, and in just a few minutes—after all, we were skilled farmhands—we had a recognizable furrow dug the width of the dam. We were enthusiastically committed to Bobby's plan now, and smiles were all around as the top of the water was only inches below the furrow's bottom.

"Wait," I said, "Let's think about this."

"Hell no, let's don't stop now," Bobby said.

"I don't mean stop, but we need a plan. I'm thinking when we dig we oughta pile the dirt near and if anything goes wrong, we can refill the trench and stop the water. Let's dig until we have one last plug to take out. That way we can see what's gonna happen. If it's flowing too fast, we'll just stop it and fill the trench back up. Okay?"

Everyone sort of grunted in response, but took their positions on either side of the narrow ditch. Soon, all that remained was removing the last plug of dirt. We had dug the trench a half-foot lower than the water level and feeling proud—the big moment was at hand—I handed the mattock to Bobby.

"To the architect of another plan goes the honor," I said, as we all bowed to Bobby.

Adrenaline surged and excitement was palpable. Straddling the trench with pick in hand, Bobby delivered one final blow downward into the already wet plug of mud.

Water began to find its way through the trench ever so slowly. The water melted its way through the dusty soil and for a brief moment, I really believed that Bobby had finally summoned forth a plan that would work as advertised.

That thought lasted but an instant.

It was amazing how fast our enthusiasm turned into panic as we watched the trickle of water—having quickly washed away the narrow trench's loose soil—turn into a torrent. Frantically, we leaped into action. Clayton with the shovel, Bobby with the pick, and everyone else with hands and feet, madly throwing and pushing as much dirt as possible into the trench, only to see the fruits of our labors washed downstream faster than we could kick more dirt in.

When all the loose dirt we'd removed from the trench had washed away, there was pitifully little we could do but observe. We backed away as the narrow trench evolved into a large ditch and then into a breach that would have made a stick of dynamite proud, eroding away the dam's softer core.

"Holy shit! Look at this," Lanny said excitedly, pointing down at the upper-end of the ever-widening gap. We all rushed to the pond side of the dam to see what he'd discovered.

The pond was dangerously low now. And beginning to get sucked through our hole in the dam came the fish we so desperately sought. Every size and species of fish in the pond was being shot through and spat out on the other side—bass and catfish and bream and a few monstrous carp and a few turtles and even a couple of snakes.

There we stood, mesmerized by the seemingly unending mass—thousands of fish gathered at the dam, awaiting their turn to be propelled through the muddy, rushing torrent. There were fish that didn't appear eager to make the trip, but try as they might—even with a valiant and violent effort, they couldn't avoid their fate. The fast-moving water pulled them backward and flung them through to what was now a waterfall shooting out the backside of the dam.

Together, three on one side of the ten-foot-wide chasm and three on the other, we solemnly witnessed the final desperation and last throes of the small body of water.

The Home's once picturesque farm pond was no more. Now, left in its place, was nothing but a sad, three-acre muddy hole. Some of the larger fish had avoided the final exodus and were now vigorously slapping the mud in a final desperate attempt to survive. The ultimate survivor and kinfolk to dinosaurs, my old friend, the lone snapping turtle, was slowly, but deliberately, making his way toward the far end, having somehow found some footing to avoid the flood. Adding insult to injury, he paused once, and turned his head toward us as if to ask, "How in hell could you boys have screwed up this bad?"

The sun was going down now, and we'd been busy for a good while. It takes more than a few minutes to completely bury yourself under an event of this magnitude.

Then we turned silently to survey the pasture below the dam. All I could utter was, "Amazing."

Before us, spread out over many acres, was the depressing result of our efforts. The evening's sunset cast a heavenly glow over the scene, with the glorious pinks and reds reflecting onto the shimmering surface of the previously dry pasture now immersed in what used to be a pond.

And as I watched the fish flopping in every corner of the pasture, it brought to mind a biblical scene. It became a divine spiritual moment. Manna from heaven lay before us. Somehow, Peter and fishes and loaves came to mind and I wouldn't have been too surprised if Jesus Himself had walked out of the woods and across what remained of the pond.

Then, the shock of reality struck.

"OH SHIT," Bobby wailed loudly, his arms stretched out in front. "WHAT IN HELL ARE WE GONNA DO NOW?"

I envisioned him as Moses parting the Red Sea—partly to remain in my biblical state of mind for as long as I could. Our butts were cooked and we all knew it.

"Well, we can't lie our way out of this'n," Mike said. "Too many people knew we was down here. We're just gonna ha'ta let the chips fall where they will."

At that, Bobby let out another piercing howl.

"Hell, we done some bad stuff but we ain't never done nutt'n worse'n this."

"For the life o' me," said Joe-Bob, "I can't 'member when we done *anything* that's gonna get us in as much trouble as 'is is."

Bobby wailed again.

"Will you just shut the hell up," Clayton said to Bobby.

"Well, I tell you what we'd better *not* do. As much as they beat us up about not wasting nothin', we better not waste 'ese fish," Mike said sensibly. "What we done's bad enough, but leaving fish here to rot in the field'll be almost as bad. I'm goin' to the barn t'fetch the tractor and trailer and we'll take 'em back with us. Y'all start piling 'em up and I'll be back in a minute."

It was the only solution. Just a sliver of shot at redemption, so we fanned out and started piling up the still-flopping fish. No one had voiced an idea as to what do with all the fish but Mike was right. We couldn't just leave 'em here.

"Maybe we can say we just caught 'em all," Bobby said.

"Well, you big dumb ass," Joe-Bob said, looking at Bobby with disgust.

"Please tell me you ain't 'at god-damn stupid. At might just work if the dam didn't have a hole in it big 'nough to drive a god-damn hay-truck through," Joe-Bob railed, with hands held high in the air.

"Damn, I had no idea 'at many fish were in 'at pond. Look at'ta size of some o' 'em," Lanny said, amazed, as he watched a huge catfish flopping in a few inches of water.

Mike returned, pulling the trailer behind the red Farmall tractor, and circled the pasture as we loaded the slippery, wiggling, slimy mess into the trailer. We weren't very discerning, and a lot of other crap got loaded along with the fish—grass and sticks and whatever else we grabbed—because not only were we in a hurry but it was hard to see in the near dark.

When we'd loaded all the fish we could find, I stood back, absolutely dumbstruck. There had to be at least five-hundred pounds of fish in the trailer. Precisely what we were going to do with them was still a mystery.

Once we hopped atop the slimy load and Mike drove us up the hill, we all became solemn. You would have thought that we were being driven to our executions. And maybe we were.

The steepness of the hill and the uneven terrain dislodged the occasional bass or bream or catfish, whereupon it would disappear into the dust behind the trailer, but no one seemed to care. It had been agreed that we would innocently drive up to the front of the cottage, and in front of God and Homer and the rest of the world, simply explain what had happened. The only reasonable alternative would be for us all to scatter to the far reaches of the earth, but we were too tired for that.

It's been said that honest confession is good for the soul, but this was going to be a total crapshoot.

"You know 'at George Wash'ton did'n git'n no trouble 'cause he told 'em 'at he was the one 'at chopped down some tree," Bobby said.

"It was a cherry tree, you dumb ass," Joe-Bob said. "And if you say one more stupid thang tonite, I'm beatin' hell outa you." Apparently, Joe-Bob had heard enough.

Arriving at the front of the cottage, Mike pulled the tractor up and killed the engine. He had decided that as the oldest, he should be the one to break the news to Homer. He disappeared through the front door.

Mike didn't return for a long time, it seemed.

"What in hell could be takin' so long?" Lanny wondered.

"Maybe Homer killed him," I said.

"Oh, my God, maybe we all gonna die," Bobby moaned.

Ten minutes later, Homer and Mike exited the front door and walked to the trailer where the rest of us were sitting atop the huge mound of fish, our feet propped on the sideboards to keep from sliding off. A few fish were still alive and one, as if prompted by some unseen director, just happened to flop off the trailer and land directly on the ground between Homer's feet. Completely and utterly stunned by the magnitude of this event, Homer just stared at the gasping fish for a while—at least a whole minute—before looking up at us.

We expected a lot of screaming and maybe a good thrashing with a switch or a belt. But Homer, known for his hot temper and harsh punishment, spoke in a calm, almost reverent voice.

"Boys, I find this very, very hard to believe. I've spoken to Mr. Loveless 'bout 'is already. This's what you gon' do first—Mike's gon' drive the fish down behind the kitchen. 'En, you gon' clean ever' las' one o'em. I don't care if it takes all night, but you gon' work till it's done—I furtha don't care if y'all don't sleep a wink t'night but you *will* be at the barn in time to milk. Is 'at understood?"

We all nodded. What else could we do? So Mike drove us to the gravel lot behind the kitchen and the knives were handed out. We were given explicit instructions about rinsing the fillets and packing them into containers before putting them in the walk-in freezer. Homer then left us to our work.

"Just like I said—we gon' get off purty easy fo' tellin' the truth," Bobby remarked, grinning. And we all began to think so, too, if this was all that was going to happen.

There were plenty of nights when we'd stayed up all night and gone to the barn to milk in the morning and survived. But I was still unsettled. This couldn't be the end of it.

It was two a.m. when the last fish was put in the freezer, and we were tired to the bone. Every fly on the hill had been feasting on the fish and us since we'd started.

When we walked back to the cottage, Homer told us to strip outside and took great pleasure in hosing us down with cold water. He made us soap up and rinsed us once more before letting us in the house.

I hit the sack, and it seemed like mere moments before Homer was knocking on our doors, hollering for us to head to the barn for the morning milking. The six of us pulled together and finished our chores. As we were walking out the dairy barn door, Homer surprised us by telling us all to climb into the back of his truck.

"They's sompin' I wanna show you boys," he said.

We opened and closed a couple of gates before I realized that he was headed down the hill to the scene of last night's crime, and we were all morbidly curious now. As Homer drove around the soggy edge of the pasture, we saw Mr. Loveless and Eustace standing on what was left of the dam, watching us approach. Homer killed the engine and told us that we should go take our medicine. We wondered what kind of poison we'd be swallowing.

Standing on the dam, Mr. Loveless looked at us then smiled and said, "Boys, you should be complemented for such an ingenious plan. It brings to mind some of the stuff we did when we were kids. It's too bad it didn't work, though."

He turned around to gaze at the three-acre mud hole that yesterday at this time had been a thriving farm pond. Contemplating for a moment, he turned to face us.

"But now, boys, we have no pond. No place for these milk cows to get a drink—and that's a big problem." He sighed and paused for effect. "So, here's what you boys are going to do for our thirsty cows. Eustace is gonna get on the tractor and repair the dam. When he's finished and the dam is in good shape, you six boys are gonna take those five-gallon buckets from the back of my truck and walk over to the creek, as many times as it takes, and you're going to refill this pond.

"It might take you all summer. I don't know, but since you emptied the pond, you'll fill it back up."

He nodded his head once and turned toward his truck. And as we watched him walk away we heard him say, "That was one clever plan. I'll give 'em that." Then he threw his head back, laughing.

I found Mr. Loveless' message hard to comprehend. How could this be? I looked at where the pond once was and began to calculate just how many gallons it must have contained. Millions—maybe billions—and I knew that I was responsible for replacing one sixth of that amount. Boy was that depressing.

With all twelve of our collective feet dragging, we trudged toward a deep spot in the creek where we would dip our buckets for the first time and return to the mud hole with the water. And so began the birth of a new pond. I reverted to my biblical state of mind again, but this time I could only imagine us as Egyptian slaves.

That day there was no laughing or joking or playing. We had been caught, tried, and convicted, and we had received our punishment. We were relatively sure that all of us, for the rest of our lives, would be perfectly happy to stand, cane poles in hand, and catch fish the way we always had.

The summer sun grew hotter and the walk to the creek grew longer. And the few hundred buckets we emptied into the pond on the first day.... well, let's just say that if they made any difference at all, we sure as hell couldn't tell.

At the end of the day, we still weren't talking much.

Bucket after bucket, day after day, we made the same trip down the same path, till the track we wore into the earth impressed even the cows. There was no summer for us that year, nothing but milking and toting water.

None of us had ever been interested in the weather forecast before, but we were now. We prayed for rain as hard as the dust bowl farmers had. We nursed blisters on both hands and, in vain, wore leather work gloves, but the lesson was still painful. Bobby even surprised the Pastor at church when he volunteered for whatever extra work the church needed in hopes that God would look kindly upon our dilemma.

Finally, four months to the day, having been helped through our undying prayers and the resulting rain, the pond was restored to its former picturesque beauty.

I always wondered what the Jersey cows thought while they watched us, month after month, as the herd waded in the shallow end and drank the fruits of our labors. Maybe they were grateful to have their pond back—or maybe they were pissed that we'd taken it to begin with, like our old friend the snapping turtle. But who the hell knew?

On the final day, we watched Mr. Loveless' truck roll slowly down the hill to the pond. He stood on the newly repaired dam, assessed our progress, and turned to us and said, "Boys, I want to thank you, and the cows thank you. You've done a good job."

That was it. He turned and walked back to his truck, shaking his head and laughing. Again.

# 29. A Terrible Day

I WAS SITTING NEXT TO LUKE IN the cab, engrossed in thought, as the six-ton flatbed rolled down the road toward Cave Spring and the Pickett farm, where we'd be loading hay and hauling it back to the dairy.

Ahead of us in the pickup were Lanny, Joe-Bob, Bobby, Mike, and Clayton. They would begin to gather the hay bales before we got there.

This was the last summer I'd spend working with Luke. I'd graduated from Cedartown High School and would soon begin summer school at Georgia Tech, in Atlanta, so I was holding tight to my memories.

The morning had greeted us as several thousand had before with the Georgia air "s'thick you could spread it on a biscuit," as I'd heard Luke say hundreds of times.

"Ain't this just a beautiful road," he said, as if talking to himself.

I chuckled. I'd often heard him say the same thing as we'd traveled this direction. I knew this route contained pleasant memories for my friend—memories he shared with me every time we traveled this way.

He'd journey'd down this same road as a kid, riding with his folks toward town on Saturdays in their mule-drawn wagon before the road had been paved, breathing dust from the wagons ahead when it was dry. His dad tried his best to keep their wagon in the muddy ruts if the weather was bad and the road wet.

"GEE," or "HAW," he remembered his father yelling to the mule, directing it to pull right or pull left when the heavy wagon slipped from the track.

When Luke shared these memories, I saw a change take place in his face. He became that small boy again, still riding to town in the back of his family's wagon, amazed at his father's ability to control the beast in front of him. The wrinkles in his face disappeared and he became that dusty-faced boy of his youth, wondering in amazement at the treasures Main Street offered— how the shopkeepers paid his friends and him a nickel a day to help free the multitude of wagons from the mud.

I never tired of listening to Luke talk about those days that still held so much appeal to him. It was a time in his life when nothing but good prevailed. I sometimes wished I had been his little brother back then so those loving memories could be mine, too.

That couldn't be, of course. I grew up in a different world from Luke's. Indeed, the world had changed, and according to him, many of the changes weren't improvements. Most of all, he'd said, it had been a kinder place.

Luke had taught me the art of acceptance over the years. I had come to accept and understand that my life and memories are my own and that the perspective is mine to alter. He taught me that my experiences could propel me upwards or downwards and that the choice of direction was mine alone. I could learn from it all and prosper, or I could be defeated by the pain and struggle, never understanding or experiencing the sheer joy that life had to offer.

Over the years, Luke had nursed me with kindness, gently lifting me upward. And because of his generosity, I now know the true value of kindness.

"Boy, I'm sho's hell gon' miss you, though," Luke said.

"Well, here's the way I see it, Luke—you have my three brothers to look after, and that's more than enough to keep you busy for years. I've already talked to 'em so you'd better get ready," I said, smiling.

"Yeah, I know, son. But I grown real fond o' you, don' know how t'account for that," he said, chuckling. "Been lota boys com'n'go since I been 'ere. You may not know it, Charlie, but you got a real special place with me. I wouldn't miss you n'more if me and Louise were your real Ma and Pa."

"Yeah, me too, Luke," I said, proud that he felt that way about me.

He'd become my father. Luke had been in my life longer than my real dad had. Most of my memories of Big Mark had faded. There were times when I felt sad about not being able to remember more about him, but my eight years with Luke were full of good memories. I often wondered what course my life would have taken if I'd never met this strong yet humble man.

Luke had been there for me when I needed him most, illuminating the dark creases in my soul. I now believe it was a divine intervention.

*I really wish that there was a Luke for every kid who needed one.*

"Luke, what do you reckon that is?" I asked, pointing to a thick column of black smoke in the distance.

Luke had already spotted it, and I could see concern on his tanned, wrinkled brow. He didn't answer, but kept one eye on the road and the other on the plume of smoke ahead as it billowed higher into a light blue, late-summer sky.

This section of Cave Spring Road followed the serpentine path of Cedar Creek. There are not only sharp curves, but also trees following the banks on this side of the creek. Their limbs hung out over the narrow road, making navigation of the route treacherous if a driver didn't slow down.

Luke hadn't said a word when it became obvious that whatever had happened was going to be directly in front of our truck when we made the next turn. He slowed the big truck to a crawl.

And the accident suddenly lay before us.

Lying in the road, scattered in front of us, were Bobby and Clayton. Mike, bleeding profusely from a head wound, was kneeling on the pavement over Bobby, holding his hand.

Beyond the boys, and lying on its side, was an old rusty, red-and-gray Massey-Ferguson tractor and a trailer. Both had crashed through a fence, lying upside-down in the creek beyond. A gray-haired farmer in overalls, who'd been operating the tractor, had been thrown to the grassy shoulder between the road and the fence. He was just now beginning to rise to his knees, holding onto a broken fence post for support.

Twenty yards beyond the tractor and in the ditch on the other side of the road was the pickup that the boys had been riding in. The truck had rolled, coming to rest on its partially caved-in roof. The shattered windshield had popped loose and was lying in the middle of the road. The nose of the truck was stuck down into the ditch, the bed sticking up into the air.

The truck's engine compartment was the source of the thick black smoke, and the fire was spreading rapidly toward the cab, where Lanny and Joe-Bob lay motionless.

"Charlie, go check on the boys in the road and the old man." Luke said. His voice was raised and deliberate. He skidded to an abrupt stop, engaging the parking break, his eyes on the blazing truck.

A breeze was swirling and I could feel the fire's heat from sixty feet away. I reached Mike and Bobby, stripped off my T-shirt and wiped the blood from Mike's face and then wrapped it tightly around his injured head.

"How is he?" I asked Mike. Bobby's eyes were open, but he had a large goose egg on the side of his head where he'd impacted the pavement.

"I think he's gonna be okay, but he says his arm's broke."

"Stay with him," I said, hurrying to Clayton, who tried to sit up.

"Lay back down, Clayton. Somebody'll be here to help soon."

"I'm gonna be okay, Charlie. You'd better go help Luke."

"If you're up to it, check on the old man," I hollered, pointing to the farmer who'd been driving the tractor.

Luke had made his way to the pickup. And in defiance of the heat and flames, he pulled Lanny through the narrow, crumpled space that used to be the truck's driver's side window. He dragged Lanny by his arms, backward, in my direction, and then dropped him as quickly and gently as he could.

"Pull'im back a good ways'n look a'ter him, son" Luke said, before turning and racing back to the inferno.

Because of the truck's position, facing downward in the ditch, the flames had begun to penetrate the cab, lapping at the seats. The thick, acrid-smelling smoke was black as night and boiling out the side windows like some escaping demon.

I was afraid for Luke, now on his belly with half his body inside the truck, as he crawled through a wicked ball of fire to reach Joe-Bob.

Luke dug the toes of his boots into the ground for traction, pulling and struggling frantically on his belly to free Joe-Bob. The truck's seat was now blazing.

The Chevy Apache pickup's eighteen-gallon fuel tank was directly behind that bench seat, and it was full.

With one last heroic effort, Luke finally freed the unconscious Joe-Bob and pulled him through the window. Standing, he picked him up in a bear hug from the back, struggling to move Joe-Bob away from the flames. Luke's and Joe-Bob's clothes were on fire.

Luke screamed as he saw me coming toward him—he wouldn't let me come any closer.

Luke was standing just ten feet from the truck when it happened. Struggling to walk toward us, holding Joe-Bob in front of him, the flames found the gasoline dripping from the upturned fuel tank.

What happened next was instantaneous and brutal.

The fireball engulfed them as if they were being swallowed by the sun.

The explosion knocked us down, turning our faces into singed, black masks and charring my bare chest.

The stench of burning hair was overpowering.

Then, inexplicably, as quickly as it had appeared, the demonic fireball evaporated into the blue sky, leaving behind smoldering remnants of the pickup and the damage it had rendered to our flesh.

I managed to get to my knees and began to scream.

I staggered to Luke, now lying on top of Joe-Bob. His clothes were still on fire and I slapped at the flames until they were extinguished.

I always thought that Luke was indestructible. But now, I feared the worst. Joe-Bob was moaning, so I summoned Mike, still bloodied from the accident and blackened from the explosion, to help me.

"Mike," I said frantically, "I'm gonna lift Luke and you pull Joe-Bob out."

I straddled Luke's back and lifted while Mike pulled Joe-Bob from under the man who had saved his life.

That was the moment reality kicked me in the teeth. Luke's body was so damaged that I was afraid to touch him. I was afraid of causing him further pain. His hair was burned away and his exposed scalp was now nothing but raw flesh. Droplets of blood flowed from his head down his charred neck. The back of his overalls had been blown away and chunks of metal and glass shrapnel were embedded in his back and legs. Blood oozed from all the wounds. I ripped at the smoldering remnants of his clothes and tossed them aside.

Until now I hadn't had time to cry. But now, the tears began to tumble. I lay on the ground beside him, stroked his face and whispered, "You're gonna be okay, Luke,"

But I didn't believe what I was saying.

Through the cloud of my tears, I could see Luke move his lips but I couldn't hear him. The burned-out hulk of the truck was popping and hissing, so I put my ear close to his lips and listened.

"The boys? The boys?" he whispered.

"Yeah, they're gonna be okay, Luke," I said sobbing, knowing the safety of the boys was his only concern even while he lay there battered and burned.

As I lay there, looking into his blue eyes, feeling helpless and desperate, Luke attempted a feeble smile and said, "Charlie, I love you, son."

My friend then closed his eyes and was gone.

For the second time I had lost the one thing that meant more to me than life itself.

# 30. The Funeral

A HEAVY CLOAK OF THICK AUGUST AIR hung over the hill and pressed upon my senses.

There are days in all our lives that we'll remember forever—some because of great events in history and others because of some tragedy so terrible that, try as we might, we can never forget, even though we might wish to. These days are imprinted in our minds—we remember all the details.

Today was Saturday, the seventeenth of August, 1968, and this was the third day in my life that, had I been able, I would have banished from my memory forever. If I could be God for just one day, I would see to it that those three days never existed. There seemed to be no purpose for them other than to torment me.

That was contrary to what Luke had taught me, though. He'd said there had been a purpose for all of the days in my life, even the day that my father killed my mother and then ended his own anguish with another bullet. It was "Divine Design," he'd told me.

I struggled when I awoke that warm summer morning to reconcile the events of the past few days.

The crushing reality of death is inevitable. That I had accepted. It had taken years of Luke's patient counseling and mentoring, but I could accept that terrible things not only happen but that we must also learn to live with them.

Hours had turned to months and months to years, but Luke had persisted in guaranteeing that I become the person that he knew resided within my soul, even though I still didn't have a clue as to who I really was, much less who I wanted to be. He could see around and beneath the trauma of all the children and find and resurrect the precious remnants—that's what he'd accomplished with me—that's what he'd done for dozens of others.

Today, we would bury my friend.

Luke's wife, Louise, had honored me by asking if I would drive her, in Luke's truck, to the church and sit with her during the service.

"You *are* his family, Charlie, and mine, too," she said.

Gammage Funeral Home had offered to drive her in the black Cadillac they reserved for such solemn occasions, but she'd politely refused. She wasn't one for pomp and circumstance. "Luke would want me to keep it simple," she'd told him.

All the children from the Home would attend. There wasn't a single child there that Luke hadn't spoken kindness to, even the little ones. There were times when I would pass and see him in front of the little kids' dorm hugging and kissing and playing with the small children. Belying his toughness, his love for all the kids knew no boundary and although they were very young I'm sure that they, too, would miss him.

I walked up the staircase to the second-floor dormitory where Luke and Louise lived and were house parents to the dozen or so girls they looked after, and I escorted Louise down to the old blue pickup.

I knew that Luke would be proud of his wife's decision to ride to the Methodist church in his old truck. I closed her door then sat behind the wheel. I could feel Luke's presence. It felt like he was right here with us. I had never been in this truck without him beside me.

I sat there momentarily with my hands on the steering wheel and closed my eyes. In my mind a vision of my friend appeared.

"This is not a day to be sad, son. Rejoice! Everything's just like it's supposed to be, just as God would have it," Luke said, and I saw him smiling at me.

I felt Louise's soft hand as she reached over and wiped a tear from my cheek. Then I opened my eyes and looked at her.

"Oh, Charlie," she said, "I know how you loved him. There were nights when he would come home all excited about how you had done this or done that. Yes, he had cared deeply about many of the other boys, too, but I had never seen him as hopeful about the future prospects for a child as when he talked of you. I wish you could have seen how his eyes would light up. You occupied a very special place in his heart. It was as if you truly were his son and he your father. You need to remember that. I want you to always remember how deeply he loved you."

I pulled to the curb in front of the church into a place reserved for Luke's wife. There was no other parking to be found for blocks surrounding the holy place where we would honor Luke.

I knew Luke and I knew how deeply he felt for his fellow man and how they cared about him, but this day, after hearing the praise from those whose lives he'd touched, one would have thought that we were laying to rest a king or a Pope or a President.

Louise asked me if I wanted to say a few words about Luke, but I declined. What I felt was beyond my capabilities of expression.

Joe-Bob, still in Polk General Hospital, told the doctors and nurses that he was going go to Luke's funeral whether they liked it or not and that if they didn't release him in time to attend the funeral, then there would "be hell to pay." His doctor knew the circumstance surrounding his injuries and finally agreed to allow him to take part in the funeral.

Joe-Bob really thought that he'd scared them into letting him go, but that's just Joe-Bob.

He stood at the pulpit. Most of his hair had been burned away, leaving him with a bandaged, shaved head. Before he'd finished thanking 'his hero' for saving his life, we were all in tears.

Lanny was there in bandages too, but he hadn't suffered as bad as Joe-Bob. Bobby's arm had been broken, just like he'd said the day of the accident, and was in a cast, and Mike's head had gauze bandages taped all over. The back of Clayton's head had been shaved and stitched and bandaged, but none, other than

Joe-Bob, had to stay in the hospital. I was just red-faced from the explosion and my eyebrows had been burned away.

Luke didn't want to be buried in town. He had been born in the country and in the country was where he would finally be laid to rest. After the ceremony at the Methodist Church, a long procession of cars drove down Main Street and past town to a small country cemetery.

These were the "dog days." The columns of billowing thunder clouds towered into the pale blue of the sky, their foundation a menacing steel-gray bottom that would undoubtedly unleash lightning and fierce rain before the day's end. The early afternoon was hot and the air was thick with moisture, but the rain would stay in the distance, for a while at least.

There weren't but fifty folding metal chairs, some under the white funeral tents and some in the sun, but there must have been two- or three-hundred folks gathered around to pay their final respects. The funeral home had underestimated Luke's impact in the county.

After I escorted Louise to the front, I turned to look back. I was angered to see that the folks Luke loved the most, as far as I was concerned, felt as if they were where they should be, in the back. I was mad about the history of the oppression of the colored man for so long that even after we'd had the decency to admit our wrongs and change the laws, everyday life was too slow to change. Especially on this day, there was no place for differences—every person here came to honor a man they loved. I yearned for a simpler world with less hate. Louise tugged at the bottom of my shirt and I bent over as she whispered a request. "Of course," I replied.

I turned and walked down the aisle between the seats and through the crowd until I came to my friend. I gave Buddy a hug.

"Come with me. You're family and Louise would be pleased if you would sit with her. You're all family," I motioned with my arms to all those in Buddy's group, "so she'd like for all of y'all to come closer."

I took Annie Mae by her arm and escorted her to the front row where she sat beside Louise. The rest of Buddy's friends gathered closely around the sides of the tent. Buddy bent over and gave Louise a kiss on the cheek then took a seat beside his wife. Louise, without turning her head, reached over Annie-Mae, grasped Buddy's hand in hers, then, with her other hand, reached and held my hand also. Annie Mae added both her hands to the mix. There we were—the four of us holding hands—four who loved Luke and would miss his presence. It was a powerful bond between those who would miss him most.

The country preacher said some nice things, but not even the most eloquent speaker nor the most accomplished writer could adequately describe the hole that was left by Luke's absence. The world had lost one of its great treasures and no one was more aware of that than I was.

The casket was lowered into a dark hole, and then, one-by-one, every child at the Home passed by and dropped a handful of red dirt onto Luke's casket. The kids then turned and each and every one kissed Louise on her cheek. Even the smallest, the three-and four-year olds who had only the smallest memory of him took part. Though these young children did not know him well, I was sure that the memories they did have of Luke were of him smiling.

I watched them and I said a prayer that they, too, might find their "Luke." I knew how blessed I was to have had him in my life for all these years.

At the end of the line was Eustace. He surprised me when he showed his tender side. As a tear slid down his cheek, he gently clasped Louise's hands and told her how he, too, would miss her husband, then he looked at me and nodded his head to acknowledge my loss with a genuinely heartfelt look. Old Luke had even gotten to him.

It was hard for me to imagine how anyone who had known Luke could have not been impacted by the man in some way. He might have been the only man on earth who's passed away never having made an enemy.

We'd been at the cemetery for an hour, and most of the mourners had gone back to their lives. Eventually, the preacher, too, said his goodbye and retreated into the world away from Luke's grave. The four of us sat in silence, on the front row in the metal chairs emblazoned with the funeral home's logo.

In a few minutes I stood and looked at Louise through what felt like bloodshot eyes and asked her if she wanted to be left alone for a while. She nodded and smiled.

"Thank you, Charlie, if you don't mind," she said. "I won't be long."

Buddy and Annie Mae stood and kissed her and said their goodbyes.

"My husband loved you, Buddy, and you too, Annie."

"I'm gonna stop by and see you tomorrow if that's alright." Annie said to Louise.

"I would like that, if you don't mind," Louise replied.

"Well, mis' Louise," Buddy said, "I spect it ain't gon' be too awful long 'fore we all gon' be t'getha agin. I'm kinda lookin' foward t' it," he smiled.

With that, the three of us walked away and left Louise to contemplate life without the only man she'd ever really known—the only man that she had ever loved.

"Chalie, I wan' you t'stop by the house fore you leave fo' 'lanta. Let Annie fix us a glass of that good iced tea of hers and we'cn talk, okay?"

"You helped to raise me, Buddy. I wouldn't leave without coming to see you, you know that," I told him. After exchanging hugs, he and Annie began the drive back toward town in Buddy's truck.

Louise sat by herself for a long while before turning and finding me in the back where I sat, giving her all the time she needed. I would have camped out there for days waiting for her, if that's what she'd wanted.

"Come sit with me," she said, and we talked for another hour before leaving. Just sweet memories mostly, interrupted by silent contemplation.

"I want you to stop by and see if there's anything of Luke's that you might want. He would be proud to know that you have some of his old things. I know you'll want some pictures." Louise said. "Buddy's planned to pick up the dogs and keep them—Luke would like that. He might need your help moving them, Charlie, if you don't mind."

"Thank you. I'd like to have a picture of him, if you have one and a picture of both of you together, and of course I'll help Buddy with whatever he needs."

"One more thing, Charlie," she said as we neared home, "you're going away to school soon, and you'll be needing something to drive while you're in Atlanta. Luke would love for you to have this old truck. I know it doesn't look like much, but he's always kept it in good shape. You and he have spent a lot of time together in this truck, and I know it means a lot to you. He would want that, Charlie."

"Are you sure?" I asked her, quite surprised.

"I have my car, Charlie, if I ever need to go anywhere. Yes, I'm sure. I've known my husband most of my life, Charlie, and when you spend your life with someone you love, then you can almost tell him what he's thinking and feeling before even he knows it. I happen to know that when he sees you driving away in this truck, that'll make him smile. Oh, he'll be slapping someone on the back up there in Heaven telling them that there goes his son."

It suddenly became hard to see the road through the tears.

This truck was more a part of my life than anything else I owned, which, to be truthful, wasn't much. I felt like I'd grown up in this old truck—it was certainly here that I had begun to be able, with Luke's coaching, to feel again. It was in this old Chevy that Luke had challenged me to discover who I was. I had talked to God in this same truck. I had witnessed Luke's courage here and I'd been educated about what really matters most in life, sitting right here on this old, worn-out seat. I had learned a lot in my seventeen years, but the most important lessons I'd ever been taught had been delivered here, sitting between the two men who knew more about how to be genuine human beings than most would ever know.

Did I want this old truck? To not take it would be to deny who I had become as the result of years of Luke's mentoring and love. It represented a connection to the most precious episodes in my life that I'd been privileged to have been exposed to with Luke and Buddy. It meant a great deal more than the transportation it would provide.

Yeah, I wanted this old truck. I would baby it and it would remain a part of my life for as long as I lived. Luke would like that.

I parked in front of the shop and walked Louise across Fletcher Street and up the stairs to her apartment in the dorm and made sure she had what she needed.

"Charlie, I know you must be as tired as I am so why don't we both just take a nap and we'll talk some more later," she said.

I suppose I needed to be told to leave. I would have stayed with her for as long as she needed, and she knew that.

I walked back down to the truck and opened the door and sat back in the driver's seat and left the door open. I propped my leg up through the open window of the truck's door and just sat there looking up at the leaves of the white oak as a strong gust of wind transformed the thick silence to a clattering of leaves and limbs before disappearing as suddenly as it had begun. I wondered if that was Luke's way of letting me know he was still with me—I smiled at the thought. I knew then that I would forever be looking for signs of his presence.

# 31. With Buddy
# After the Funeral

A WEEK PASSED. I SUPPOSE I'D BEEN contemplating life without Luke, but it was hard to remember what transpired in the last seven days.

I know that Luke had forced me to deal with feelings that I'd tried my best to bury and now the process was again at hand—I wanted everything to just go away—I hoped that I might awaken from a bad dream, that it had just been a joke gone horribly wrong and that Luke hadn't died. But try as I might, I couldn't shake the sadness that surrounded my days.

It had taken this entire week to come to terms with the fact that Luke was really dead. He had fought to help me meet my fears head on, and I wished that he were here now to hold my hand and lecture me one last time on the benefits of facing down whatever challenge I might confront.

"Don't give into the fear, son. With faith you can overcome anything," I can hear him telling me.

But I wasn't the only one who felt his absence. Buddy had spent almost his entire life as Luke's best friend. An odd pairing, I'd thought many times, considering the time in history that these two had been destined to meet and grow up together.

I use the phrase "grow up" loosely here. The two were still "growing up" the day of the accident that took Luke's life. The odd pairing of these two best friends had enabled the spirit of youth to dominate both their lives. Although the two of them had grown old, their souls were still alive with the unending promise and hope of young men. I'd heard both Louise and Annie, the two who knew them best, say of these two that "they'll certainly grow old, but they'll never grow up."

I had promised Buddy that I'd stop by before I left for Atlanta, and today I'd fulfill that promise. I'd begun to miss him terribly after a couple of days, and I knew it was time to visit my friend.

When I pulled to the curb in front of Buddy's humble unpainted dwelling and killed the engine of Luke's old truck, I sat for a moment. I don't know why, but I was surprised that everything was the same. Annie's begonias were still blooming in their worn-out coffee pots. The kids were still in the narrow street, playing, and the neighbors were still in their porch swings, hollering back and forth. I know how I had changed inside since Luke died, and I thought that maybe the whole world had changed along with me, but that wasn't the case. The world around me looked different somehow, but everything was just as it had been—the only exception being the hole left in the hearts of those of us who had loved Luke.

Buddy's neighbors who hadn't attended the funeral all knew what had happened. They also knew about my relationship with Buddy and Annie Mae, and when I finally opened the door of the rusty truck, several of them stepped from their porches and walked down into the street and greeted me with hugs and condolences.

I was enveloped in a sea of kindness and warmth—a tender moment of unselfish compassion. I sensed that I would never feel alone again.

A beautiful, gray-haired colored woman took my face in both her hands and pulled me down and gave me a kiss on my forehead. I could see tears welling in her cloudy, dark eyes.

"We love you, boy. We all sorry fo' yo' loss," she told me before releasing my face, then she nodded as if to reinforce the truth of her statement, and her group of friends nodded in agreement. Several were there that I'd seen at the funeral, some I knew and more that I didn't, but I knew that Luke had been a friend to all of them.

I shook hands with the men and was hugged by all the women and thanked them before I turned and walked toward Buddy's house. It was an uncomplicated, genuine display of kindness from folks who didn't know me other than to say hello, and I felt privileged to have them in my life. I felt an overwhelming sense that my family had just grown larger. I understood and felt the importance of community amongst these neighbors.

Buddy and Annie Mae were standing on their porch. When I reached the top step I looked into Buddy's face, his cloudy, teary dark eyes an indication of the depth of his sadness.

"Hey, son. How you gettin' long?" he asked as he grasped me by my shoulders and stared into my eyes before wrapping his long, skinny arms around me and pulling me against him in a tight hug.

"Fer jes' a second I thought you's old Luke comin' t'see me one last time when I saw his truck turnin' a'coner," he said, smiling. "Ain't ne'er ben'a who' week go by fore I seen 'at old truck come 'roun. Fact o' matter is, I don' believe a who' week e'er went by 'out me seein' Luke, e'er since we was youngens," and he peered into the distance, searching through his memory.

"I don't know how I'm doing," I answered. "And I don't know what to do next. I just feel sad and empty."

Annie appeared and embraced me in a hug that I'd come to know well. The love within her flowed through me like the current of a fast moving river.

I know what love is now. Maybe I knew something of love when I was a small child with real parents, but that memory had faded over the years. Luke and Buddy had both spoken of God's love, but the pain in my past had prevented me from understanding that. I had spent years enveloped by a shroud of anger and mistrust until they had come along.

Luke at first, then Buddy, began to show me the true meaning of the word. I say show, because that's what they did and the only way I could have ever learned. Luke always told me that the teaching was in the doing—it was his way *and* Buddy's.

The stirring, intense emotion caused by Luke's passing was awakening something in me, and I could feel the change taking place.

Long ago, I had a need that had gone unsatisfied and now, here I was again. The difference now, though, was that I was in the presence of someone who could help fill that need. I had found solace here today, in the company of an old colored man and his wife who, I knew, both loved me. They would open their home and their hearts to me unquestionably and take me in as one of their own, if need be. I had never felt as *wanted* as I did here today.

"Come on in," Annie said as she took me by my hand and pulled me through the screened door that Buddy held open, "and I'll fetch you boys some iced tea."

I took a seat on the old couch and Buddy sat in his home-made, weathered rocking chair, the hickory arms worn as smooth as porcelain from years of use. The only light was from a floor lamp. Illuminated above the lamp was the large picture of Dr. King. Next to Buddy was a small table upon which was a collection of worn, yellowed old-timey photos from long ago. Buddy noticed me looking at them.

"I been digging up ever' picture I'cn find o' Luke since he passed. Boy'd 'ese rustle up a passel of memories," Buddy said, looking at the stack of photos.

He scooped the photos together and handed them to me.

"I don't rightly 'member who took 'em all. I b'leve Luke's daddy had bought some kinda camera and I think he musta took most o' 'em, cep'tin a ones he's in. Been a long time now, but if I's to recollect right, Luke had told me his daddy paid a dolla' for a Brownie camera 'at made these square pitchers. They's pitchers of Luke's daddy and my daddy and our mommas and me and Luke. Been a long time now."

I was amazed by the small square photographs. Luke and Buddy were both little kids. I had never thought about either of them being young, but here they were in these old, worn, yellowed pictures—two skinny little kids playing in a creek and climbing a tree and sitting on a tractor. Two innocent, barefoot children—their arms around each other's shoulders, smiling from ear to ear and having fun. Pictures of them grinning without their front teeth—snapshots of their innocence frozen in time from long ago.

To them, they were never different—they had grown up together in the same world until ugliness reared its head and told them that they couldn't attend the same school. But there were other pictures here—pictures of them later in life at each other's weddings and a few of them together in the Army, always in the perennial pose with their arms thrown around the other's shoulder. Nothing had ever come between these two friends. Even though man's law had often dictated their separation, no law could have prevented their bond of friendship.

I was mesmerized by the photos. While I was drawn into the world these two had shared, I was struck with the enormity and sadness of Buddy's loss. The loss I felt was great, but to have grown up with Luke and been a part of his life for seventy-some-odd years was hard for my seventeen-year-old mind to comprehend.

"I'm gon' be awright, Chalie," Buddy said, reading my mind. "And you gon' be awright, too. You see, son, Luke ain't really gone nowheres. He right here wif us. He lives in you'n me and all 'ese folks who loves him. As much as 'at man loved you—you think he just gon' go and leave you w' nothin'? Naw, son, he done left you wif'a whole bunch'a his love. And the rest o' us, too—plenty 'nough to keep us going."

Suddenly, the tears were rolling down my cheeks.

"Yeah, but I just wish that we could go hunting again, one last time," I said, "I want to be able to talk to him for a few more minutes. I sure do want to tell him how much he means to me and how much I love him. I just wish it hadn't happened so suddenly. God, how I miss him, Buddy."

I wiped my tears away with the back of my hand. Buddy took his handkerchief from the top pocket of his overalls and wiped his eyes, too.

"He knows how you feel, son. He listenin' right now. You see," Buddy said, leaning forward in the rocker, "Luke done did ever-thang God wanted him to do. I know God put'im 'ere t'save 'em two boys from 'at fire. While he's waitin' f'that t'hap'n, he done taught you all you need t'know. He taught you t'love and f'ogive and introduce' you to his God. Oh, Charlie, Luke wa'posed to be in yo' life—that weren't no coincidence. There ain't no such a thang in God's world. You gonna take all he done taught you to wherever you gonna go and put it t'good use. He always gon' live in you, Charlie, jes' like he's always gon' live in me. All things happen jes' like 'ey 'posed to. Always 'member 'at boy. Okay?"

I was glad that Buddy was part of my life—I needed him now. I cared as much for him as I had Luke. I just hadn't spent as much time with him, and now I'd be going away to school.

"We ain't had much time t'talk 'is pas' week, son. Will you be kind enough to tell me 'bout'a details of 'at day?" Buddy asked.

It hadn't occurred to me that Buddy might not have heard a firsthand account of what had happened the day Luke died.

"I'm so sorry, Buddy. I should have come sooner and told you. I've just been having a hard time."

"I unde'stand son. I'll unde'stand if you can't talk 'bout it now."

I needed to talk about it though, and so I did. Without leav-ing out any details, I described what occurred that day, from the beginning. Buddy would interrupt frequently to probe for more detail. He was interested in things that I thought insignif-icant—Luke's every word and even his facial features—I believe he was searching for clues as to whether Luke might have known it would be his last day on earth.

When I reached the end of the story, Buddy seemed to be im-mersed in deep thought, looking away into a place that seemed to put him in touch with his friend. There were several minutes of silence.

"He really did what God put 'im 'ere t'do. He died a happy man, son. He saved 'em boys. And I know you'n'me bof would like one las' huntin' trip—one las' visit wif our good friend but he don' all'e 'ad time t'do. Last thang he don', Chalie, he wanted you to know he loved you and he told you 'at t'make sho' you know'd it. You was impotant to 'at man, son. I need t'tell you sompin," Buddy continued. "You been impotant t'me, too. I watched you growin' up in'ta a mans gotta a lot t'giv'. You got a gift son, and ain't no doubt in my mind that you gon' be able t'hep a lot of folk. When you come back to visit yo' brothers, you come stay right'ere wi'me and Annie, iffin you need a place. We'd be proud to have you, son."

I was finally at home in my heart.

"Thank you. I'll take you up on that when I come back."

Buddy and I sat there talking till we'd said all we needed to say. I had needed this visit. I knew that I would soon miss his and Annie's immediate presence in my life.

"When you leavin' f'school?"

"I've got about two weeks, and then I'll be packing up to go."

"I don'tol' Louise 'at I'd come by and pick up the dogs. Kin you hep me t'mar, move 'em n'fix 'em a new pen out back?" Buddy asked.

"Sure thing."

"Oh, one mo' thang—gon' be 'shamed to put 'em dogs up 'out some runnin'. How 'bout you'n'me takin' 'em out t'mar night in 'at old truck o' Luke's and actin' like fools one mo' time?" and his face lit up in a grin. "I know old Luke'd like 'at. We'll go talk to him some," Buddy said with a twinkle in his eye.

I grinned, too.

"Ain't nothing I'd like to do any more'n that," I said.

# 32. The Green Buddha

BIG MARK AND MY MOTHER, ANNIE Laurie, were dead and had long since been laid to rest—so had Luke and my friends Cecil and Lydia.

Two of my high-school friends had been killed in some crazy war we were fighting in Vietnam, and we'd wept and mourned their passing as their flag draped coffins had been solemnly paraded down Main Street. They had grown up together here and joined the army on the "buddy" plan. They had been only eighteen when a Communist mortar shell had dropped into their foxhole. I suppose their parents were consoled by the fact that their deaths had meant something—at least that's what the telegram from President Johnson had said.

The Beatles had taken America by storm in '65. They had even performed in Atlanta. We'd all been captivated by their music while feverishly trying to write down all the lyrics when their songs were played on our six transistor radios.

Yeah, I'd say a whole lot had happened in the seventeen years since my birth. Some of what had happened I would have changed or stopped from happening had I been able. Then again, I had to smile while remembering what Luke had told me more than once, "We ain't in charge of that." His blue eyes sparkled as he'd smile and point skyward as if to remind me who *is* in charge.

Even the Trailways bus station a block off Main Street had changed. The WHITES ONLY signs had been taken down. The sitting area now accommodated whites and colored folks alike, but they still remained on separate sides of the room while awaiting their transport to the myriad of small towns beyond Polk County. It had been determined that a white man wouldn't, in fact, die from drinking from the same water fountain that a colored man had drunk from so separate water fountains were no longer needed. The bus station had even removed one of them to save money. The class of 1968, my class, was destined to be the last all white class at Cedartown High School. Yeah, change had finally reached all the way to Polk County, Georgia.

This morning I asked to be awakened at three-thirty with the boys who were assigned to the dairy. I wanted to have time to get some things done on my last day at the Home. I was apprehensive about something I'd needed to do for years—something I'd chosen to avoid doing for a long time. Today it would get done, finally.

The pre-dawn September morning was warm and accompanied by a soft drizzling rain. Under the street lamp at the ball field, a thin fog lay on the wet grass like a white, fuzzy blanket.

I had been saying my goodbyes to the boys for days now. Yesterday I had gone to the barn for the last time to wish the cows well, even old forty-nine, who's well-placed kick had been my initiation to milking my very first morning there, years before.

I didn't feel like a boy anymore—in fact, I hadn't felt like a boy for a long time. I had become a man already—not because I had wanted to necessarily, but because the events of my life had prematurely forced manhood upon me. I'm not sure that since my mother and father died that I was ever a boy again—I believe that the horror of that night irretrievably robbed me of most of the joy that children have in their lives and stripped away the insulation provided by boyhood innocence.

But I'm not sad about it—it is what it is. I had dealt with more pain in seventeen years than most folks experience in a lifetime, but it didn't kill me. Maybe it would have if not for my love and concern for my brothers, and Luke and Buddy. I'll never know.

I harbor no illusions though about what might have been had I not met and been taught the lessons of life by a pair of great men—two men who deserve their mantle of greatness, not based on wealth or position, but rather that sort of greatness acquired through humility and selfless giving. I was a welcome recipient of countless gifts of guidance and wisdom and direction from Luke and Buddy. They never asked for anything in return except that I give to others what has been given to me.

Light began its slow interruption of the morning's darkness. I walked out to the front porch of the cottage and took a seat in one of the chairs, sheltered from the rain. Eventually, the sun began to peek above the eastern horizon, turning the dawn's raindrops into a shimmering curtain of sparkling crystals. I was fascinated by the slow birth of a rainbow—one end penned to the ground, at first, alone. And then a plume of pure, unmixed Divine color burst forth into the heavens before returning to earth and planting the other end of the arch into the ground of a faraway pasture, completing the masterpiece.

Maybe the unfolding beauty inspired it or maybe, again, it had everything to do with the timing, but I was stunned to find my spirit engulfed by a feeling that everything was as it should be.

I was instantly struck with the awareness that everything that had happened in my life was the way it should have happened. Luke had once told me that "there is nothing that happens in God's world by accident," and suddenly, this last morning here, I understood.

For nine years I'd been convinced that the world I had been living in was a temporary place, at best, with the only constant being my brothers presence in my life. They were the only things in my life that had stuck around for long. People—even parents and the ones you're closest to—came and went, bringing or taking with them a small measure of joy or pain, whatever the case might be. Friends died or moved on and new ones would arrive in my life and fill the void until they, too, for some reason or other, would be swept away in the perpetual recycling of souls and places that we'd called home. Because of the fleeting nature of everything that had passed through my life, I hadn't yet begun to believe wholeheartedly in the most important message that my two friends had tried their best to deliver to me. This was about to change.

Faith—that's what Luke and Buddy had been trying to teach me for years, but I hadn't allowed myself to believe that anything that concerned me and my brothers could work without my help. Self-sufficiency had been my mantra. After all, I had gotten us through the hard times, hadn't I? I had told God, who's help I'd never asked for, that we were going to survive in spite of what we faced, and we had. That was through sheer perseverance, wasn't it? Surely self-reliance hadn't failed me.

For the past few years I thought that my brothers and I had survived through our sheer will to live, but this morning the answer came to me as quickly as a searing bolt of lightning through my soul. What I'd thought was real was cauterized and cast aside. I had the sudden realization that I hadn't accomplished all that I had claimed, at least not without help.

I had made the choice to be mad. Yeah, that's what it really had been—a choice, and now I was tired of it all—just plain worn out from the anger. Like I said, maybe this morning it was just the timing, but I realized that I didn't want to drag the anger with me as I moved on. It was a yoke that had defined me for most of my life. It was now time to lay it aside.

Luke had told me before he'd died that God had graced Big Mark with forgiveness. He'd said that it was necessary for me to find a way forgive them both—Big Mark *and* God. For years he'd tried to help me understand that, but I'd rebelled at the prospect of forgiving either of them. Leaving here today encumbered by the weight I'd been suffering under didn't seem to be an option any longer. Forgiveness finally found a crack in the hatred and seeped through.

I would be here for a few more hours. And in the end, just like Luke had tried to teach me, it would come to a choice—I could learn to forgive and choose to live a life of joy or I could remain a prisoner, wearing the irons of anger and the bitterness of dead dreams and defeat.

My choice was made—I would leave here today no longer shackled by the anger and fear I'd struggled with since arriving here with my brothers. Luke was right—but then, he had always been right.

I have no way of knowing why things happened like they did that last morning, but I was okay with that. For the first time since I was a little boy, I was no longer afraid.

I had spent days packing. What I couldn't fit in the front of the truck, I gave to my brothers. Danny was almost my size now, and he could wear the clothes I couldn't take with me. Mr. Loveless had driven me over to Georgia Tech a couple of weeks ago for orientation, and I knew I wouldn't have room at school to store much, so everything I owned was packed in the floorboard of the truck and on the seat beside me.

The rain stopped and the morning's clouds began to burn away, revealing a blue sky and promising a day of late-summer heat.

I was finally packed and ready to go. I said goodbyes to all the boys. Homer, and even Eustace, stopped by to wish me well. I had spent a couple of hours with Louise the night before, and she had talked about how she knew that Luke would be proud of me before making me promise to write to her from school.

My brothers all walked me to the old blue Chevy that I'd always refer to as Luke's truck and helped me load a few remaining things.

"Danny, this is on you now," I said, taking hold of his shoulders. "I'm gonna be gone so you gotta look after 'em okay?"

"Sure thing, Charlie. You ain't got nothin' to worry about."

"He ain't gotta look after us," Little Mark said. "We're almost grown up now."

"Well, we've all come a long way but while you're still here I want you to stay out of trouble, okay? And I want you to study hard so you can go to college, too, alright?"

"Yeah we will, but Charlie?" Jeffrey said.

"What?"

"I'm gonna miss you, Charlie," and he started to cry.

"All of you come here," I said as I dropped to one knee and gathered my brothers in a tight circle around me. "Listen, I'm only gonna be sixty-two miles away, and you'll have a phone number where you can reach me. I promise I'll call sometimes, too. Y'all just started a new school year so stay busy, and you can write to me and I'll write back. Danny's got my address and phone number so he can call in case of an emergency. Now, come here."

We all hugged, and in spite of knowing that the time had finally come for me to leave, I wanted more than anything to stay with them for just one more day.

"Look, I'm gonna miss you, too, but everything's okay, and I'll call as soon as I get to school."

With that and a final hug, I sat in the truck and started the engine. In the rearview mirror I could see my three brothers waving as I drove down the hill. Danny's red hair was a shining, sunlit beacon. I watched them until I rounded a corner and they disappeared. A warm tear made its way down my cheek and onto my chin before dropping onto my blue jeans, leaving a small, dark spot.

I pulled to a stop in front of Buddy's house and shut off the engine. Before I could even open my door I heard him holler from his porch.

"Well, I guess you all growed up now and headin' fo the big city. Can't say's I been lookin' fo'ward to 'is day, but we all gotta leave the nest sometimes. I'm proud of you, son. Come on in and say bye to Annie Mae else she gonna be hoppin' mad."

I was fortunate that Annie was feeling generous with that heart-stopping hug of hers. For a full minute she held me with her face pressed against my chest. I looked down and stroked her gray hair and knew that this old woman loved me as her son. And I loved her just as much as the mother I'd lost.

"Charlie, I fixed some food fo'ya t'take wi'you. Ain't no tellin' what they gon' be feedin' you ov'ere. They's a basket of fried chicken and some conbread and a jar o' tea when you git thirsty," Annie Mae said.

Buddy walked out to the truck and placed the cardboard box containing the food on the driver's side floorboard. "Gon' ha'ta ride 'neath yo legs, so's you'cn reach it case you get hungry," he said.

"Come on and let's set a spell." He walked the three wooden steps onto the porch. I sat with Buddy on the porch swing. Annie Mae took a seat in her old porch rocker facing us.

I told them both what I'd experienced at dawn as I sat on the porch of the cottage.

"Yeah, I'd ha'ta'say 'at's Old Luke payin' you a visit just so's you git yo' thankin' right 'fore you leave. I done tol'ja he gon' be lookin' a'ter you. I bet he done been talkin' to God Hisself 'bout you already, sho nuf. You ain't got one thang t'be worrin' 'bout. Old Luke's probly already a angel b'now and I spect it ain't gon' be long 'fore me and Annie git'ta see'im agin. Then we's all gon' be lookin a'ter you son, an you ain't gon' be able t'do nuttin' wrong," and he laughed as loud as I'd ever heard him laugh.

If I'd had any reservations or fears about leaving they vanished.

"Nosirreee," he said when he finally stopped laughing, "We all gon' be lookin' a'ter young Chalie," and he stood and grabbed me by my hand and pulled me to my feet. The old man I'd come to know and love embraced me tightly. "I'm sho gon' miss'ya, son. So's when you come home you make sho'ta stop by and see me'n Annie. Okay?"

"Yeah, well, I'm gonna miss both o' you real bad, too."

Annie stood. I guess this was just a day for tears because she was bawling as she told me she loved me. She kissed me on my cheek, and I promised I would return soon.

"Now you be drivin' slow. When you git'ta Atlanter then you best be pa'in 'tention. 'Ey te'me they's some crazy-folks up 'at way. We sho'do love you, son. Now git goin' so's you ain't drivin' a'ter dark."

He stepped back and looked the old truck over from bumper to bumper.

"Ain't it sompin you drivin' off'n Old Luke's truck," Buddy grinned and closed the door behind me after I sat behind the wheel. "You goin' by t'see Luke 'fore you go, ain't you?" and before I could answer he said, "Yeah, I suppose you better or he gonna be mad," and he laughed. "You best be careful out 'ere now, son." His dark, scarred hands still gripped the door. He reached in and squeezed my shoulder before I drove away.

I looked in the mirror and could see Buddy and Annie Mae, arm-in-arm, standing in the street waving to me. I found myself saying a prayer for them to the God that I had lost touch with a long time ago.

*\*\**

It was early afternoon when I pulled into the small gravel parking area outlined by old telephone poles lying on the ground. The country cemetery was deserted and quiet.

Luke's grave was still covered in flowers left by folks whose lives he'd touched. Some were fresh and looked as if they had been left today or maybe yesterday. The headstone hadn't been installed, but there was a small funeral home marker identifying who had been laid to rest here. Someone, probably Louise, had left a folding metal chair beside the grave and I sat down, staring at the small mound of red earth. A pair of dragonflies settled on top of a flower vase while katydids screamed at me from the tall surrounding pines.

"I'm leaving today, Luke. I wanted to tell you thanks for everything." I said then laughed. "But you know how I feel. I wouldn't have made it without you, old friend. I'm ready to move on now because of what you've given me. I just had to stop by and tell you that, okay. And I sure do miss you, Luke. Damn, I miss you. But I'm fixing to go do something you've always told me I should."

"And I sure could use your help just one more time," I said, rising from the chair. "Come on old man and take one last ride with me, okay?"

Feeling the presence of Luke's spirit, I drove back through town and down Main Street before turning onto Highway 278 toward Atlanta.

The first town I came to was Rockmart.

Although my father had been born in Mississippi, it was near here that he and my mother had been buried.

Before I'd left the Home I'd asked Mr. Loveless where my father's and mother's graves were.

"I knew you'd want to know someday," he said. "I just didn't know when," he said, as he drew me a map. All these years they had never been very far away.

"There's something else, Charlie." Mr. Loveless reached into a file cabinet and retrieved a large yellow envelope, handing it to me. "I think it's time you had these. That night, when it was finally decided that you and your brothers were coming home with me, I gathered these few things from your house. I thought that one day you might want to see them. I decided not to give them to you unless you asked about your parents." I opened the flap of the envelope, seeing pictures inside and closed it. "Forgive me for not giving them to you sooner," he said, "but for many kids, it's best to leave well enough alone until they're ready to remember, and now you are. Do with them what you will, but they belong to you and your brothers."

Not opening the envelope, I placed it on the dashboard of the truck before saying goodbye and driving away.

Just inside Rockmart's city limits I pulled off the highway into a large cemetery between two tall stone columns flanking the entrance and traveled down a slight hill on a narrow blacktopped lane to where Mr. Loveless said I'd find their graves.

I found them tucked under the shade of a group of tall crepe myrtles. The white and pink blossoms from the trees had fallen, covering the granite marker. Brushing the petals away, I could see their names cut into the stained gray-stone slab. Above my father's name was "MAJOR—USMC." In spite of what he'd done, I felt a tinge of pride for the man he'd once been.

I didn't know how they'd come to be buried here. Maybe the military had been responsible. One day I would seek the answer to that question, but that day it wasn't important. I had mixed feelings when I found out that they'd been laid to rest together—

somehow that didn't seem right after what had happened, but this was before I'd ever had any intention of forgiveness.

I had no interest in coming here before. Until a few weeks prior, I'd never even been curious about where they'd been buried. But it had always been unfinished business. I knew that I would continue to shoulder a burden if I didn't leave it here, as Luke had urged, so I'd made the choice to find them.

If God, as Luke had once questioned, could forgive my dad, then who was I to continue to hate? He had asked me that question many times in the past. Hating Big Mark had been easy, yet the road to forgive him had been long and hard.

I opened the envelope Mr. Loveless had given me and removed the dozen pictures it contained. Sitting on the ground, spreading the pictures before me, my memory instantly reconnected to a past that was all but forgotten. All the snapshots were from happier times: four brothers together on a porch swing—Big Mark and Momma, smiling while embracing—all of us together at some lake—all four of us boys sitting on our parent's laps, me missing a front tooth. Only in my dreams had I seen the joy in our earlier lives—pain hadn't allowed such conscious memories for the past nine years, but now, in these old photos from long ago, was evidence that joy *had* existed. We *had* been a family once—a loving, happy family.

I replaced all the photographs except one of my smiling mother, alone.

Sitting in the tall, dry grass beside the gravel-covered grave, I began to pull some of the weeds that had grown up through the gray pebbles. I hadn't rehearsed—had no idea how to begin, but as I laid the picture on her grave, the words began to flow.

"Hey Momma. It's been a long time, I know. I just want you to know that we've been okay. We've made it, in spite of everything. Danny's all grown up; he's almost as big as me, and Little Mark's so smart—he's never made anything but A's in school. You'd be so proud of him. And Jeffrey—everybody loves him, and he's a good kid, Momma, and growin' like a weed. I bet he's gonna be taller than the rest of us before it's over."

I looked at her photo and tried to remember how she looked and her smell and the softness of her skin, but nine years had robbed me of much detail.

"We've missed you so much, but we're all okay now, so don't worry. I have a friend who's up there with you, Momma. His name's Luke. If you run into him then get to know him some, and he'll tell you how it all turned out. He's a good man and I wouldn't have made it without him—none of us would."

I paused, considering what I'd say to my Father.

"You know something, old man—I've hated you since that night—hated you so much it damn near killed me—there were days when I really thought it might. But I have to confess something: I never once considered the pain you suffered from what you'd gone through—what you endured in the war and had to live with. I had a good friend who helped me to understand. And I'm sorry you ever had to suffer.

"I came to find you and tell you that I forgive you for what you did to Momma and to yourself. It's taken me a long time to be able to say this, but I hope and pray you'll find some peace now so you can rest. I believe I can find some peace now, too. You'd be proud of your sons now, Big Mark—we're all still proud of you."

I sat there with them for a while in silence—my mind pleading for memories—too few revealing themselves. But somewhere, buried under a mountain of anguish, there *were* good memories—the photographs an indication of happiness somewhere in my past. But I'd been too busy surviving the past nine years to recall them, and now, my memory was clouded and fleeting at best.

And then I stood up and wept, thanking God. And that's how I became a free man—unburdened of hate and awash in the hope that Luke had promised me was just waiting to be embraced.

I began to walk away then stopped and turned back.

"Oh, I almost forgot. I brought something for you, Marine. I don't need it anymore. I thought you might like to have it back. Thanks for letting me keep it for you all this time." With that, I removed the small jade Buddha from my pocket and walked back and placed it on the marker above my father's name.

"I love you both. I gotta go now, but I'll stop by again someday."

I turned and walked back to the truck. Before opening the door, I looked up into a pale blue, cloudless Georgia sky, smiling as I wiped the last of the tears away.

Sitting behind the wheel, I glanced up. Stuck in a seam in the visor was a picture of me and Luke together, both grinning, when I was much younger. *I wonder how long it's been there.* "Thanks Luke," I said, looking at the old photo. "Thanks for everything, old man. I've a ways to go, but I'll come by to see you when I get back."

The engine in his old truck purred as I moved down the highway toward a new beginning, and a warm breeze blew through the open windows of the rusty Chevy. When I passed through Rockmart the next sign I saw read, "ATLANTA—54 MILES."

That day was my introduction to that big world I had feared so much since I was nine years old.

Yeah, it's still a big world—even bigger than I imagined. The only difference now was that I was no longer afraid of it. I don't know what life has in store for me, but I was okay with that.

There's just so much hope out there—plenty enough for everybody with some left over.

Just like old Luke said.

# Epilogue

WELL, THAT'S THE END OF MY story. But I don't want to leave you without including a few final notes.

During my first year at college, I made many weekend trips home to see my brothers and Buddy and Annie Mae and Louise. Every trip included a visit to the small piece of hallowed ground in the country cemetery where we'd laid Luke to rest.

The rusty metal chair that sat beside his grave is still there, its smooth seat worn shiny, attesting to the many who've visited and sat for a while, no doubt absorbing the spirit and love of the great man whose name is now etched into a humble granite headstone. A generation would pass before any rust could invade the seat—such was the impact Luke had made in the lives of those who loved him.

Buddy and me took to running the dogs whenever I had a long weekend at home, accompanied by my brothers on many occasions. Danny struck up a relationship with Buddy, and before long, Buddy had taught him the art of successfully shaking coons from treetops.

While away during the late autumn of my sophomore year, Buddy called to tell me that Annie Mae had slipped away, her frail body having succumbed to illness. Her passing came suddenly, following a sharp bout with pneumonia and was quite unexpected, he'd said, or he would have informed me sooner so I could be by her side with him.

Before she passed, she asked Buddy to be sure to tell me how much she loved me. I still regret not having been there that day.

So, in Luke's drafty old Chevy truck, with the purple leaves of the west Georgia sweet gums still clinging stubbornly to their branches, I made the trip home to Cedartown to lend what comfort I could to my friend.

My first stop when I reached town was Buddy's house. A crowd of well-wishers stood on the street and porch, collars turned up to protect them from the cold wind, while trying to hand roll cigarettes from stained-leather tobacco pouches. When Buddy heard my name called out by his friends, he stepped onto the porch and welcomed me inside.

*This is home—this is where I'm supposed to be. This is the essence of life, what I feel right here, right now, and I'm comforted in the presence of my friends.*

The house was a busy place—the black, cast-iron, pot-bellied heater being force-fed stubby oak logs, keeping the autumn chill at bay. Several old women were busy in the kitchen preparing food, enveloping the four small rooms in odors of collard greens and cloves from sweet hams and homemade apple pies baking.

After Annie Mae was laid to rest beneath the cold red clay, Buddy and I returned home in Luke's truck, and he made an unusual, but very specific request.

"Chalie, son," Buddy said, "I wan' you t'promise me one las' thang, okay?"

"Yessir," I said. "Anything you want."

"Well, when I go, I wan' you t'see tuit ' I git burnt-up," Buddy said, referring to having his remains cremated.

"Ain't no problem," I said.

"And 'en, I wan' choo t'take sum-o'-my ashes and bury 'em o'er by Luke. Jes' a bit, mind you, and all'a rest by Annie. I don' recken she'll mind 'at," Buddy chuckled.

Buddy followed Annie Mae to Heaven a year later. Yeah, I'm a believer in Heaven now—"Gotta be sompin' ater this," Luke and Buddy both said.

With one final smile and a wink, Buddy said he was "goin' home t'see Annie'n'Luke," and then he traded this world for a more peaceful one. I was fortunate to have been by his bedside, holding both his scarred, skinny hands in mine when he took his last breath. I miss Buddy terribly.

And I honored Buddy's request—several weeks after his death. With my three brothers in tow, I interred a handful of his ashes beside his friend. It was only fitting that Luke and Buddy share the same piece of earth in death as they had in life.

These two men had been my teachers—they had purposely spent years making sure I was educated about life and honor in the most important schoolroom of experience. But unlike others, they had never told me what I should believe; they simply asked me what I thought and how I felt as they unselfishly displayed their noble character before me, allowing me to determine a course for my life.

I'm older now—already into my seventh decade. My brothers are all healthy with families of their own. My kids are grown, and I have three beautiful grandchildren.

Even though they don't understand yet, I'm already telling them the story of Luke and Buddy. It's a joyful tale, full of wonderful memories that I'm sure they'll appreciate one day.

Over the years, I've been asked many times why I smile so much. The answer is because I'm aware of just how much I've been blessed. But according to my two old friends, we've all been blessed—all of us—*every last one of us*. It took a lifetime for them to help me understand that.

I pray that you discover *your* blessings and you find *your* smile.

One last thing: if you have children or grandchildren or nieces or nephews, love them and be grateful for their presence—they're a gift and should be treated as such. If you don't have any kids in your life, find a child somewhere and make them feel wanted. It's the most important need they'll ever have—of that I'm sure.

God Bless.

# Acknowledgments

THIS BOOK WOULD NEVER HAVE BEEN written if not for the work and support of two people: my beautiful wife, Mary, and my friend and fellow author, Jedwin Smith. For years I had this story smoldering inside me until one day, while driving through Dahlonega, Georgia, during the Dahlonega Literary Festival, Mary stopped her truck in front of the Atlanta Writer's Club tent and strongly suggested I get out and talk to author George Weinstein, who was manning the table. She knew it was time for this story to be told. George headed me in the direction of Jedwin Smith, and the rest is history. Jedwin nurtured and taught and edited and edited some more. He removed parts of the book that I just knew Steinbeck or Faulkner would have admired, and then edited again. When he was finished and I was sick and tired of seeing red ink, a book lay before us containing a story that has always been in need of a good tell. I spent three years with him as Jedwin taught me the craft and gently nudged the very emotional, intensely private events in my story from the safety of my memories to their very vulnerable place on paper. Then Mary and Jedwin both gave me the courage to proceed. Thank you Mary for believing in me when it was hard for me to believe in myself.

Along the way, there were others who helped me to achieve my dream. Daniel, Mark, and Jeff, my three brothers who have shared their lives with me, way back then (and today), were a valuable asset as they prodded me toward the finish line. I love and thank you and I'm grateful that we're as close as we are.

Danielle Wirtz, my sweet cousin, exercised her talent on the computer laying out chapters and whatever else she did for this computer illiterate. You rescued me from a bundle of confusion and misery and for your help and support, I thank you.

George Weinstein was, and is, a valuable friend, and I'm glad he's part of mine and Mary's life. It seems that every time I needed to ask a question, George was somehow part of the answer. A great author in his own right, George helped when I didn't like all that some literary agents had to say about my work by telling me that "literary agents are a dime a dozen. If you don't like one, there are thousands more!" He encouraged me through a very vulnerable stage. He was there when it was time to publish and sent me in the direction of his publisher, Deed's Publishing, and I soon had a relationship with Bob, Jan, and Mark Babcock at Deed's, who've become my biggest believers.

I need to mention a classy lady who was a friend to George and me, Polly Neal. Polly was a past president of the Atlanta Writer's Club, but more than that, she supported writers like George and me with undying encouragement and loyalty. We lost Polly in December, 2013 and her generous spirit will be sorely missed. God Bless you Polly Neal.

Author James Rollins gave me advice which was contrary to the writer's mantra—"Don't send a query," he advised, "Just send the whole damn book. Either they'll like it, in which case they have it there in front of them, or they'll dump the whole damn thing in the trash." Thanks for the advice, James, as dubious as it may be.

I don't get to Atlanta much, as I prefer to stay here in my beautiful mountains, so I don't see many of my writer friends as much as I want. There were those I felt a bond with: Chuck Clark, Chuck Johnson, Ron Aiken, and many more. I wish you all the best, and thank you for your input.

There are hundreds of thousands of us "orphanage children" out there, and we all have our own story to tell. This book isn't now, or ever has been an indictment of the Homes we all grew up in. Homes of many faiths were scattered all over the country doing the best they could, from as far back as the Civil War, providing a roof and a full belly and an education and God knows, some of them even loved us as their own. People with big hearts who instilled hope—it must have been as hard for them as it was for us. Thank you for the courage to accept us.

I want to especially thank two friends for their help and support: Gary Willis and his wife, Chris, who were there when I needed them. Thank you both for your love and support. And Ronnie Tillery and the rest of the Tillery family. We grew up together and got into trouble together, and now we'll grow old together. I thank you and your brothers.

And thank you to all Bill W's friends out there as we "trudge the Road of Happy Destiny" together. It's been a wondrous journey. God Bless.